How To Bring A Boyfriend Back From The Dead

HOW TO BRING A BOYFRIEND BACK FROM THE DEAD.

Jim McLean

Published by Twisted Word 2011

Twisted Word
Suite IX, 136 Narbonne Avenue,
London, SW4 9LG.

www.twistedword.com

A Catalogue record of this book is available
from the British Library

ISBN 978-0957092105

For Victoria, endless love.

"Love's not Time's fool, though rosy lips and cheeks Within his bending sickle's compass come: Love alters not with his brief hours and weeks, But bears it out even to the edge of doom."

William Shakespeare, Sonnet 116.

1

"Is anybody there?" asks Portia Maxwell, like it is the very last time ever.

"God," she says. "IS ANYBODY THERE?"

She has already scraped the heel of her snakey lemon Manolo Blahnik's three times on the wobbly floorboard under her seat. She has groaned two ghastly ghouls, exhaled noisily through her nostrils, thrown herself sharply back in her seat and even tried rolling her eyeballs back inside her head. Now she is crunching the bones of the customer on her right's brittle old lady's fingers while her restless left hand is squishing the flabby jelly around Vivienne's knuckle-duster sovereign rings.

This question she is asking. It isn't mainly for the customer who needs to talk to the dead. It isn't for the ears of the four other shadows huddled in darkness around her walnut dining table, hands joined, breathing each other's breath, each praying a personal catechism.

Neither is it a question for the ears of the ever hereafter gone befores. The Dead.

Portia doesn't go into the Psychic Deli's dark and dusty séance room merely for the waiting to see what might come through from the other side of it. Fate should never be allowed to play a hand in business. And anyway, the spray-on cobwebs murder her asthma.

Portia. If you could freeze frame her in the darkness with flash this is her still life. Pink hair fluffed like candy floss. Emerald green contact lenses. A honey yellow trouser suit, with trims of white lace on cuffs, lapels and trouser leg bottoms. Roberto Cavalli. More lunch at Harvey Nicks than an angel at deaths door.

The question she is asking is for Aurora. Spooky. Space girl. The new waitress with the far away eyes, the juicy lips and the hippy dreads. The girl with the slow west country drawl who arrived late this lunchtime and has lost herself frothing cappuccinos out front instead of sending Portia some signs like she was told to. That's why she is having to make do with the basics of flicking the neon fairy lights, buried in the walls and ceiling, on and off with the thumb switch under the arm of her chair. It explains why she has no cd of ambient ghoulish rattles and wails. Why there isn't even dry ice.

Portia doesn't look to Vivienne to bail her out. Even if her chubby hands were free, whoever heard of anyone whipping out tarot cards right in the middle of the monthly séance?

The best she hopes for is that the SOS pulse she has sent out around the table means Vivienne is pumping someone else's hand too and that, really soon, someone in the darkness will have an idea of what to do in this absence of routine administrative support.

Next door, Aurora is lost in millions of tiny rainbows blistering the surface of foaming milk. She has made cappuccino, she has made latte. She has warmed croissants, sliced cheesecake and she has grilled veggie bacon sandwiches. She has decided she doesn't like any of the dusty old paintings decorating the place and she would rather have a French feeling. She has done some special Glastonbury twirling on her heel moves beneath the ceiling's gold leaf constellations and wondered who painted them, particularly the scary giant Orion chasing the Gemini twins with a large club. She has turned the television set off - Sky News is running today's disaster story in Afghanistan - and put Classic FM on instead, coming in halfway through something nice and dreamy that sounds like Chopin.

She plays with her hair for a bit, sucking the ends of some dreads.

The rainbow bubbles give her an idea for beads made from plastic coated with clear nail varnish so that they might look as if they are made from mother of pearl, when she has this sensation that someone is standing too close next to her.

The way customers sometimes do when they are feeling a bit ignored so try to get inside the body space of the person they want to see respond in a surprised human way. Jump up, or drop everything, just to serve them.

So instead, she looks even deeper into the rainbows. And through the colours floating on the oily contours of bubbles, under prancing Sagittarius, she begins to make out the form of the person right there who is blocking out the light from the front door. Aurora sees how the words Psychic Deli from the window make a perfect accidental halo around the dark silhouette of this person's shoulders.

The conversation from customers at tables one, three and seven falls silent. The bubbles start to burst and the syrupy sweet air they let out warms her face.

The walls in this place, these dusty paintings, they don't just have eyes - they have voices.

At first Aurora thinks the scream is steam blasting out the nozzle under pressure. Then this person, this middle-aged man wearing a yellow and pink checked rugby shirt, is walking out the door. No, Aurora blinks against the daylight blurring in. The man is walking *through* the door.

But, all the time, this screaming.

It is coming from the room on the half landing. And rolling out after it, propelling shrillness into the café, is the huge bulk of Vivienne waving her stubby hands in the air over her red curls, spilling a tarot deck wildly across the floor, and the screaming coming over and over from her stuck open cave mouth.

"S'weird," says Aurora.

Vivienne runs over to Aurora, grabs on and buries her tearful face into her orange t-shirt. Ochre blossoms bloom there between sobs.

"Hurr. Hurr," she eventually says, pointing upstairs.

People are trying to get in and out of the room before one another and at the same time, crowding the door until the boomerang that Vivienne has become bursts a way through for Aurora.

"I said get an ambulance," the voice of Portia says from under a table. She is gasping, punching her fist into the chest of someone lying on the floor.

Bending over Portia is this old woman, blind yet gawping, absorbing the scene, her white unseeing eyeballs pulsing, a black saw of a smile to match her dress, this black lace number with veil fresh out of Gone With The Wind.

Aurora blinks at her to be certain she is really there, really one of the breathing persons in this room and not an old ghoul come to cause mischief and rants. Cos if she is, she'll be packed off to Kingdom Come and make no mistake, turning up here on Aurora's first day before she gets a chance to warm her way into the place.

Quick as a flash she tugs on her lucky crow's foot key ring three times. Nothing changes, not even the room's temperature.

"An ambulance," Portia hisses.

One look and Aurora sees the whole picture. She sees it from every angle. It fits, it is complete. Like the

4

Battenberg cake shirt the man on the floor wears.

Portia is punching. "Who knows the kiss of life?"

Aurora says. "No need. The gentleman has departed."

And slowly, like it might be a serious mistake to punch an obviously dead man just one more time for spoiling her day, Portia draws herself back onto her knees. The sugar has gone out of the day and her pink floss hair is wilting. When she needed something to happen, this is not what she had in mind. She would never have betted on Sid standing up and screaming like that, then thumping down on the table, with all the weight of his body, and then the two or three seconds of him writhing on the floor clutching at his chest.

OK. There was a moment there, a whiff of a time, she had felt sort of pleased someone was doing something. Well. Maybe not pleased. Relieved. But now, now she has to deal with this. This embarrassment.

"Mrs Pugh, I am ever so sorry."

Aurora is reassured when Portia straightens up, takes the old lady by the arm and leads her out the room. Spectres don't get led away so easy.

Still, if you were truly unlucky, you might get a tricksy one that deliberately let itself be led around.

"Not at all," blind Mrs Pugh says. She smells of dusty flowers when she passes. "Not at all. First signs of life I've seen at one of these things."

Vivienne is sobbing snot into a mobile phone. She asks the room if an ambulance is the right thing to call if someone has just died.

"Contacting the dead," Mrs Pugh says. "It's a terrible business."

Portia nods, steering everyone out the room. "I'll get you a sherry shall I?"

Mrs Pugh bares her chipped teeth at Aurora. With her black pearls and dead garden smell, she looks as happy as can be to have been there the day someone died.

As if she has at last found proof that it can be done. That Sid's falling down dead was a result of the meddling going on in the room. And that the line between the living and dead might actually be a blur in time and space that can be crossed over and over again.

And that she is closer to the answers she needs from the grave before slipping off into one herself for eternity.

With a rolling white eyeball stare she says it straight at Aurora. "I'm looking forward to next time. Aren't you?"

2

An ending and a beginning. This is creation.

In the dead of night, beneath an endless sky, with a light easterly and the lapping Thames taunting the burnt out shackles of the Cutty Sark, the regenerated terraces of Royal Greenwich trace a new meridian between time and space as much as east and west.

The darkness holds its breath.

Then, ahhhh. You can see it frost up the columns of St Alfege's. The tombstones line up silvery in the graveyard the instant the neon strip of the Psychic Deli spits across the road.

A little further, a traffic light on Romney Road freezes Stop. The walls of Wren's hospital run blood red once more.

And when the crystal towers of Canary Wharf exhale, the London night draws you upwards. Put your thumb against this sky and it obscures a million pinprick suns. Spread your fingers apart and light years of galaxies drift in and out between the bones and the flesh. Make a fist and you can punch a black hole all the way back to eternity.

Along Croom's Hill the sound of a piano drifts over slate roofs, one key tapping a low soliloquy in this comfortable suburb of grey and beige painted clay. The tail of one note wraps itself around the dark branches of a chestnut, nestles among silver fronds of birch.

In all this vastness and silence, of all the nights that have gone before, thundering and rolling with the significant pendulum of time, there is only this night. The night Mohammed was purified then filled with knowledge and faith by the archangels as he slept? And the journey from Mecca to Jerusalem by winged Buraq? All gone with the scent of jasmine.

The night of the last supper? Finished with the dregs of wine and a stale crust dropped in the dust of Calvary.

On a night like this Queen Maya dreamed of a beautiful white elephant carrying a white lotus flower in his trunk. He touched her side and wriggled into her womb. Later she found herself squeezing the branch of an ashoka tree while giving birth to a little buddha.

Or perhaps it is Maha Shivratri, the moonless night of Shiva the destroyer, dancing the tandava of primordial creation, preservation and destruction.

Once, on a night like this, God even passed over the Hebrews.

Tonight. Consider only this night as, effortlessly, the ordinary becomes extraordinary.

Croom's Hill is as entitled to a beginning as the muddy reeds of the Euphrates or the remote darkness of deepest space. It is neither a place where people come to celebrate, or die. It is a place people visit in order to go on to other places, usually via the Dockland Light Railway interchange.

The houses shield their occupants with shrubby gardens. Internally, the partitions in these homes are coming down. The subdivisions are being taken out. In this conservation area, where you cannot take out a single brass screw without replacing it with another, every rotten cubist Georgian window demands an expensive certified reproduction replacement.

New wrought iron railings sprout from under privet.

These gardens with plastic playparks next to budding camellia. The restored summer houses and conservatories. The retro, fashionably dim electric gas-lantern street lights. You can imagine you hear the whole neighbourhood sighing it into the night: Money.

But all you can actually hear is this one note, this one piano key being struck from inside this one villa, the biggest and smartest house in the whole place. It is set back up a gravel driveway framed by a couple of cherry trees in blossom.

In this light, the blooms are anaemic.

Behind their screen of ivy and climbing roses, the first floor balconies have bow shaped metalwork. The front porch, its oak door with decorative leaded glass lit from inside, gives little shelter from the cold night air.

The person standing there, in the half darkness, lights up a cigarette. And she becomes an instant miniature Rembrandt. This nurse, acclimatising to the air, cups her hands around the flame. Pale light momentarily reveals the details of her leopard skin turban, white shirt and dark ski pants. It gives us her thin wrinkled lips and long fingernails, the smooth clear varnish, and it flits across the faces of two carved winged figures hovering over the door.

She draws deeply, our nurse, intentionally. She blows smoke mingled with the steam of her own breath up to the stars. She loves terminal breast cancer support when it reaches this stage. When the customer is ready and the family takes her into their confidence. It is simply a pleasure.

Nurse flicks cigarette ash into an empty amitriptyline carton and considers the simplistic beauty of a handful of tricyclic antidepressants and a polythene bag. The pills are merely a sweetener, to calm things down. A plastic bag over your head means it is impossible for the lungs to breath oxygen. In her experience, it only takes about ninety seconds to pass out and around four minutes to die. No need to even tie the bag at the bottom. Even a loose bag will effectively seal off the mouth and nose. It is clean too. There is no forensic means of detecting any evidence from a bag once it is removed.

Anyway, nobody ever wants a post mortem with these terminals.

She is not waiting for something to happen, this nurse. She savours what will happen. What she does not know is that when her taxi comes she will take it to the lights on Romney Road before remembering that she has left something. In less than fifteen minutes she will be back here to collect the purse she slid under the fancy table next to the phone.

By then the job will be over and the customer's husband will be distraught. He will run his hands through his shoulder length grey hair. He will twist his wedding ring round and round his elegant long fingers. He will tug at the neck of his grey turtle neck sweater, nervously smooth the creases of his charcoal slacks. He might cry out and probably slump over the piano keys in despair. Or succumb to a surge of creativity and play beautiful sad music into the morning.

Nurse smiles her cracked smoker's lips. She is experienced enough in these matters to know that he shall desire her most delicious extras to comfort him in this time of sorrow and weakness.

Inside. In the minute it takes James Earnest Hammington to go into the kitchen, fetch ice from the fridge, pour a very large malt whisky and return to the piano room, his wife is flopped on the sofa. He can taste the lavender, rose and cinnamon of the scented candles flickering around the room.

The incredible shrinking woman is almost withered to nothing inside her dressing gown.

New. Perched on her head she is wearing a bizarre hat, a green plastic bag turned in around the edges. He will never know that it took almost all of her remaining strength to pull that bag from under the cushion where the nurse had placed it for her.

"Miriam," Hammington says. He kneels beside the woman who is becoming a skeleton right in front of his eyes. He touches her hand and says, "What's this?"

She can barely open her eyes, even the soft lamplight burns them, and her voice is a whisper. The drugs are pushing her to sleep. He leans close.

"Time," she says. She lifts a finger upwards. "You do it."

And Hammington sucks in the air. They have already said their farewells and he knows what it is she needs him to do.

He leans forward and kisses her on the lips, on the sunken eyes, on the clammy forehead, then smoothes her hair off her face. He says he loves her.

She coughs, a dry hacking gasp, and says she loves him too. "Play," she says.

Hammington nods his head, rolling down the plastic over her face. The dark green with gold writing polythene hood.

"My darling sleepy head," he says. "Sweet dreams."

It is done.

And yet, as he sits beneath the triple candelabrum at the piano, next to the framed photograph of himself looking younger and more handsome in a tuxedo, he feels completely undone. He has a voice going over and over again in his head. It is Oscar Wilde, only Oscar Wilde gone all wrong.

He can't take his eyes off of it.

"A Harrods' bag? A Harrods' bag?" this voice says again.

With all this repetition, it begins to sound like Herod's. There is all this plastic in the world, all these supermarket chains, music stores, clothes shops and self publicising takeaways. And the brand she goes out to is Harrods. Or Herod's. It makes a snug fit.

Perhaps she has one more minute left of consciousness. Two hundred heartbeats of life. The biggest metronome ever and he, Hammington, one of the greatest concert pianists of his time, should have something sad to play. His soul should melt in anguish, outpour something wonderful and heart rending, excruciating to listen to. Albioni's Adagio. A tearful piece by Satie, or the exiled Chopin. Handel's Death March of Saul.

But nothing has prepared him for this moment.

His mind creased, Hammington finds himself tapping the piano with one finger.

Slow, soft, measured.

"Elton John," Miriam says.

Her voice is suppressed, stifled by drugs, polythene and asphyxiation.

"Daniel," she says.

She is quite comfortable on the sofa in front of the living flame fire.

And without thinking he strokes out the melody until he reaches the bit when the song soars away from the typical pop ballad and stretches, it reaches out and touches you inside. He taps a chord. He is a concert pianist who cannot sing.

He judders out, "God it looks like Daniel."

Then straining together, James Earnest Hammington and his wife Miriam, soon to be deceased, sing a harmony for the last time.

"Must be the clouds in my eyes."

Slowly he realises he has been singing alone. There are no more notes left.

So he sits and waits for a while to pass.

And he thinks.

Not of their years together, the thrill of romance, the

places they visited or the children they have raised. He does not even linger on the knot of loneliness he feels in his stomach. As he looks at her lying there, stretched out and dead, he could be at ease with it all.

If only it wasn't for that bag.

If not the head of his dear Miriam, he wonders what a Herrod bag should hold?

The head of John The Baptist, of course. A Jewish king, some dead first born, three wise men. Gaspar, Melchior and Balthazar. Gold, frankincense and myrrh. A prophecy on the coming of the saviour of the world. A latin phrasebook. Some astrological charts and a road map of the ancient middle east.

Hammington gets up, taking the candelabrum with him, and opens the French doors to let the night in.

As if from out of nowhere, the lights go out. All the air, the life of the candles, the muslin curtains, billows out into the garden. The muslin, whipped to a tempest, smacks him across the face as the house exhales to the infinite sky.

And there is a hammering at the front door.

Hammington, his immediate thought that his wife is lying there dead with a poly bag over her head, relights the candles from the fake coals and pulls the bag off her head.

The door is hammering so that the hinges shake.

He worries that this could be the police at his door. So he hurries to tidy up some of the pills lying by Miriam's side. He flicks some back in their container and some in the bag he stuffs into his pocket. He puffs up her pillow and he clasps her hands together on her chest. That looks too dead, he decides, so he takes one arm and rests it by her side. He buttons up her nightshirt. Tidies her slippers, her spectacles, stands her bottle of vodka next to the sofa. Then he runs over and flicks the light switch off and on, off and on a couple of times. He swears at it. But nothing happens.

The power, or a fuse, or something has gone. It is dead. Maybe, he finds the cigarette lighter and fires up a candle stub, just here or maybe in the whole of the city, he doesn't know.

And still the hammering at the front door refuses to go away. That hammering. It knows you're inside, the determined blows that tell how much the person out there is simply not going to stop.

So imagine Hammington's surprise, the look of confusion and worry, when he opens the door. He waves a dim candelabrum high over his head and squints out into the gloom. His eyes strain for movement beyond the pool of light.

Nothing.

Then he has a vision that makes his heart miss a beat. A thought that while he stands here, the music room is wide open to the garden.

He is already turning to run in the instant he hears something behind him, back in the room where Miriam grows cold beside the fire. And as he turns, his foot slips perfectly through the noose formed by the brown leather shoulder strap of a small bag he has never seen before. This noose tightens around his ankle. The bag wedges itself under the brass lion claw pedestal base of the early nineteenth century mahogany and maple card table Hammington inherited from his grandmother.

Up this close by dying candlelight, pink terrazzo flooring is beautiful. The marble chips are an ice flow.

Until he hits a cliff of black patent leather.

"You really needn't grovel," says a woman's voice.

Hammington takes in the clear plastic eight inch heel and two inch sole, the yard of leather boot, upwards a cloud of fur that stretches into the shadows.

Could this be Miriam gone to hell by some mistake and already come back to taunt him?

"Been having little party in darkness?"

This time he picks up on the eastern European accent and the theatrically low voice. Clambering to his feet, he chokes his way up through the familiar decay of Christian Dior. Poison. It smokescreens the meticulously torn fishnet stockings, black tutu and velvet bodice, so that he can't bear to linger or stare. It wafts around the folds of the full-length silver sable coat.

"Ramana," Hammington says to the blood red lips at his eye level. He guesses she is about Miriam's age, but her body is toned like an old dancer's. Her powdered white skin has only a faint smell of sweat. Her shoulder length black hair has a designer white lightning bolt of a skunk's streak. Her breath is sweetened by alcohol.

"Where did you come from?"

"I make my own entrance," she says.

"It's really not a suitable time," Hammington says. "It's really not."

"Hammy, my dear. I think it is. We need to talk," Ramana says. She leans into his face, presses a finger into his chest.

He takes a pace backwards towards the door and says, "Alright. But in the morning. I'll call you."

This woman, this panther, stalking him with deliberate steps that have him fumbling backwards.

"No need to call. I was at a party in neighbourhood. You know, I hear some ve-ry in-ter-es-ting news," she says.

"Oh yes?"

"Yes," she says pressing him against the wall, leaning into the candle flame. "That impresario Hammyton doesn't want his Ramana any more. That great pianist Hammyton has decided to find new representative. Is true. No?"

Up into her black eyes he says no. Well, yes. For god's sake, he means yes. He is in his own home after all. He

15

says he means yes there is some truth to it. "I need an artistic change in direction that's all," he says. "Can we talk about this tomorrow? I'll call you."

Ramana leans tighter into the struggling candle. She hisses. She almost spits out the flame. On the wall behind her the black shadow of a cobra rises to strike.

"You see," Hammington says, pushing her away. "This is exactly what I mean. You come into my home in the middle of the night. You torture me with your questioning. How can I be creative when you behave like this?"

She tells him that he must know he will never find a better theatrical agent than Ramana Queen of Evil.

"That's another thing," Hammington says. He thumps his flat hand against his head. "All this Queen of Evil stuff might do for walk-on parts in low budget movies. But it simply isn't acceptable for the Albert Hall, or The Carnegie, or anywhere in the classical world. I don't know why I let you talk me into it in the first place. I don't want an agent anymore. I don't care if I never work again. And you've got to face it. You're a laughing stock."

Ramana has been drinking champagne all night in the West End. And she is not accepting laughing stock from a nobody.

Doesn't he know she was born on the cusp?

She could have been a star, she says.

Unfortunately the craft of real acting lay dying.

She was unlucky, the full potential of television drama had yet to be revealed.

When she was working on Countess Dracula, The Witches, Plague of Zombies and The Devil Rides Out, where was he? Tinkling on a bar stool, that's where.

When he was nothing she was on first names terms with Fontaine, Cushing, Lee and Mower.

And she says, "Look at this place I got for you. It's a palace. Let us go ask your missus Hammyton if she will give up all this, for your art."

Hammington says this can't happen, not tonight. "Miriam is not well, she's sleeping," he says.

Ramana is staggering towards the music room. "Nonsense. I spoke with her a moment ago as I came in through here."

Hammington tries to get in front, to block the door. "It's not possible."

He had touched her dead skin. He was too afraid to kiss her blue lips although he had respected her silence.

For a moment they press together in the doorframe. He has the warmth of Ramana's breasts on his face.

"Your heart is small, Hammyton," Ramana says. "I feel it beating like a bird. Everyone wants to be a star. Not everyone is big enough. That's why you need me."

She pushes straight over to Miriam and sits down beside her in the firelight. She speaks to Miriam, but Hammington cannot focus on the words.

Everything was going fine. It was all going so damn fine.

"This really is not a good time," he says to the back of Ramana's head. "Will you go now?"

Ramana is holding Miriam's fist. She is up close to her face, straining to listen to a whisper.

"Really. Go." He hears his own voice tremble.

Then she turns to Hammington, in thespian surprise. Holding out in her open hand ten capsules prized from Miriam.

He cannot begin to think how this must look. His head spins with the details. How Miriam lies dead with all those pills. The alcohol, the darkness, the polythene bag hanging out of his trouser pocket.

Miriam has given Ramana the power to destroy his career. Or worse, bind him to her forever.

Perhaps it was the effects of the stressful day mingling

with the whisky, sharpened by adrenalin. Or despair, a pent up scream that eventually forced a way out. Perhaps it was merely something he had wanted to do for a long time. The weight of the candelabrum felt solid and precise as he brought it thumping down onto Ramana's vulnerable upturned head.

Effortlessly the ordinary becomes extraordinary.

It always takes a minute for an electrician to reset the power supply after a surge. In the instant that Hammington's arm begins to come down, the electricity starts its run to oblivion. In the next instant, the shaving of a moment, the traffic lights on Romney Road blip to green. The office towers fill from bottom to top and overflow with light. Across north and southeast London a new cycle begins. And at almost exactly the same time, in a music room not far away, a total of fifty incandescent high wattage bulbs burst into life in the Hammington's hand cut and polished Swarovski crystal Grand Entry chandelier. It is a beautifully blinding instant.

Ramana instinctively lifts her arm. She need not have bothered. Hammington's aimless arc swings past her arm and thuds against her coat. The force ejects a small book from her pocket. This filofax missile whizzes across the room, knocks Hammington's tuxedo portrait into the guts of the piano, then follows it down to a hellish discord.

Ramana is rising to her feet as Hammington sinks to his knees. His face crumples. She casts the amitriptyline against his chest.

"You worm," she says.

Hammington rolls away the candlestick in disgust. His stomach tightens, uncontrollable.

He crumples and cries aloud like an animal.

Ramana has the sleeve of her sable rolled up to the elbow, her arm plunged into the piano. She can see it, but her precious book lies just beyond fingertip reach.

She pounds the piano with her fists. Kicks at it with her built up boots. The emptiness of her black eyes burn into Hammington's soul and she says, "You dare to lift your hand to me? I should crush your skull beneath my foot as Ra-Antef in Curse of The Mummy's Tomb. Fire nails through your eyes as I endured in Horrors of the Black Museum. Rip out your throat, as Vampire Lovers, demand the Gorgon turn your evil heart to stone. If I only had my book I would repeat such words of death that would so destroy your heart you would gladly crush your own skull into the dust of The Mummy's Shroud."

"This isn't a B-movie," he says.

But on a night like this her words make perfect sense. They cut through his tears and wither his will to live. In this entire world without Miriam, he will forever now only taste despondency.

He is convinced. It would be better to destroy himself.

And that is simple enough. As Ramana tip toes to reach deeper into the piano, he feeds himself on the pills lying all around. He falls amongst them, licking them off the floor, pecking them from the folds of Miriam's nightdress, gathering them from under the sofa. He washes mouthfuls of them down with Miriam's vodka.

Ramana has shoulders and head inside the hull of the instrument. She is almost there. Beyond the silver frame of Hammington's conceited portrait she can touch the book's red leather binding with a fingernail. It leaves a small impression. She is almost there. Inside this piano coffin of wires and dust, she can barely breathe. Just one more inch.

And there is a hammering at the front door.

Ramana has to push herself out.

She expects to see Hammington with his head in his hands, wiping his red eyes on his sleeve, ignoring the noise. What she actually sees is him lying down next to his wife, foam coming out of his mouth. She sees more pills on the floor, the empty vodka bottle.

The door is hammering so that the hinges shake.

She hisses and spits, slams the piano lid down hard enough to set the wires burring. She kicks Hammington on the leg. "You bloody fool," she says. Then she pulls her sable around her, she gathers her folds of fur and swirls out into the garden, rolling off into the night like invisible distant thunder.

The dedication of a nurse can never be underestimated. Our nurse, returning for her little bag, smoothes her shirt tight over her figure. She straightens her leopard pattern turban.

She gives up hammering at the front door, usually continued a touch longer for the benefit of near neighbours.

She already has a key. And the house is silent and with every light ablaze.

She loves terminal breast cancer support when it reaches this stage. It is simply a pleasure.

In the piano room, the customer and her talented husband. The customer is comfortable and dead. Her husband is groaning and choking a little and nurse believes he has a frightened look in his eye. He is trying to speak. He wants to tell her something. He rolls his head from side to side a couple of times, twitching. The meaning of this is unclear.

Too late for all that now, she tells him. "All the spilt milk in the world that can't be put back in the bottle. All the broken eggs that can't go back in the chicken," she says.

She smiles. It wont take a minute and they will be together again. Peace at last. She just needs to unfurl this green plastic bag hanging from his pocket.

3

The new owner comes bouncing downstairs, still in their dressing gown. Full of anticipation, glowing with pride at their fine new acquisition. They can't wait to see the painting hanging above their fireplace in daylight.

And there it is.

Only now, stained in the oil glaze beneath the impassionate eyes, ta rah:

TEARS OF BLOOD.

At this point the art collector is willing to believe a friend has done it as a joke, crept in and Picasso'd them.

By the time they get dressed and take another look, the tears have gone. They put it down to a trick of the light.

But the next night the whole house shakes. In the dead of night the heavy frame of the painting has worked loose from its industrial strength fixings and crashed to the floor. Upside down against the mantelpiece, the face in the portrait has a satanic grimace.

The night after this and a woman starts to cry. It seems to be coming from behind the painting, from inside the wall.

The art collector on the phone is having a worse time than Portia Maxwell, director of the newly formed Psychic Deli Detective Agency, expected.

But she could do without the stuttering and complaining.

She needs to hear what is happening on television.

Portia Maxwell jangles her office keys until her new personal assistant tears herself away from frothing milk for someone and looks into her office. She points to the television, holds out the phone and mouths silently, "What is that?"

Aurora, with a milky moustache, shrugs.

Portia scribbles into thin air. She mouths, "Get the address."

And Aurora bends over the television screen, to get a closer look at the blurred images. Then she stands up and says, "It's alright. It's a plane crash in China."

She clicks the remote control twice. A purple cartoon mouse tap dances across the screen of the muted television.

Gas explosions, children playing with matches, spontaneous combustions and fatal electrical faults. Murder, suicides, and the inexplicable death of priests. Planes crashing into buildings, fishermen lost at sea. Phantom pregnancies, sudden illness, homes that no one wants to buy. These are the latest road signs of Portia's life. With all the treasure trove of disasters in the world, she can't afford to miss the next big thing. But how Portia wishes that the new owner of the Portrait Of A Woman 1892 would stop for breath.

Understandable, if they truly had blood streaming from the eyes of their painting. Or the heavy gilt frame creepily worked itself loose and crashed to the floor. Or it spun itself upside down still attached to the wall. Whatever way this art lover looks at it, the painting always reveals the Face of Evil.

The woman crying in the chimneybreast is a new one. But soon it will be the blazing red eyes that stare at them in bed at night. And then the face that looks back at you from behind the mist of the bathroom mirror.

An old woman's cancerous flesh rotting off in strips.

To the art lover, Portia Maxwell says, "I agree it sounds like a very serious case. We may be able to help although, you must appreciate, a refund would be out of the question since you would need to prove beyond all reasonable doubt the painting is actually haunted.

"Win a case like that and that painting would be worth a fortune. Imagine the media frenzy. The galleries, the scientists, the people who'd die to own it. Lose the case, however, and your painting will be worthless."

After a pause she says: "No one in recent centuries has ever proved a haunting in court."

And, she thinks, I employ the sole single person who could probably put me out of business.

It is a fine painting, Portrait of A Woman 1892. Unsigned. Late Victorian English School, a follower of Whistler. She stands sideways, looming out of a grey brown background, in full length red satin dress and ermine stole. She has black curls of hair tumbling over her shoulders. A cigarette smoulders in an ivory and silver filter. Portia knows it so well. She's sold this work five times in the past two years.

Another painting, the pre-Raphaelite Redhead With Dove And Skull, possibly by Rossetti, and blood running from the bath taps. She's sold that one eight times in three years.

The walls of the Psychic Deli make an excellent gallery. They attract just the right sort of person.

To the art lover she says, "Just a minute" and hits a button.

Portia. An impressionist's vision today in a silk ankle length dress from Monsoon, a blizzard of maple leafs in pastel pinks, blues and greens. A string of brown kukui nuts around her neck completes the organic ensemble.

And to Aurora next door she says, "Aurora? Darling?"

Then louder she says, "Spooky?"

She has more important things to do than this. In two hours she needs to be selling the 18th century French cradle in mahogany with supernatural gunshots and the screams of a murdered infant echoing around the canopy. Then there's the 18th century Venetian painted glass mirror, complete with the vision of the laudanum suicide. Both splendid additions to any quality home seeking that finishing touch in haunted antiques.

Aurora comes in, folds her arms and says, "What?"

Portia says, "I want you to run over to" ... she finds the notepad on her desk ... "to 32 Croom's Hill. There was a double suicide last month. A concert pianist and his wife had cancer. House clearance is tomorrow."

A red hammer squelches the purple mouse.

She writes the address on the back of a business card that says Psychic Deli Detective Agency in gold lettering and hands it to Aurora.

"Now don't get carried away. Don't go praying for lost souls or star crossed lovers."

Aurora takes the address. "I'll see if there's anybody there."

"Whatever." Portia waves her hand over her head and says, "So long as you insist that any ghouls possess something collectable."

Portia Maxwell ignores the call on hold and says, "Any vibes at Sotheby's?"

And Aurora lifts her shoulders to her ears. She huffs out a big sigh, fingering the yellow and blue beads on her rat's tail hair extensions, and says, "There was definitely one thing. It had energy. It was very gentle and refined. This burr elm commode, it had the most beautiful warm colour."

And Portia says, "Sod warm colour."

She wants to know about the hand that grabs you from out of nowhere and tries to pull you down to hell. Or the teeth that bite and won't let go. Forget the precious family heirlooms that only sell once a century. Screw rarity value. Screw gentle and refined energies, cold shivers and shy spooks that only pets can see. What she wants is blood curdling screams, spectral gunshots, whispers that lure children away with strangers.

That wrapped up in something chichi.

Like the bronze and ivory figure in the window of a semi-clad maiden by the Gladenbeck foundry in Berlin, incised Gladenbeck Berlin on the back of its base. It stands on a mottled rouge and white marble plinth, chipped on one corner where the statue embedded in the owner's skull. New owners are guaranteed sleepless nights rich with murderous screams.

Like the mid 19th century American rococo carved rosewood tripleback sofa, with floral and fruit-carved crest, carved moulded stiles, padded scrolled arm supports, carved serpentine seat rail, husk-carved cabriole legs. Perfect in the séance room. Probably originated in New York, like the body with multiple stab wounds that folds over it.

Or the gold pendant necklace signed by Bulgari. Eighty circular-cut and oval-shaped rubies weighing exactly 33.00 carats in total centring upon a unique two carats heart-shaped Burmese ruby, adorned by pavé-set diamonds and ruby boules, that will garrotte the person wearing it until they cough up mouthfuls of blood and bleed to death.

Portia strokes her hair. It's all nonsense, she tells herself. Of course. There is no underworld, bursting with trapped souls screaming, reaching up to grab you and pull you down to share their hell with them.

Unless, that is, you want to believe in such nonsense.

Unless, that is, your world is weak enough to be inflamed by the imagination of those who believe in such things.

People like Aurora.

Anyway, whatever, Portia keeps the Bulgari locked up in the safe for protection.

One day she dreams of turning off the television, closing the café for good, ditching the obituary columns and macabre auctions, no longer dreaming of the most horrible hauntings known to man. Why do spooks never do anyone any good? Like you come downstairs and all the housework is done and there's lipstick on the mirror that says You Are Welcome. Or a place just gets this really happy environment for no apparent reason.

"I need you to take Bobo out for a walk first," she says, pointing at the ugly little pug sleeping in the corner of the gallery window. She hands her empty teacup to Aurora and says, "And try to show some respect for the dead. Wear a hat or a veil or something black when you visit Croom's. I mean something classic, not like that scary star thing you always wear."

Aurora pulls up a black leather cord around her neck until the pentacle with an amethyst evil eye pops out the front of her shirt. "It's a pentacle. It wards off evil. Jimmy T gave it to me."

And Portia says, "That weirdo."

She says, "You should use it to scare him off."

And Aurora kisses the pentacle and drops it so it hangs against her chest. "He says it will protect me." The evil eye is smudged with black lipstick.

"Oh, and before you go," Portia says, "get me Quentin Greer on the phone."

Aurora screws up her face. "I wish you wouldn't do this. Black art is bad karma."

Listen, says Portia. She'd love to leave the art world far behind. "Just as soon as Spook Detectives starts paying."

Portia takes the call off hold and says, "Sorry to have kept you." She says the options are this. The art lover can instruct a lawyer if they really want to.

"Or," she says, "we can come to a confidential agreement that I will sell the painting for you for a commission."

At this point, sometimes the art lover wants to say no. But after the evil upside down face appears again and the agonised howling comes down the chimney, or the owner gets the rancid flesh in the bathroom mirror. Well. There is no real alternative.

This owner, naturally taking time to consider the implications of any decision that meddles with concepts like right and wrong, says, "And you won't tell anyone about what happened?"

And Portia says, "We'll just say the red dress clashed with your décor."

If anybody wants to know, tell them you're switching to abstracts. Say you loved that painting like it was part of the family.

She says, "All the rest is classified."

From the next room Aurora says, "I've got Quentin Greer holding."

On the silent television screen the resurrected purple mouse is slicing a dazed cat with a chainsaw.

Portia drops her keys, hits a button and says, "Quentin!"

She mouths *Bye* at Aurora and nods her head in the direction of the window. She plays an imaginary piano with one hand.

The television cat's head, body and legs reassemble themselves only they are an all mixed up mutant.

"Quentin, you and Charmaigne wont believe it. I have found simply the most perfect painting for that dining room of yours."

The gallery door has a little bell that chimes when it opens, chimes when it closes.

And she says, "You're going to love it."

4

Aurora finishes an ice cream. She is sheltering from the sun beneath the pink blossom of a cherry tree in the garden of 32 Croom's Hill.

She is also loitering around a bit because she needs to be in the right frame of mind. She has to be receptive before entering.

As she tunes in, a young couple come out of the house arm in arm and walk backwards towards her down the granite chip driveway.

Smiley Linford from the letting agents, who Aurora has now met several times, is waving them off the premises. He is chubby, middle aged, with a penchant for tight fitting three-piece pinstripes.

The young man nods his head appreciatively towards the elegant twin pillars framing the sandstone entrance of the villa. The girl reads the inscription carved into the banner carried by the two carefully restored cherubs flying above the door.

She points at it then reads it out loud. "All the stars hide their diminished heads," she says.

Then she says, sighing, "These people must have really loved each other."

Aurora twists a dreadlock around her finger, and pops the end in her mouth.

This is 32 Croom's Hill. A double suicide. There are roses up the driveway to the door. Yellow on the left, white to the right. The lawn rolls smoothly around the side of the house. A solitary garden gnome fishes in a small pond. Nearby there is a timber-decked patio with potted geraniums and French windows.

The couple consider the property from the driveway for another minute, they exchange goodbyes with Linford, then turn and walk away slowly into the street. They are so focused on the property that they do not see Aurora standing under the tree. They are still arm in arm when they pause on the corner of Croom's Hill for a last distant view of the grey slate roof.

The former residence of concert pianist James Earnest Hammington and his wife Miriam. Both deceased. Debunked. Gone.

A breeze moves the sweet scent of blossom around Aurora. Something touches her face.

The temperature seems to rise a couple of degrees. When Aurora bites her knuckle hard she can barely feel it.

Stillness falls on the garden.

It's oppressive. Her legs take root in the soil.

She sees things in black and white.

Then she hears it.

A piano. Playing something slow, sad and quiet. It's a tune she has heard before somewhere. Probably on the office radio. Gymnopedie, by someone called Eric Satie.

The music comes from behind the locked French windows but it steals around to the front of the house like cigar smoke.

It reaches out to where she stands. Holds for a few seconds. Then drifts away to nothing.

All the colour comes back into the day.

"Blimey," Aurora says.

She rolls her eyes up to the sky and blows out a big sigh. "Spooky music."

The standard approach to visiting houses like this is that you prepare yourself. You gather all your best most powerful charms about you, in Aurora's case her pentacle choker and crow's foot key ring, and you don't rush. You need to be calm. You don't go into any room you feel you shouldn't. And you never scream. That only makes things worse.

The physical can be straightforward. If there is a pool of blood and a knife spinning on the kitchen floor, try to find out discreetly if everyone can see it or if this is a spectral manifestation.

Not normally difficult.

If the vision is a shadow floating above the bed, or there is a swirling black hole in the fridge, remember gawping will simply draw attention to yourself.

Some spirits will really home in on a communicator. That can spoil your day.

Shouts, jangling chains, rattling keys, blood curdling screams, murdered groans, take them in your stride.

Importantly, confirm that the person showing you around the property has authority to do so.

More importantly, confirm that the person showing you around the property is not the deceased.

This happened once. Aurora thought the sweet old lady was, well, a bit on the grey side. But not dead.

Accept that it can be tricky. It's not every business transaction where you feel for a pulse when you shake a person's hand.

Linford has left the front door open and is beside her under the tree. "Well, I hope you're not going to tell me this is one of *those* places," he says.

"Definitely," says Aurora. "It is very strong. Very dark."

Linford used to be a schoolteacher. He squints back at the house and scratches behind his ear, where his black hair is going grey. He doesn't see anything unusual.

"Were you playing the piano a minute ago?" asks Aurora.

Linford puts both his palms flat against his chest, opens his eyes wide and pulls his mouth down at the edges. "Moi?" he says.

"Thought so. It was coming from that room with the nice windows."

"Well," says Linford, suddenly all excited. "What are we waiting for? Let's go."

He leads her past the pillars into the hall, drenched by sunlight pouring down through a domed cupola. The floor is like glass. To the left an elegant staircase with a balustrade of wrought iron musical notes leads to the upstairs bedrooms. There are fresh flowers cut from the garden on a glass table. Along one wall runs a stanza of black and white photographs of men wearing evening suits and wing collar shirts.

Aurora walks behind Linford. Their footsteps sound like beats on a muffled snare drum.

"I love this place. It is just so classy," Linford says. He would live in it himself he says if the rent was not double what he could afford.

"And then there is, bam bam boom, the music room," he says, standing aside to show Aurora in.

The room runs the length of the house with French windows opening out onto the patio. An upside down wedding cake of a chandelier is showering crystal rainbows onto the walls. A huge piano stands in the centre of the room. The lid is closed.

Linford sits at the piano and runs his hands over the dark wood.

"It's a Steinway model B grand. The kind concert pianists play. Isn't it beautiful? Costs about fifty grand."

Aurora has her crow's foot in her hand. The air in this room is like breathing syrup.

Linford is larking about. He flips up the tail of his pinstripe suit and slowly dances his hands along the piano keys pretending to play.

31

His fingers trace black and white on the keyboard. Black and white. Black and white.

The colour is draining from the day.

Linford's feet are pumping the pedals. His legs are working hard. He brings his face down to the keyboard and splays his arms out either side like a crucifixion.

"This is where they found them, you know." Without looking up at her he says, "Mr and Mrs Hammington."

Aurora is tugging on her crow's foot. It is way too warm in this room.

"Sitting at the piano. Pills and vodka. She had cancer. So he did her first, then did himself."

Linford hits a weird series of notes then plays them off one another with discordant harmonies.

"Had a poly bag over his head. Couldn't bear to live without her. You could say he died broken hearted," Linford says, swaying. "But that wouldn't be the whole truth."

The average medium sized piano has about two hundred and thirty strings. Each string has about a hundred and sixty five pounds of tension. That makes the combined pull of all strings approximately eighteen tons. Aurora feels all the pressure on her temples. It squeezes her head and makes her feel sick. Linford and the piano grow small and distant. Down the wrong end of a telescope.

"One of these things sold in the States for over a million dollars couple of years back. It was all painted with classical scenes on the lid and had ivory and mother-of-pearl and stuff," Linford says.

"The musos that played it all signed it inside to leave their mark. There was Richard Rodgers of Rodgers and Hammerstein, Sir Arthur Sullivan of Gilbert and Sullivan."

Aurora needs air but the patio doors are locked. Her hair is standing up.

Linford thumps the keys with his forehead. "There is no perfect way to play Beethoven's thirty two piano sonatas. No matter how hard you try. It is an Everest. That's why there are so many imperfect recordings.

"The great maestro, Solomon tried. He worked out a way to do them all perfectly. It was real blood sweat and tears. He dedicated years of his life to their study until he was note perfect. His interpretations were free of distortion. His concentration on slow tempos was unfaltering. His playing had a majestic sweep that made other pianists sound routine.

"Then just as he was almost finished he suffered this massive stroke."

The striking of the keys, the pumping of the pedals, stops. Aurora cannot remember Linford ever talking about unfaltering concentration on slow tempos.

His head rests on the piano keys. The eyes are shut. He could be talking in his sleep. "Those sonatas, opus ten number three, opus ninety and opus one hundred and ten were the last thing he ever played. He was left paralyzed for the remaining thirty two years of his life."

He says just listen to Solomon's finale of Waldstein. The music moves with microscopic accuracy. In the following rondo, the four-bar tune flows so easily that it sounds andante, though the marking is allegretto moderato. But it has the rhythmic and dynamic potential to let the rondo achieve overwhelming power.

Linford is levitating off the stool and moaning. His groans sound far away and hollow. Little blue sparks crackle between his fingers. His eyes begin to pulse with light.

As though he has a lighthouse in his head.

When he looks at her, Aurora is zapped by two powerful beams from his eyes and a blast of air from his mouth that smells of blocked drains. It almost knocks her down.

With one hand on her crow's foot and another reaching for her pentacle, she focuses on the piano through the whip of air and buzz of electricity.

The great beast of a piano. The lid is snapping open and shut like jaws. The keys rattling in great munching swoops from down low to up high.

She takes a step. The whole thing rears up on hind legs at her like a horse.

Linford is spinning, eyes beaming out rays of light. Aurora reaches out her crow's foot to touch him but her arms are weighed down by a hundred gravities. It takes all her strength to lift a hand. It seems to take a lifetime to lift and aim the key ring into the jaws of the snarling piano.

There is a frazzling blue flash. Then a sucking up of all the energy in the room, an implosion more than an explosion.

Daylight returns.

There remains a strange smouldering smell.

Aurora realises this is coming from her hair.

"Blimey," she says, rubbing the ends of one frazzled rats tail between her hands.

Linford, wearing a new crop of white hair he hasn't seen yet, looks up at her from the piano. He picks the crow foot off the keyboard with a puzzled expression.

He holds it out like it is something nasty and says, "This one of yours mate?"

5

This should have been a love story. Our love story. Aurora and me. The Jimmy T and Aurora showboat. But somehow all the holding of hands, the tenderest silent moments, the shared smiles and passions, the love that makes love wonderful, it doesn't make it through to here. To the where I am now. Don't ask me where. You're not ready for that yet.

Many of the smallest details have already moved out of the reach of memory and now my imagination wants to remould reality.

Add to that how, when it comes to the truth, there is always the complication of individual perspective and you might start to understand my case.

So I'm telling it as I remember it. In real time, as best as I can while I think it over.

They say the world is full of miracles but the miracles that most people see are, in truth, only things they can reach out and touch.

I'm in this café next to Aurora, people watching. She has dyed her hair red and wears big sunglasses. Every so often she blows on a charm she wears around her neck and uses it to tickle my nose.

"Jimmy T," she says. "I love you."

But when Aurora holds me close, despite it all, I am uncomfortable that she still loves me.

Anyway.

This isn't a story about what's happening in my life now. Me, Aurora, Portia Maxwell and everyone at the Psychic Deli. What I need to focus on, what I need to explain, even if

I have to start over from the beginning, is the truly amazing thing that happened. How we ever got to be together here in the first place.

6

this relates to me in the here before I was dead, not the after now.

The Red Rooster bar clings onto the cliff like the parrot on Long John's shoulder.

Yanis too stares out into the plum dark night and points over the med to where the horizon crackles open, momentarily slit by a distant crimson. This distracts the half dozen tourists sitting around patio tables.

"That's Syria," he says to me, pointing with his loaded corkscrew.

"Jes-us," I say.

The coast is only sixty miles away. If over there lies the road to Damascus then Cyprus, specifically here in northern Cyprus, is the last lay-by. It is the penultimate stop before somewhere more interesting.

That sums up my life, my withering. With a degree in archaeology, while I am here I should have been down in the dirt with the others rebuilding the Roman gymnasium at Salamis, or scouring for links with Atlantis (in my imagination at least), then out tracing the steps of Crusaders on mountain goat paths. But since the only job I can get is stuffing dead animals for the Natural History Museum, I would rather sit on my hands at present thank you very much. Not that I am entirely lost to history though. In the end I became a taxidermist because: one, I always wanted to work with animals; two, that, plus the lure of the macabre. In Mexico the dead roam free on the Day Of The Dead to pass their wisdom to the living. So here I am, a conduit for wisdom if you like.

I have not come here for friendship or for love. I have not come here for frolicking on the beaches, although I did once consider an eighteen thirty sand and booze holiday somewhere in the touristy south of the island. But that was before I grew wise to the attraction of the unattainable. Now that I know my limitations, I happily brought my mirror sunglasses for undetectable letching and, I have to admit, I have perfect technique.

Only when you become aware of it does time pass too slowly. Crazy ideas begin to take shape. Perhaps role acting beneath this tree, this centre of the universe for idlers, was a challenge to the spirits that run this place and the deep feelings that waft around the sandy soil and pomegranate trees.

It is baking hot and if it wasn't for the tourists I might have given up on my navel gazing. Then I would have missed it. The changing.

This trip was meant to be solitary from the start. I had always promised myself that when I hit thirty I would give myself a timeout to consider all the options. So here I am, holidaying under this thing they call the Tree Of Idleness, to celebrate my uselessness.

I took a room at the Tree of Idleness Inn overlooking the ancient abbey at Bellapais and for seven days plumped myself in the shade of their mulberry tree, scratching that day's new growth on my chin and swigging bottles of Bud after lunch. The coach parties come and go all afternoon, and I pose by turns as a philosopher or a writer to enhance their tourist experience and freeload the odd beer. But by dusk the game is over and the locals descend on their café to reclaim it with salads from the groves, jugs of icky sweet red wine and a lazy conversation.

We all waited. Counting the seconds after every flash. No sound of an explosion came.

"It's the Americans. They're using new stealth bombs," says someone at another table, their nervous laughter sounding outlandishly English. Everyone except Yanis laughs. He pours me a glass of house red, his eyes two halves of the one black olive.

I worry it might be true.

"It's not the Americans is it Yanis?"

"No, no, no," he says, quiet for only me to hear. "Let them worry. It keeps them drinking. This is only a far off storm."

He smacks the cork back into my half done bottle with a deliberate little thunderclap of his own.

"Are you certain?"

"For sure. My brother is out there fishing. I spoke to him," Yanis touches his mobile phone attached to his belt.

I am struck by the vulgarity of sitting snacking char grilled artichoke drizzled in fresh olive oil and the sweetest rosemary while Yanis's brother risks his life for tuna. I visualise him alone in his little brightly painted wooden boat, an evil eye on the prow, locked in an ancient life or death struggle with the tempestuous elements.

"I wouldn't go out in that for tuna," I say. I ask for more crusty bread.

"Sometimes it is not always the fish that are the catch," Yanis says. This time he touches the side of his nose. "Remember, the worst of seas and the darkest of skies can be the best of friends."

Did the Saviour ever take a holiday in Cyprus, a thirty something like me, in retreat from the Holy Land? I'm thinking about this and other things like it, such as why I have started smoking Winstons when I have been on nicotine replacement patches for three months, when from out of nowhere some girl flops down on the bench beside me fluffing at a fly bothering the jelly baby beads in her hair.

Here, in the pupil of the tree, the Buds are warm as soon as they come out of the cooler. So I drink too fast and think of Lana. Lana. Lunch at the Tree of Idleness has just finished and I am lost down the front of the waitress's shirt as she wipes the tables. Lana is from Kyrenia and drives up the dusty hillside to Bellapais by vespa everyday. She has dark cinnamon curls but, unfortunately, she also has a faint moustache.

Then this new girl turns to me. Where did she come from? I didn't see her having lunch in the restaurant. I do that move where you half take off the sunglasses, peering over the top, and I see she's wearing faded jeans with a trendy cut across the knee and a white t-shirt with a print of a giant turtle face on it. The face is smiling banally and the words Loggerheads Are Cool pop out like cartoon screams around its head. On her neck she's got a string of little white seashells on a purple thread. The shells have a pink tinge from her skin. The skin of her leg is also new arrival pink. It might be something to do with the sun filtering through the leaves above, but she has these amber coloured eyes with a blue ring around the iris that you sometimes see on animals like a lizard or a goat or an alligator, that remind me, for certain, of something ancient.

"How can you bear to smoke in this heat?" she says, jingling the little gemstones on her bracelet when she waves her hand up and down under her nose.

I am not a smoker, in my heart of hearts, but here I go defending it. "How can you bear not to? It keeps the pests away."

"I'm not a bug," she says, settling into the dapple on

40

her face. "And if you really want to keep away from insects you should try sitting in a citrus grove. They don't like it there."

She pauses. I sense her slowing. Maybe it is the Bud. Or maybe it is the influence of the tree.

"But it is very nice here," she says in a whisper, as if suddenly she is talking to another person, someone sitting between us, up-close beside her.

I say, "It is."

I pick Aurora up at her hotel. She is on a fortnight's eco holiday to save the turtles. She paid her own flights and Turtle Watch gave her a room in the trendy sounding Hotel Eco which she shares with comrade ecology warrior Lotte. Their hotel is a squat and prickly arrangement of concrete cubes and satellite dishes nowhere near the busy little harbour of Kyrenia with its cafés. The Russians built it as part of their cold war economic push into Turkey. Now, apart from the eco warriors being parachuted in, it is a tourist free zone. I cannot decide whether the environmentalists are here to save the turtles from extinction or boost the crumbling economy.

Eco's verandas are a messy charity shop of dried out bedclothes, t-shirts and dried out people.   Local youths hang about the reception desk, smoking and playing table tennis. Aurora thinks they are being put up by social services. Proper paying guests would revolt at the rundown air conditioning and walls that sweat at night, she says. The brochure gave it seafront views, but a wave of concrete blocks overlooks the small rooftop pool.

Eating out with Aurora is an experience. We are in the Beijing Star and I don't know where to look. She scoops her arms around, flopping them forwards at the elbows. She says two kinds of turtles lay their eggs near here, the green turtle chelonian mydas and the loggerheads, her favourites, the caretta caretta. They drag themselves across the unspoiled beaches that form the frying pan handle of the island, moving in this unbelievably clumsy way out of their natural element. All that dragging, all that sand in your eyes and mouth, then all the pain of turtle egg laying.

"It's anguishing," she says.

And while the rest of the Med got tourism, Cyprus got war. Aurora says the only good thing was that it remained an undeveloped natural haven for the turtles. "They've been swimming around the oceans for more than a hundred and fifty million years," she says. "They were doing fine until we came along mucking about with the environment, destroying their habitat."

I say things will be better now we have her ecological army.

Aurora leans over her prawn cocktail, half hiding her mouth behind a glass of lemony New World chardonnay. "It's worse than you think. That's why I brought you here."

From behind the screen of our quiet corner table the Beijing Star appears normal enough. "What do you mean? Surely it's not turtle soup?"

"No stupid," Aurora says. She's smiling, but it is only day two night one and she is already calling me stupid.

"It's them," She drops her hand, lets it brush against mine. I get this tingle in my fingers. Then she nods towards the only other people in the place. She says, "The Chinese are coming."

According to the placemats, this is first Chinese restaurant in the north. The red lanterns dangling over each table, the stork posters with stringy zen writing, perfectly matching cutlery, it all has the feeling of being fresh out of the packing case.

"Coming to take us away? Ha Ha. Ho Ho."

"Worse than that."

She clasps her hands around mine and glances sideways at the two Chinese men at the other table, an odd but perfectly legitimate combination of an older fat man and a thin man.

There's this tingling again and I feel the hairs stand up on the back of my neck.

"Listen," she says.

Foo wears his hair cut tight on the nape of his neck but jags up a long spear at the front with egg white. He saw the effect in some western magazines. He thinks the image makes the joint more sophisticated, in contrast to its faux Chinoiserie, the silly lanterns and traditional prints.

"Stop posing like a bloody rock star or something," Chi says, in the way a certain boss can talk to his staff like he is one of the family.

"Film star," Foo replies, emptying a plate of cigarette buts into the tin bin beneath the bar.

"Wannabee," laughs Chi, waving a freshly dismembered prawn tail at him. And he sighs. For that is what young single men alone in the world are allowed to be. It is a comfort for them to be dreamers.

Chi nudges the barman in the small of back as he squeezes past into the kitchen. He tuts and shakes his head. Wan has disappeared again. With no chef, he has to see to the deep fried spicy tiger prawns.

The air in the kitchen was bad because it was hot and the fan was broken. The high notes of decaying flesh were concentrated around a worktable where three large carp heads pointed upwards like the Sydney Opera House, bobbing along on a mushy sea of vegetable skins and prawn shells. Wreaths of chicken skin tumbled across the floor where Wan had thrown them in the general direction of the overflowing bin. There, the biggest fly party of the summer was in full swing amid the various entrails.

Chi found two dozen defrosted tiger prawns in a basin in the sink.

He pulled the soft legs off one large shrimp.

"These are good and fat," he called through to the bar. He picked one up and held it against the bare light bulb, savouring its translucence. Keeping the shell on the prawns, Chi lined them up into two irregular rows of legless soldiers, black eyes staring into black eyes. Chi always prepared prawns like this, hoping in a miserable way that if the spirit of a prawn could comprehend he would see that his fate was not unique and understand, in the mirror image of his own death, both the futility and beauty of prawn life. He was impotent, but at least he was juicy.

"Whoever the hell's out there better get me some wine before I die of thirst," yelled Chi.

Foo stuck his spiky head through the serving hatch.

"I'm Max. I'll get you some wine."

Chi saw that this was how it was going to be from then on. Foo was gone, Max had arrived. The hair was going to be up.

He dried the prawns one by one and piled them into a bowl.

"OK Max. None of the plummy local stuff either. Get some French."

There was a whoop from next door. Chi smiled as he spooned the prawns. "Rice wine is better for cooking anyway," he said, pouring a splash of Shaoxing over them. Then he added a glug of light soy sauce and a couple of teaspoonfuls of corn flour, turning the prawns in the marinade.

"Max has found this, or this." Foo clanked two bottles together. "Semillon or Chardonnay? What's it to be Chi?"

"We'll start with the Semillon, Max-Semillon of course," said Chi, pulling two glasses down from the shelf. He spilled the spices onto the table - a star anise, fennel seeds, cloves, cinnamon bark, and a handful of black Szechuan peppercorns - and using the flat blade of a cleaver, rolled the heel of his palm over it time after time, until he crushed them together. He added a dozen crystals of raw sea salt, crushed some more, paused to wipe the blade, chopped a little, then crushed the spices again.

Chi worked the cleaver while Foo hacked the cork free.

Chi reached out his glass, grunting at Foo to pour. The spices in the pan made Foo cough.

Chi laughed. "Here's to you Max. And that old Foo, where ever he's gone to."

"I never liked him anyway," said Foo, gulping the cool wine.

Chi removed the spices from the heat then turned the flame higher on an oil-filled wok. It started to smoke.

"What plans for Max?" he asked as he dropped five prawns into the wok to deep fry. "Does this new name bring a new man?"

Foo gurgled the wine on his throat and studied Chi's narrow back as he scooped the spices into a bowl. The boss, fifty, small, grey and calm, had been good to him.

"You've been good to me boss," he said, feeling a surge of sentimentality. "But one day I'd like to be boss myself."

"One day you will be. Way things are going here." Chi hesitated a second, then scooped the golden brown prawns from the wok with a slotted spoon. He laid them on paper to drain and dipped another five beneath the surface of the sizzling oil.

"Maybe I could run one of the new casinos you've been talking about with them."

"Maybe."

A flame kissed the lip of the iron bowl.

Chi unearthed two shards of spring onion and started slicing. "OK Max. Where do you see yourself in five years?"

"I want to be rich. I want a Porsche."

"Convertible?"

"Sure. And an American girlfriend. A pop singer. One that sticks her boobies out and wears nun costumes on stage. That sort of girl, you have to be rich for."

"So Max wants sex. And a Porsche."

"And I want to travel the world to see the great places. New York, London, Paris, Egypt's pyramids."

"Wow. That's a good holiday."

"And everyone knows who I am."

Chi tipped the remaining prawns into the oil. "There's hundreds of millions of Chinese out there. All us boys can't all make it with the same Yankee baby."

Foo looked away. He did not know. Something inside told him that he was better than all this, that there was opportunity out there waiting for him to grasp it, that his destiny was great. But he did not know.

Chi's calm voice rolled on. He enjoyed cooking prawns and these looked spectacular. He spread them evenly on two square blue-glazed earthenware plates.

"My philosophy," he said, pouring a little of the hot oil over the chopped onion leaves, "is that there will always be mouths to feed and thirst to quench. Eating never goes out of fashion."

He garnished the prawns with the onions and handed Foo a plate. "That's for you. Bring the wine through."

The back door slides open and Wan, the usual cigarette dangling from the side of his mouth, meat cleaver in hand, tells Foo to chill out. "All you need is a glass of Shaoxing and five minutes on the kitchen floor with Yao."

Yao appears from somewhere behind the bins,

smoothing down her hair, hitching up her too tight jeans. The smell of rotting vegetables and flesh, her skin gritty with street dust.

She thumped Wan on the head. "And that is why you are always going to be last in line. On this earth and whatever stinking planet it is you come from."

A little sweat trickled down Wan's neck. He ran his thumb along the edge of his cleaver, staring tensely at Yao's breasts.

"Maybe just one more little stir fry then. Something special for the customers." His tongue flicked out-and-in like a snake. Wan hissed. "Sweet little pork belly. Sweet little shrimp."

Yao got behind Foo, draped her arms around his neck and taunted Wan. "Now, here's a nice young man who knows how to treat a lady."

Foo could tell Wan had been drinking. So when he made short chopping thrusts at Yao with his cleaver, he stepped back.

Wan was less than half joking. "That bitch Yao. She comes in here, we feed her for free, she fucks our customers and she tells me I'm stinking. Who does she think she is?"

Carefully, letting Wan see he was smiling, Foo turned Wan around and pushed him out the door minus the cleaver. Wan did not resist.

Wan gave him a serious look. "You make it up to the boss for me, eh?"

"Sure," said Foo. He handed Wan a bottle of rice wine. "Take this shit and go home."

When the door closes Foo collects his prawns and follows Yao into the Beijing Star. Chi is in the corner booth with the two men who have now finished their meals. They are smoking from the one packet of Marlboro Lights. Both are in baggy cream linen suits and Panamas with an ivory coloured ribbon. The shorter, older, fatter man has pushed his hat back off his forehead so that he can frequently mop his bald head with a soggy handkerchief. The other's face is hidden to the nostrils by hat brim. Out from under this a thin pencil moustache sprouts above white rat's teeth. Foo glimpses badly pockmarked skin on the man's face.

Foo, son of LeCheung of Shanghai, met and shook hands with Dr Sun and LM.

"LM?" he asked, then wished he hadn't for fear of being impolite.

The scratchy moustache rose to allow a little smile. The head tilted back and Max felt easier at the sight of the man's brown Chinese eyes.

"Love Missile. My parents were part of a Mongolian commune dedicated to the space race. Father was a rocket engineer. He believed that the future lay in rocket propulsion, which was quite right."

Chi's laugh settled Max, who had shuffled a bit uneasily through this introduction.

"We tend to use our initials these days, but I have three sisters. Space Launcher, Nose Cone, and Saturn Five. My brother is Mission Control. He has two daughters, Google and Yahoo. See how times change?"

"No bad thing," agreed Sun. "I know a dentist in Kowloon called Fear."

The men laughed together, Foo eating next to Chi, LM and Dr Sun, sipping iced water and the Beijing Star's best Chablis.

Chi says they are in Cyprus as part of a trade delegation. But his real purpose, his secret mission, says Dr Sun, is to write a movie about life in old Shanghai. Dr Sun's talents as a writer, rather than his medical skills, would at last be recognised. It was to be an epic love and murder story, set against the opium trade and city's 668 brothels, of the British Club, the Whangpoo River and the magnificent

Yangtze estuary.

"Murder," says LM, who evidently knows the script, "was never so beautiful. Death was never so sweet as when life depended upon it."

Dr Sun laughs. "You know Max, when I was a boy, about fifty years ago, just down the Chunghua Road in the old city, a few pennies would get you a nine year old virgin for an hour?"

"Price has changed I bet," says Yao, stirring her coca cola.

"Everything has changed. Think of The British Club, where the great taipans sipped their stengahs and dreamed of their empire ruling the waves. I know it's a hostel now, but imagine," Dr Sun draws a square in the air "how in the film the Japanese are moving in, taking over, cutting the legs off the tables and chairs for their short arsed officers. As if that was ever going to be permanent in our Shanghai.

"Think of that day, the last old boy out kissing his China beauty farewell." Dr Sun stood up and saluted the young English couple who seemed totally engrossed in one another at the rear of the restaurant. "So-long-honey-I'll-be-back-with-the-fleet-by-Christmas."

He tumbled down again, laughing. "Ahh. Her oriental beauty is stained by salt tears. After all, her whole life is going out that door with him. She's invested everything making him happy. When he goes, it's back to being a whore or a concubine for her if she's lucky. But she understands. She realises he will not take her with him. The great and powerful European has a lot on his plate. One tear runs along the crevice of her lips. Until she licks it away, tasting the misery. AND THEN SHE SMILES."

Sun yells out in a climax, throwing both arms above his head so suddenly Foo and Chi miss a beat in their eating.

"What's she got to be so happy about?" asked Foo.

"She knows it's going to look good in a movie somewhere," jabbed LM.

Chi waved a hand in front of his face. "The Japanese came. That was no laughing matter."

"No, not a laughing matter," Sun sobered up. "Not for our girl, our courtesan. Let's call her Lilly. Today, it's Lilly anyway."

"Our Lilly, however, is very good. She has learned a lot with her Englishman gentleman. Remember, she is a tiger from the streets of Shanghai who has clawed her way up in life, killed her rapist father, drowned her own bastard daughter at birth. That sort of thing. She's tough this one."

Cool as he was able, Foo blew a stream of cigarette smoke over the doctor's head.

"And when the Japanese arrive, there's a gecko general that needs his home comforts to come back to after being out chopping off heads all day. See? Lilly does. And she learns some more. That to survive is more important than dying."

Dr Sun mops his face with a napkin then wipes inside his hat.

"One night this general goes berserk. His men have been getting shot at in the old town. The prisons are full to bursting, you know, he can't get his favourite sake imported. So he's chopped heads. Chop, chop, chop. All day. He's raped little girls. Forced water and hot chillies up their fathers' nose. Put on those favourite shoes, the pair with metal spikes for toes, and kicked the prisoners all over. No joy.

"So he takes it out on Lilly. He asks her again and again. Demands she tells him what he wants to know. Who are the communists? Where are their leaders? Lilly is so afraid, she's seen the film of Japanese soldiers cutting people in half and tied-up prisoners being fed to the dogs.

"Yuk," Foo says. He can barely contain himself with excitement. "And then?"

"And then love comes to the rescue. A young man, perhaps a lowly barman like you Max, has secretly worshipped Lilly from a distance. She is too important for me, he thinks. But he tries little things. Like eye contact. Or, when he serves her a drink, his hand will rest momentarily too close to hers so that the tiniest hairs on his skin brush against hers. Gradually she notices this handsome young man. And amid all the pressure and terrors of their lives, in Shanghai they find true love."

"So do they run away together Sun?" asked Chi.

"Yes. But it is not so simple. They know the Japanese will hunt them down. So they have a plan. Vowing to love one another for eternity, Lilly tells her cruel master that the young man is a communist leader. At first he is furious and grabs for his sword. But Lilly is persistent, here. She has to be. And she convinces the general that one communist is not enough. Let her infiltrate, gain his confidence, and she will present him with the entire Shanghai communist party. She wins the day." Sun sat back like a defence lawyer resting his case.

"I don't get it," says Foo.

"It means they can spend time alone together," says Chi. "But how do they get out of it?"

Dr Sun crossed his arms. "I'm still working on that part. But remember, Shanghai was a terrible place. I have one ending in mind. The secret lovers meet in his house, always watched from outside by the Japanese. It is a terrible time. They are so afraid, but risking all for love. With immense stealth, they prepare a tunnel underneath the house that will take them well away. Then, as the time draws near, they collect a couple of bodies. A man and a woman, there are plenty of them in open pits all over Shanghai. They steal the bodies to the house, up the tunnel so the Japs don't see them, then set fire to the lot of them and escape back down the tunnel."

"Where do they go Sun?" asked Chi.

"I don't know, get a boat up the Yangtze. Go find the real communists. Or maybe it doesn't matter. You know how these arty farty films are. They run away together into the night leaving the blazing house behind them."

"Anything's possible. Maybe the war ends the next day," says LM.

Foo could hold back no more. "Who plays Lilly?"

"Hush! Big business likes secrets," whispers Dr Sun, looking around the Beijing Star. "But if I get the cooperation I'm hoping for, we're looking at a big star. A big American star."

Foo's mind swooned. Chi felt him tremble and was a little embarrassed for the boy.

They moved onto the case of Buds stacked in the cooler.

With all the story telling, no one noticed exactly when the two customers left. But the hippy English girl and her zombie boyfriend, who Dr Sun diagnosed as drunk comatose, left behind the correct money.

Dr Sun goes for a pee and when he returns he has Yao on his arm. She sits on Sun's knee, laughing with the men, playing catch up drinking two Bacardi's and coke to every Bud for the men.

"It's fucking amazing," says Foo. He waves another empty can of coca cola up to Yao's face. "The money they make from this stuff would make us all millionaires."

"Why rely upon black capitalist sludge when we got other resources?" says Yao, pointing at her crotch.

Dr Sun slips his hand up the back of Yao's shirt and Foo watches the podgy bump move like a spider around her body until it comes to rest over her left breast. It starts quivering. Yao, thinks Foo, isn't so bad. She is about thirty, slender enough, but has a bad inward squint in her right eye. Sometimes when you thought she was looking at you fiercely she was, in fact, looking in totally the opposite direction. She had a good mouth, he thought, only too used to rough kissing and too often bruised.

Dr Sun jiggled her up and down on his lap like a child, but the effort caused a fresh eruption of his sticky sweat. "We all have our business interests at heart now, don't we?"

"If you say so," Yao says in a little girl voice. Foo sees her squeeze her buttocks tightly into Sun's groin.

Next time Foo looks, Yao is kissing Sun full on the mouth.

LM leaned forward and inspected the couple closely for a few seconds then winked over to Foo.

"Big tongues," he laughed.

All three stare for longer than is polite. When Dr Sun made jerky movements with his hips, it was Chi who cleared his throat first.

"Ah. Funny thing about Coca Cola, Max. These characters, here see?"

Foo read out loud: "Can Mouth, Can Happy?"

"Yes. But."

Chi scrawled imaginary characters in the air which Foo and LM tried to follow.

"The original, in American, see it wouldn't read like this. In the original, it says: Bite The Wax Tadpole."

LM grasped the thread. "Yankee slogans often lose in translation. It's the same with Kentucky Fry Chicken. Have you seen the posters? I saw them in Hong Kong. Old Colonel Saunders, he's telling the Americans: Finger Lickin Good. Translate that and you get: Eat Your Fingers Off."

"I also heard, and this is true," said Chi, "that this beer called Coors, from Canada, once had a slogan

Turn It Loose. They meant, go for the wild time, have fun living now. That sort of thing. But when they sold the beer in Spain..."

Chi waves his hand in front of his face, forcing the words out through laughter "...it was: Drink Coors, Get Diarrhoea."

Chi gasped the words out and disintegrated into a wheezing fit. LM shrieked and thumped his fist onto the table. Foo choked, belched, coughed and hooted. "Stupid fucking Spanish."

Dr Sun heard the laughter like rumbling thunder on a hillside very far away. Yao was some kisser, he thought, and she was gonna be a great fuck. That's if he could keep it up. This time, yes, don't tense up now, yes, he tried to relax as her big wet tongue rolled round and round the hollow of his mouth, there was definitely something stirring down there in the dark, damp, previously assumed dead part between his legs.

Yao, sensing the time was right, pulled him to his feet. "Outa here boys. We're going for stroll."

"Goodnight. Tomorrow, tomorrow, tomorrow," Sun says to everyone.

Squinty Yao looks into the room and out of the door at the same time. "Night night," she raises a hand at Foo and Chi. Then she leans over to LM and kisses his ear and says: "You wanna come fuckey me too?"

LM keeps three fingers pressed against his temple.

Outside the night air is still and warm. Sun props himself against a wall, beneath the orb of the red silk lantern decorated with a cartoon monkey in the branches of a Heaven tree hiding from a contorted but fierce stalking tiger. Bugger the sexual adventures. Sun simply knows he could sleep soundly under such a mystical blood red full moon.

Yao hisses and tuts. It is two fucking am. She looks, hands on hips, up and down the deserted street. Sun lurches forwards with a finger raised and calls out to a phantom taxi. Yao catches him as he trips on the kerb. "Let's walk. It's not far," she says. She slips her hand inside his rear pocket and steers his buttock.

"So what kind of doctor are you, Sun?"

"I am a doctor of life," Sun replies.

Yao steadies him, squinting ahead and to the dim lanes that yawn for her. "Me too. Guess we're the same. We make people happy, right?"

"Uh-huh."

"And life's too short for time wasters, huh?" Her hand massages Sun's wobbling buttock.

"Life is too short."

Two streets from the Beijing Star, they fall spiralling down a lane. Sun skids over a rusting paint pot and sprawls on his back. Those distant blurred stars. He is concerned that he cannot recognise the constellations. He cannot even find that blistering red moon he saw a minute ago.

Yao is kneeling beside him undoing his fly. "Life is too short Dr Sun. But the night is warm. And we must make the time work for us. Now what you going to give me? What you got in there for Yao?"

Her head lowers and Sun feels the warmth of her mouth. He looks down on her bobbing black head and wishes, oh dear, how he wishes he could just relax. Get it over with. Let her have it.

Yao is thinking the same thought.

Sun clears his throat. Talking helps him relax.

"I am a doctor of genetics, Yao. I study the genetic structure of natural populations. It is as dangerous to be conspicuously above a certain standard of organic excellence as it is to fall short of the standard. Science has proved this through study of organisms such as snails, lizards, ducks and chickens."

Yao responds to Sun's mumblings, what she assumes are her patient's groans of delight, with vigour.

"Humans are not exempt from selection for optimum values. The ideal birth weight, that which has the highest proportion of survivors, is eight pounds. Any more or less, ah, nah, the smaller the numbers which survive between birth and one month of age. Genetic death is the enemy, not actual death. Genetic death is sterility. Not being able to find a mate. Genetic perfection, lack of genetic death, never happens. Environmental changes, see, take care of that. Get smug, wow, ahh, nature teaches you. The peasants. The peasants. Used to eat their children. In the famine, gnaw at the bones of their daughters. Especially daughters. Like you. Oh. Yao. Steal babies. Sell it as rabbit meat. Or pay fines for, for having more than one child. Mothers spraying milk from their nipples when they hear a child cry in the street. Selection. See? Yao. Do you see? China is too big. Too big. Nobody knows how many lost daughters. Thousands.Thousands.Thousands."

Sun bit his knuckle and closed his eyes tightly as Yao held him in one hand.

"Man has forty six chromosomes. Twenty three pairs. Twenty two are autosomes. One pair, sex chromosomes. In males, sex chromosomes are X and Y. Females it's two X's. Y makes a man. Like Y-Fronts. That's how I remember. It's sex. Sex, sex, sex."

Yao has to put her spare hand over Sun's mouth to stop the screams as he orgasms. She feels him judder just once, then he lies still beneath her. She thinks, that wasn't too bad. Then she wipes her hand clean on his trousers.

She smiles at Sun. "Now I've given you my medicine doc what you going to prescribe me?"

After his first ejaculation in ten years, Sun is slipping in and out of consciousness. Yao did up his fly.

"That's a good doctor. I thought you didn't like me, first. Little Yao was worried you prefer to play Flower in the Back Garden, with Mr LM."

She tapped Sun's jacket pockets for his wallet. Yao took a twenty from the wedge of US dollars, held it out for Sun to see, then put the wallet back in his pocket.

"Consultation fee," she says. "I think maybe you need come clinic again soon."

Beneath the violeting morning sky, propped on a pile of rubbish, Sun watches Yao's silhouette disappear out of the alley. He takes his wallet out of his jacket and puts it under his hat for safe keeping. The stars were almost blanched by dawn.

Sex, he told himself, was still a mystery. He wondered what phase the moon was in, what time of day ejaculation had taken place, the wind direction, whether the right or left testicle was involved and if it was at all possible for his semen to make its way through Yao's stomach and into her womb. Maybe there was something, a solitary spermatozoa, wriggling right now on her finger. Waiting for the big chance.

Inside. Chi trusts Foo to lock up in return for being allowed to sleep on the premises.

LM plays with the dregs of a Bud. His face is red and puffed from drink, but he is not absent minded. He dips his finger into the wine and outlines an equilateral triangle on the table. Foo recognises the triad symbolism.

"You know who," LM said. "Man, Heaven and Earth. The Heaven and Earth Society, the Three Dots Society and the Three Harmonies Society. What about you Max?"

Foo takes the glasses from the table and wipes it clean with a cloth. "I have heard about these things. But I do not understand them. I know there was a man who had a magnificent coffin delivered to his home. The next day he gathered his family, sold his business and left the village."

"A student of Tzu," laughed LM. "Subdue the enemy without fighting. What about Green Gangs? Blue Gangs? And then there's Red Gangs. The Hung League. The Restoration Society."

LM takes off his hat, strokes the brim, puts it back on. "Old Shanghai has not all gone forever you know. Have you even heard of the Blue Villa?"

Foo puts on a dumb face. "Is this film research?"

LM laughs. "Film research my arse. Or Sun's arse. History? Don't tell me it has all gone away. It is still there, only the world has evolved and moved things around a bit. Don't tell me you never heard of Blue Villa? The girls then were very young, twelve maybe. Exquisite in loose silk trousers, jackets with high wing collars up to their cheekbones. The nights were legendary. Do you think legends can simply die?"

Foo had read somewhere about fabled nights at the Blue Villa, where curtains of hundreds and thousands of blue macaroni shaped glass beads screened every window and doorway. Perched on a hill secluded by a wall of old maples it was now the home of a wealthy cobbler and his family. Foo wondered if the cobbler was a foot pervert who had actually bought the villa because of its history of making sport from crippled feet. How cruel love seemed. He had never understood anyone wanting to fondle and suck deformed feet, even if it was a national pass time. They would stroke, sniff, lick and linger over a girl's twisted feet for hours. The more deformed by bandaging the better. He had heard of a girl losing a toe or two in the buckling process. Give him a breast any day. Not a foot.

At the Blue Villa there had been spectacular nights with thousands of performances of toe sucking. The peasants who could not afford such delights were equally besotted by it. If they ever managed to get their hands on one of the girl's tiny silk shoes then they would surely have sex with it before handing it back.

Another favourite was eating almonds from the girl's toes. They must have been jammed in first, Foo thought, because the foot was dead. As soon as he could, some guy'd pop her tiny feet onto his shoulders, stick her Gold Lotus big toe in his gob, and suck furiously until the moment of Clouds And Rain.

"That was all a long time ago," Foo said.

LM nodded and rubbed the back of his neck. He tilted the brim of his hat lower than ever across his face.

He said: "Say, I got you into the movie."

Foo's heart skipped a beat.

"Nothing too big, but a start. Maybe you'd keep an eye on the American girl or something. Ya'd like that huh?"

Foo smiled and waited. He was good at waiting.

"Well, it's yours. If ya want it. All you got to do for me is a small favour."

"Such as?"

"We are sitting drinking and talking here like there is no tomorrow. But what if I was to tell you that there is a tomorrow coming and that this tomorrow is going to rain down so much money on us like it will be a gold rush? That this barren dusty nothing is the new gold coast? All along here, there's an adventure wonderland of opportunity. I expect you'd say give it to me, I want part of the action, of course."

Foo tried to smile without looking stupid.

LM picks at his sharpest rat's teeth. "The new Blue Villa will be just along the road a little way from here. That stretch of olive groves that reach down to the sea? My accomplices are already buying the land. I have seen the plans for hotels so grand they have skyscrapers for car parks, marinas you can only dream of. Golf courses with gold plated holes.

Restaurants where the famous celebrities will hang out, casinos with fountains of champagne. This is all going to happen, for real."

Foo thought about the undeveloped potential of this paradise.

LM says: "The Med is the playground of the rich and famous not this wilderness from the Dark Ages. Evolution is on its way, Max. Soon there will be a pleasure paradise here too. Money is coming."

LM winked.

"Big stars, you know Maxxie, they want looking after. They demand. We supply."

Foo scratched at the root of his quiff. The way LM said supply, winking like that, he knew precisely what kind of supplier LM was on about.

LM pursued him relentlessly. "Chi and Yao, they'll be begging you. Come sit here sir, please fuck me for free sir."

Max grinned at LM's falsetto impersonation of Yao.

"Sure they will. What you say? I need a Shanghai boy I can trust."

Max dropped his towel on the bar.

"When do you want me to start, boss?"

"Tonight."

A crash at the door and Dr Sun flops onto the floor, grey skinned, complaining how tight his chest feels.

"Too much Yang food. I feel like I'm going to explode," he says, then lets rip a rasping fart.

Sun praises the clever American sonofabitch who had come up with the idea of pumping ice-cold air around multi storey buildings.

"I'll prepare something for Sun's Yin," Foo says, heading into the kitchen. "Spinach and Tofu soup," he calls out.

Sun winces and puts an arm over his face.

Foo feels strangely alive as he slices a handful of spinach leaves into squares.

"First I will make my own stock, as Chi showed me," he shouts over his shoulder. "Some chicken, some pork, water, ginger root, spring onion, little rice wine, hmmm. It's all good stuff, Dr Sun."

Foo assumes the silence from the restaurant means Sun is being comforted by LM.

The wok's contents boil. Foo dices the tofu into centimetre cubes and stirs them in with a tablespoon of soy sauce. When the fluid returns to the boil he washes the spinach. He allows the soup to simmer for two more minutes before adding the leaves. He sighs in delight as they turn a beautiful emerald green. All this simmers one more minute, allowing Foo a moment to find a plain china bowl and a broad shallow spoon. He skims the surface of the soup with a small ladle until it is clear, then adds a pinch of salt and a little pepper.

"Tara! Beautiful spinach and tofu soup," Foo beams into the restaurant as he presents the dish.

Then there is this beautiful sad pieta. More than a still life of men in cream coloured suits by candlelight. LM is kneeling on the floor beside Dr Sun holding his hand, head bowed, the brim of his hat so low it touches his chest. Sun is grey and lifeless.

It goes through Foo's mind how Sun had scored with Yao on the first night, how he had dreamed of making the Shanghai film a reality. Now he was going into business with LM and Sun had died right there, of something or other, while he had made soup in the background.

LM places the hand flat on Sun's chest. "Just like that. All the dreams over. All the potential gone. Guess we will never see that Shanghai movie now."

Then LM's face turns evil rat and he fixes Foo. "One more thing," he says. "If you deal for me, you must never use for yourself."

Foo closed his eyes. In the distance a moped strains on

61

the hill up from the harbour.

Maybe it was drink, or death, or the whole crazy night rolled into one.

His eyes stayed shut.

Foo poised, holding a bowl of steaming soup over the body of Dr Sun and Love Missile, the Beijing Star swimming in and out of focus, the whine of a motorcycle becoming loud as a huge bloodsucking mosquito, its passengers crazy bike riding bugs with feathery antennae trailing the juices of their victims. The deep night revolves on this wonky axis of time and place and at the bottom of this wobbly whirlpool there is me and the rock I hold onto for dear life. This rock, this saviour, prevents me from being swept away along lines of infinity to forever nothingness.

When I open my eyes I'm curled up tight as a foetus on a bed in this sticky hot room. I cannot tell if I'm drunk, or if I've been slipped something trippy. There's girls clothes, t-shirts socks and bras and odd bright pink, striped yellow and white and green pieces of swim suits, mainly bottoms, all over the place and sandals with little tartan ribbons, beads and a brand new soduku puzzle book and a snakey entwine of belts that wriggle out of a suitcase onto the floor. There's an iPod and a book about turtles next to the bed and a pad of Hotel Eco notelets. There is also a juddering nausea and, I cannot stop it from happening, I puke there and then and empty all over Aurora's lap.

"Sorry," she says, apologising to me. "It can be like that."

She strokes my face with a cool damp towel and hands me a glass of water clinking with ice cubes.

"Don't worry though. You'll get used to it."

7

Everything outside the car was lilac. Lilac with no horizon, from the ground to the point right overhead. Not a pale lilac, more an ultraviolet. The way an ultraviolet light shines through clouds of dry ice.

The sea through the hills. The tarmac and the line up the middle. Lilac. Surging, rippling waves of lilac swaying in the hot wake of the car. From the stubby grass verge to the lilac evening sun. Lilac radiating lilac light into the car. Onto me, Aurora and Lotte.

"Linus usitatissimus," Lotte says.

"Bless you," I say. "Gesundheit."

Lotte digs a knuckle in between my shoulder blades. "Nein, dolt. It is flax, as far as the eye can see."

Aurora is driving the turtle lover's ambulance, a beat up VW camper van rigged out to save stranded turtles who have tripped over onto their shell and become stuck in the sand, or maybe suffered a broken flipper. I sit up front twiddling the radio dial and Lotte is leaning between us from the back seat.

The VW is a hand painted cube of water world, with funky orange and green smiley loggerheads frolicking among giant clams and technicolour seaweed. Someone painted lobster eyes around the twin exhaust pipe. The expandable roof is the hull of a boat.

Aurora has a map of Cyprus opened on her knees. The road is this lilac line on the map.

"It is so natural. Untouched nature," says Aurora, looking out at all the lilac with her lilac eyes. "I'd love to have been here, you know, two thousand years ago, living in natural harmony with all this."

Lotte blows out through her nose, arches her whole body back stretching long golden limbs and rolling her steely eyes. Her hair is a gelled up Bart Simpson frizz of gold. Her mouth is too big for her face. She screws this up at Aurora and says, "What natural harmony?"

Lotte says to me, "There is no harmony between man and nature. Only degrees of exploitation."

Aurora says. "People can only live with nature as best as they can in the times they find themselves living."

Lotte points out the window. The trees over there, she says, are Sweet Chestnuts, *Castanea sativa*. The Romans brought them with them for food. Those green bushes we passed back there were Alexanders, black lovage, *Smyrnium olusatrum*. The Romans brought them over too.

This landscape we call nature is actually devastation.

Lotte says, "You English. It is funny how you are more familiar with the potato from South America and the Rhododendron from the Himalayas than your own plants."

All this flax she says is being grown for the plastics industry. They can even make windscreens from the fibres.

Aurora frowns out of the window. "You mean all this is genetically modified?"

"At least flax is primarily for industrial purposes rather than human consumption," says Lotte.

"If some transgenic flax, genetically modified seed for plastics or drugs, happens to drift along mistakenly into commercial flax lines, instead of landing on someone's dinner plate it probably only ends up in a can of paint or a sheet of linoleum."

"Yeah, but say you're painting the ceiling and suddenly it turns into a car windscreen?" Aurora says.

"That can't happen," says Lotte.

"Who knows with all their tinkering around?"

"Can that happen?" I need to know.

"That can't happen," says Lotte.

She says think about a line of flax that can produce plastics or drugs. Think of crops of biodegradable plastic. Then you can grow cars. So when it breaks down you simply park it in a field and it rots away. Or pharmaceuticals produced without having to harvest plants from the Amazon basin.

That's why Europe subsidises farmers to grow more than five times as much flax than before. We've had Butter Mountains, Beef Mountains, Wine Lakes. Now we have Flax Fields.

Aurora says in the real world Lotte is finance director of this firm, World Assets. They make money by finding trendy new applications for existing materials.

"I just love flax," Lotte says.

She's slapping the back of the seats, pounding the headrests, smacking the windows. "Flax, flax, flax, flax. Flax, flax, flax, flax."

Aurora talks to the mirror. "So. Your scientists turn these beautiful plants into plastic cars and call that progress?"

"What's new?" Lotte says. At the end of the ice age, she says like she was there and watched it happen, the Mediterranean basin filled with floes of melted ice and Cyprus pulled away from Turkey and Africa to become an island. Millions of years of isolation resulted in many unique Cypriot species, particularly plants, which were found nowhere else in the world. Then along came citrus orchards and tourism that displaced the fauna, which you can now only catch a glimpse of in the mountains and the Akamas Peninsula.

"That's geology," says Aurora, looking out the window. "It doesn't mean exploitation is any kind of harmony."

"Geology," Lotte says, like it is a dirty word.

She watches the Discovery channel and says she knows how rich copper deposits were discovered in antiquity on the slopes of the island's Troodos range. Geologists speculate that these deposits may have originally formed under the Mediterranean Sea as a consequence of hot, mineral-laded water swelling through a zone where plates that formed the ocean floor were pulling apart.

"And what good did all this geology do? Well, about 8,000 years ago the locals had flint and stone tools. At the Stone Age site at Kirokitia they excavated fifty little circular huts, homes where the living existed happily with their dead ancestors buried beneath the floor. They found 26 skeletons in one house.

"By 3000 BC the descendants of these people had copper weapons. By 2000 BC their metalworking was advanced enough to produce bronze. Cyprus was rich in copper and trade throughout the Mediterranean was booming. Or? You could also call it an arms race. So thanks, Geologists."

I ask the vibrating skyline, "Who won that cold war?"

Lotte rests a hand on my shoulder and says, "Well they did not do tourism, but if you look at ancient Egypt some people believe Cyprus is the lost state of Alashiya. They can't prove it. But it was rumoured to be somewhere in the eastern Mediterranean. They traded their copper and cows for the pharaoh's silver and ivory."

Aurora is concentrating on the road, squinting at a sign through the lilac dust. On the roadmap there's circles around five beaches where we can find turtles. Aurora has drawn a line through them to make this huge pentacle hovering over Cyprus.

Lotte says to the back of her head, "Scientific analysis of clay tablets sent from Alashiya to other rulers confirms Cyprus is a good match."

I say, "Perhaps only the clay came from here. Alashiya could as easily have been Syria, or Turkey."

Lotte's breath is close to my neck. She says, "You must be one of those people who needs the seeing to believe in. What do you want, a letter written on papyrus?"

Aurora says, "There is a nature older than trade wars and political rivalries."

Lotte curves her arm across my shoulders. "I'm telling you, flax is hot. Pop it in a pill and it helps reduce bloating, sore swollen breasts and crankiness. During the menopause it reduces hot flushes, dryness of the skin and vagina, depression, mood swings and mental fog. It even combats sagging breasts."

She says breast cancer, prostate cancer, uterus cancer and colon cancer. Constipation, cholesterol, endometriosis, high blood pressure, stroke, arthritis, lupus, multiple sclerosis, anti ageing, anti oxidant, stress.

"Flax is high in Omega 3 essential fatty acids, high in fibre and high in lignans, which help the body balance its estrogen and other hormone levels. It has up to eight hundred times more lignans than other vegetables or grains. The fibres in flax keep your colon clean and keep your waste moving so it doesn't rot inside you. It even works for pets."

Aurora stares into the driver's mirror, stares into Lotte's full set of lilac teeth.

Lotte says she has ambitions to move into endangered species, like the turtles. For the time being, World Assets has a plan to make millions helping cows. "We've found a way of transforming plastic waste into a liquid petroleum feedstock."

Aurora does something that turns on the headlights. She says, "So we grow a crop, turn it into plastic, then make it into a goo we feed to animals. Can't we just give them the flax?"

Lotte says the dangerous thing is, eating too much flax

is poisonous. "But imagine, no more landfill sites full of plastic getting blown around fields, choking horses."

Aurora wants to know what exactly genetically modified means. Lotte talks to the back of her neck.

"The one thing you've got to understand is deoxyribonucleic acid."

"DNA," says Aurora.

Lotte says right. It is in all living things. It is where an organism stores genetic information and gets on with the metabolic processes of life. All this with only four chemical bases along the length of DNA molecule.

I am surprised. "Only four?"

"Four. Adenine, cytosine, guanine, and thymine. They get all rearranged and the sequences they form is the specific genetic information."

So it is all in the genes, says Aurora.

Lotte sits back, unfastens a couple of shirt buttons. "You identify the genes you want to enhance. Block the ones you don't want hanging around."

"Sounds great," I say.

"Except," says Aurora, "for cross pollination from GM crops. The potential damage to human health, the environment, the wildlife and farming traditions here and in less developed countries."

"Yeah," Lotte says, looking out the window. "And man-eating turnips."

Herbicides won't kill them, Aurora says.

"Yeah," Lotte says, opening her shirt down to the green bikini top. "Like reform schools are full of Giant Hogweeds."

Anyway, she says, climate change is going to reshape everything. Plenty of animals and plants are going to die out naturally.

Lotte slips her shirt off. I start pressing some more buttons on the radio but cannot find anything cool.

She says, "We're relandscaping the world. Forget

saving red squirrels, eradicating dutch elm or myxomatosis. If you've got a spare ten K put it where the clever money is. World Assets."

"O Yeah," Aurora says. "So you can be a multinational millionaire."

Out of her shirt pocket Lotte produces a cigarette and says, "Do you mind?"

Aurora says yes.

And I say, "Nope."

It's her shout.

Lotte takes a zippo out of the shirt pocket and runs it up the back of Aurora's seat to light it. She blows lilac smoke around the dashboard.

Aurora finds some dance music on the radio, opens a window and says we are almost there.

Lotte leans over Aurora's shoulder, looks at the map and says, "Hey. What's with the black magic?"

Aurora says the pentacle is the sacred symbol of Wicca. "Right side up, which is how we wear it, the pentacle stands for earth, air, fire, water. Human spirit surrounded by the love of the goddess and god. When the pentacle is reversed, which is what I think you are talking about, that's when it becomes a Satanist symbol representing earthly matters being more important than God."

Lotte stretches over and takes a pen. In the middle of the circle she draws two eyes, a nose, a smiley mouth.

Several miles are driven in silence.

Her eyes squinting against the smoke, Lotte leans over to Aurora's window and flicks out the glowing remains of her cigarette. She tells Aurora not to worry, it's a biodegradable butt.

"You people," she says to Aurora, "you want sustainable forestry, right? An end to child labour, big businesses to pull out of third world countries ruled by military dictatorships, life saving drugs for all at affordable prices? "

"Don't you want that too?"

"Of course," she says. "But be realistic. You need shareholders with a global conscience to be able to do away with personal greed."

Aurora adjusts the rear mirror so she can eyeball Lotte. "There are more appealing human endeavours than biological vandalism for the sake of corporate self interest."

"O Yeah?"

"Yeah."

"Such as?"

"Such as. Boycotts."

Lotte holds out her hands. "Please. God. Let's boycott boycotts."

She says A is for Adidas, for kangaroo skin football boots. B is The British Heart Foundation, for testing on animals. Continental airlines for transporting monkeys for research. Dior for using models who appear dead or drugged, and in or near cars, so glamorising drunk driving whilst eroticising the victimisation of women. Esso for doing more than any other company to sabotage international action on climate change. F. Forests. Tropical Hardwoods for the destruction of biodiversity and habitats involved in logging, except hardwoods with forest stewardship labelling.

"That's a T," says Aurora.

"Whatever," Lotte says.

Then she says G.

GlaxoSmithKline, for animal testing. H is for horses. American Home Products for using horses in the production of drugs for hormone replacement therapy. Israel for flaunting

Aurora says, "Not listening to you," and puts a finger in her ears.

for flaunting United Nations resolutions, international humanitarian law and the fourth Geneva convention. So ignore their oranges. Or coriander. Janet Jackson because of her duet with dancehall star Beenie Man whose lyrics advocate killing gay people. K. I don't know. Boycott the King of Tonga's birthday party since he is the last monarch in the Pacific. Lufthansa, they transport monkeys too. Morgan Stanley Dean Witter for funding the Three Gorges dam in China, for flooding important habitats and displacing over one million people.

And boycott Nike. They abuse workers' rights in factories in East Asia. O. Support the Ogoni people of Nigeria campaigning against Shell for a fair share of profits from oil extraction and better environmental standards. P. Procter and Gamble for more animal testing. Q. Boycott the Queen and anything to do with celebrations of her coronation.

Aurora pretends to fall asleep at the wheel.

Reckitt Benckiser for testing household goods on animals. Seaworld, who have captive performing orcas. T. Tobacco. Philip Morris for its continued production and marketing of tobacco products. Unilever, more household products tested on animals. Virgin for their drinks production plant in a disputed area outside Jerusalem. W. Let's boycott World Bank bonds and demand an end to socially destructive world bank policies. X, Xerox for attempting to make a monopoly on computer systems. Yellow, because it is a colour I don't like. And Z. Zoos everywhere.

And Lotte says, "You might as well boycott life. I could go through the alphabet again and give you a different selection."

"Please. No," I say.

"Oh," Aurora says, pretend waking up, "has she finished turning this beautiful evening into a dreary wet decomposing plastic Sunday full of corporate greed?"

"All I'm saying," says Lotte, "is you have to take people with you on the journey. That's why World

Assets sees technology as the key to change."

Aurora turns around in her seat and punches Lotte in the chest. "Boycott World Assets."

"Hey," I reach over and cup a hand over Aurora's clenched fist. "I for one am desperately motivated by personal survival."

"You know," Aurora says to Lotte, "since we are where we are, the ancient Greeks had a spell to silence someone. They'd sew up a snake's mouth and feed it to a goat."

"Burp," Lotte says. "I read somewhere that to cure a headache caused by someone droning on, like a me for instance, you need the semen of a horse as it drips from a mare's vagina."

Everybody screws up their face.

Aurora tells us the Greeks, the people who invented democracy, knew all about good and bad magic. "White and black. The right hand path," she lifts her right hand. "And the left." She lifts her left hand and pokes Lotte in the stomach with the right. We nearly drive into a ditch. "Today you'd call it science."

"Back then," says Lotte, "religion was all deities and blind faith. Now the faithful have science, they can reach out and touch the proof in genetic engineering, new medicines, space travel."

Aurora takes a book out from her knapsack, hands it over and tells me to start reading aloud. It's dog-eared, bursting with little scraps of paper she's been scribbling on. She calls it her mirror book and says this is where she collects magic spells and rituals. It's a Wicca thing. It keeps track of experiences she hopes will later reveal connections or meanings.

Birth, I say.

According to Pliny, fumigations with the fat from hyena loins produce immediate delivery for women having a difficult labour.

Lotte sniggers. "Sorry, there's a waiting list for hyena

on the national health service."

I say, What?

A drink sprinkled with powdered sow's dung will relieve the pains of labour, as will sow's milk mixed with honey wine. Delivery can also be eased by drinking goose semen mixed with water, or the liquids that flow from a weasel's uterus through its genitals.

Lotte sticks her tongue out, glances in the mirror, looks at me. "Where does she find this stuff?"

Aurora says, "If you really want to know, I can recommend a friendly pet shop."

"This is disgusting," I say.

Pliny also recommends smearing the afterbirth of a bitch on the thighs of a woman to help slide out the infant, being careful to ensure that the dog's afterbirth has not touched the ground.

Aurora says all this is as true today as it ever was. She says putting a vulture feather under a woman's feet aids delivery. So does sneezing. Celsus recommends drinking hedge mustard in tepid wine on an empty stomach during a difficult labour.

She nods at me to turn the pages.

"Curses."

Deathbed curses are the worst, Aurora says, and mostly done by effigy. The closer an effigy looks like the victim, the more the victim will suffer when the effigy is harmed or destroyed. This is called sympathetic magic. As the effigy is harmed, so the victim is harmed. When the effigy is destroyed, so the victim dies.

Aurora says, "They knew even way back then that love was not all about flowers, boxes of chocolates, or sending lovey dovey cards with teddy bears..."

"I like teddy bears," I say, even though I do not.

"..it is wishing profound inner turmoil and pain on the body and soul of the object of your desires. That's how you get what you want."

Aurora is leaning over, reading the next page aloud. Greek spells to attract a lover are called *agogai*. They are like a sneak attack. A jinx to ruin a relationship is a diakopoi.

"Hey! Keep your eyes on the road," I say.

So I find myself saying, "The Egyptians had Apep, a monster who was the enemy of the sun. The magician would write Apep's name in green ink on the effigy, wrap it in papyrus and throw it on a fire. As it burned he kicked it with his left foot four times. The ashes of the effigy were mixed with excrement and thrown into another fire."

Aurora says, "It was as good as making an atom bomb to them."

"So," Lotte says, huffily folding her arms across her chest, "you think modern science is updated superstition?"

"Faith and magic," says Aurora. "Genes and plastic."

She touches something to wet the windscreen and set the wipers clearing the dirt.

Aurora turns up the radio. The dance music.

8

Turtle Beach car park is lit up by a giant neon loggerhead with a beaky human smile. Every thirty seconds it lifts off its red top hat.

We park the Turtle Ambulance as close up to the light as we can, squeezing in between two empty four by fours. We are the biggest dazed moths on the beach.

This is all there is to witness the baby turtles making it to the sea. Aurora is saying surely they could have found a better way of signalling a world heritage environment zone.

Lotte is saying African elephants, Siberian tigers, sperm whales. Big game shoots and organised culls. "We could harpoon turtles, sacrifice a number under license every year to scuba clubs. The fees cover the cost of setting up a long term sanctuary for the ones that are left."

"If," says Aurora, yanking the keys out of the ignition.

The sand kicks up like talcum powder as we head out into the moonless night along a path through the dunes. We are guessing where to put our feet. Here, if stumbling half blind you reach out, your hand gets speared on the tips of the razor wire grass growing along the path.

But still we walk like dinosaurs, crashing, flailing with our useless little hands outstretched, drawn towards the crush of the sea.

Surprisingly, the sand is undulating and the sea is flat.

Then Aurora whispers to me that we are not messing

about on sandy ridges. Where I fell into the grass was a chemist shop. Where Lotte lifts up her shirt with a whoop and bares her little breasts to the sea air is in the foyer of the Rassian Hotel. Where we stop to comment on how the turtle's apparently disembodied bowler hat flashes over the sandy dunes is a general store for the chalets with pools that sprout opposite the car park. All the way down to the sea is such a driveway of bars and cafés, our ears should be offended by the mishmash sounds of music and television and people. All the way down to the sea and the marina where the halogens on football stadium size masts pick out the gold trim on bobbing white Benetti, a fleet of Rizzardi and a Guy Couach for charter. And the mass choir of the little yachts, the singing of their wires trembling all night long, not hopeful, gets lost in the deep of compilation drum and bass cds.

"Over there," she points.

And from out of the lapping darkness a grey silhouette drifts towards us. The night, fuzzy with flashing turtles and Aurora's phantom disco lights, casts a spell across the water. And in an instant there she is: a double decked Phoenician war galley with bronze tipped battering ram, square sail dropping and oars up for landing.

This girl, she has my head spinning. I can't say if it is this night, or ten years from now, or some other night two thousand years ago.

A man shouts out from the dunes behind us and the galley makes a turn and drifts out of sight into a convenient patch of sea mist. This time as it re-emerges there is a distinctly diesel roar. Out of the shroud an elegant Mediterranean playboy broadside appears, a million quid worth of Arno Leopard. The burring throttle eases back.

Someone jumps off the stern into the foamy water and

someone else throws over what looks like a bundle of rags and splashes in after it. Then another person, and another, leaps into the chest high water. Soon there is a small army storming ashore towards us holding up their poly bag, clothes or child the way invaders bear rifles, or Phoenician's their swords. When they reach shallow water they try to break into a run. Some fall splashing head first. The sea froths, swallows up tonight's catch.

This man at the wheel of the boat waves right at us and shouts: "Yos! Yos!"

I'm looking at Aurora. She is looking at me. Lotte is right at the edge already getting wet, stretching her hand out, dragging someone ashore.

I should be helping but I'm not sure what to do. It is in this moment of hesitation, filling it, that a voice booms out behind us: "Ya! Ferdi." I know this person.

Yanis strides towards us arms outstretched. His companion stays in the shadows of the dunes but by the pale cotton suit and rat faced silhouette, I guess it is LM.

"Mr Jimmy, my friend. Lightning. Thunder claps," grinning Yanis bashes his fist into the palm of his hand. "A wonderful night for the beach, and the tiny baby turtles, with your beautiful friends."

"Except it got a bit busy all of a sudden," Aurora says.

Yanis shouts Ferdi again and lifts his fist to the man in the boat. "Camur!"

His arms press down on my shoulders. He says, "That's my brother. I'll tell him to hurry up his friends and leave you in peace."

"Oh, the guy out in the storm?"

"Yes, he has been fishing."

Aurora says, "Your brother is a fisher of men."

And in that moment I know what she says is the truth. I know it but, I am watching LM circling in the shadows, I wish Aurora hadn't just blurted it out.

Saying something, even if it is true, can make it dangerous.

Yanis glares at her. "There are many fishes in the sea. These friends are ..."

"Kurds." Lotte helps an elderly woman fold onto the damp sand, and then says, "These people are Kurds. No passports, no visas, and by the time you've finished with them no money either."

And Yanis says, "They are travellers. We are the tourist agency for these Kurds, the Africans, the Arabians. We arrange adventure holidays. It's not so bad as you say."

More people are staggering ashore. Someone in the darkness shouts out "Europe!"

And then, near where the straggly line of shadows meets the edge of the waves, Aurora points an outstretched hand.

At a rock.

A little rock that rolls with the sea and then flips itself over and moves under the next wave, then disappears. Another moving rock follows, and then another.

"Loggerheads," she whispers.

We get to where we can watch this awkward procession of hatchlings take to the sea. Some have sand in their eyes, some get bowled over by a wave and flip frantically, or lie exposed on their backs until a second or third wave turns them right way up.

"We can look but we cannot touch," says Lotte.

"No. We must never interfere with nature," says Yanis.

So, I am thinking, what a strange world.

Looking out into the dark night, at all our faces huddled around the sand, lit now and again by a neon turtle and the glow of cigarettes someone passes around, I am wondering why does it have to be like this? How can it be so heartbreaking to reach the shore and so painful to take to the sea?

9

It happens to anyone. A baby can die all of a sudden in the arms of its mother. It can die in a car seat, crushed by an airbag. You don't consider safety devices to be harmful.

This is the way my mind goes. It is so damn, damn hot, sitting under this tree of *stifle*ness. I've been waiting for Aurora for hours. It feels like a don't show but I'm hanging in there, despite the sweat clouding my reflectospecs and the ants running criss cross over my hand to get to somewhere urgent up in the bark of the tree.

I don't know if they've got lungs. Ants are so small to have lungs like us. But if they do, I'm thinking these guys are sticky with syrup on the outside and gloopy with red hot dusty air in the middle.

I wish I could think of a different job. This is no life for a trainee taxidermist. If I was a copywriter I would give you liquid plastic nanoglobules that keep hair shiny and tangle free. Say, now go drive that convertible Peugeot across the Sahara. Live your dream.

Until, probably, the laptop would cauterise my eyesight and deep fry my sperm. My eyes burn enough with conjunctivitis already. Some days I am the weeping Rasputin. I don't put photographs up on walls because I don't need National Geographic images of Peruvian Indians to escape. And I don't need naked people to remind me of what is for sale. After all, modern man believes in his own insignificance and his biological death. To be immersed in life is to be steeped in death.

As I said. It happens to anyone. A baby can die all of a sudden in the arms of its mother. It can die in a car seat, crushed by an airbag. You don't consider safety devices to be harmful.

A true creative simply cannot accept reality, not for a moment. Not even by going to the cinema or watching television. They know reality is merely a process. Above all, a creative knows modern man does not really exist. If it looks bad, or the angle does not work, they shoot another take. For the creative, life is left lying with the awful dregs on the cutting room floor.

How we must look to God. From a distance everything looks really great. The big picture is a neat little circuit board of tiled roofs, parks and motorways. Busy streets and meaningful lives beneath huge advertising billboards of glamorous people doing wonderful things with the latest fashion, tastes and technology at their fingertips. Only it is all presentation and impact. God must be exhausted dealing with the messed up agony locked up in the minutest details.

Rat face offered Lotte a job. "If you think you can save the planet you got the job," he says.
Lotte is now conservation director for Red Med, which she says should change its name to the North Cyprus People's Development Agency. They will save the turtles, save the whales, save the world she says. Only, I've seen what good she is going to do already.
"It is now only sandy beach. A beach like this needs people. This island needs an economy," LM tells me.

Aurora says the unspoilt natural beauty is more valuable than a hotel complex. "It is bigger than just this island. It is globally important. Like, like..."

"United Nations," I say.

"Yeah, right. Like the fucking UN," she says.

LM is a twitchy nose rat face. "Then ask your global power to shut me down."

That shut Aurora up. It left her with a faraway look.

The ants have discovered the dribble of my Stella and are having a rave at the bottom of the bottle. I shouldn't complain. The bar, with a heavily stacked refrigerator, is just over there.

Bet Laurence Durrell didn't have warm beer problems when he was here. For him, Bellapais and its ancient ruined abbey were a testimony to those who had tried, however imperfectly, to grasp and retain their grip on the inner substance of the imagination, which resides in thought, in contemplation, in the Peace that had formed part of its original name. Even the winding streets of the village seem a study in introspection. Ancient wisdom tells how anyone seated beneath this age-old mulberry becomes lazy and unwilling to work. But then, it is a celebrity tree. It is right up there with all the other famous trees, from the Garden of Eden to Robinson Crusoe's Banyan tree house.

It is while I am holding my glass bottle up against the sun, creating a Stella tsunami for the ants at the bottom, that I see clearer than I have done for some time.

Over there, under a tree, sitting alone. It is Aurora.

The down on her lips is wet with Evian, not perspiration. An annoying length of hair tries to curl into the side of her mouth, but gets flicked aside. Aurora rests her back against the tree, watches Jimmy T stand up in the shade of the mulberry, make a disconsolate shuffle to the bar, collect a beer and plump back down again.

"As you were saying," she says to no one.

A swallow squirts out from the space beneath the abbey roof and disappears over the sandy fields towards Kyrenia harbour.

Aurora nods. "I see. So-o-o you're saying this..."

And she laughs.

When Jimmy T recognises her laugh he will hold his bottle up like a sniper's rifle, trace down the neck, work along the line of laughter, straight to her heart.

There he is. He takes a sip.

What's she doing over there, talking to herself?

"We were, I thought, supposed to be meeting beneath the Tree of Idleness," I said, plumping down beside her.

Aurora shades her eyes, looks up into my face. She glows with the sun.

"Glad you could make it," she says.

She's a funny one, but the most interesting person I've met in a long time. She puts her arm around my neck and pulls me in.

"God. You're going to be so famous."

"What for?"

She pushes me away laughing. "You dope. For helping save the planet."

I shrug a bit. Turtle Beach is ten miles away and from up here you can picture the skyscraper hotels and imagine the ski jets cutting across the bay.

"If it takes a global power to stop LM's casinos clotting up the pan handle, we'll need to dig one up," she says.

"How are we going to do that?"

She explains how what we do today matters so much tomorrow. In just the same way, what they did in the past ripples all the way down into our today, which as well as being our own tomorrow's-come-true or haunting, depending on your point of view, is also the distant tomorrow of those far away in history persons.

"Alright, I suppose so," I say. "Pity most of our time gets lost in the past."

She stands up and points high into the branches of the Japanese pagoda tree we sit beneath.

"Those people long ago, they were just like us. They looked for messages and left clues, same as we do," Aurora says. "We simply need to know where to look."

"Why do I get the feeling you are building up to something?"

Aurora stands, her back against the tree. She takes two steps, turns and looks down at all the dust we've been kicking up.

"Let me introduce you to, dah-dah, the true Tree of Idleness. And boy, is it time for you to get busy."

All those hours sitting under the wrong tree. All those believers worshipping the ambience of the nothing tree. Self-analysing away the days under the snickering to itself tree, the mocking tree. The Tree of Idolness.

Aurora has me digging like we are in Egypt looking for pharaohs and gold. Every spade full she bends over and fingers through the soil. When I ask her what she's looking for, she replies: "Turtles of course."

"Hen's teeth up here," I say shovelling.

"Maybe once the sea was nearer. They worshipped the sea, you know?"

Someone at the café asks what we are doing, digging up their landscape. But it is too hot and they leave the crazy tourists alone. I feel like going home too, or at least to a seat at the bar. I'm down about a metre. In fact, I've started counting down the shovelfuls from ten, promising myself a blast off at zero. When I hit seven with a weird scrape Aurora shouts "Stop!"

Next thing the ground opens up where I have just

been digging and the earth unexpectedly implodes.

"It's a chamber," Aurora jumps down into the pit.

Down on our knees, heads bumping together, eyes stinging with sweat and dirt, it's hard to see without falling through into the darkness.

Aurora has grains of sand between her teeth when she lifts her head and smiles. "Phone the United Nations."

We didn't get United Nations. We got Sky TV, the BBC, the History Channel, Discovery Channel, Fox TV, CBS, The London Times, The Guardian, Washington Post, New York Times, Le Monde and a dozen others. And what they got us was a special environmental dispensation from the Culture and Heritage Secretary of the European Union banning development of Turtle Beach pending further extensive archaeological investigations.

What we had found was Turtle Cemetery. Hundreds of mummified turtles killed in rituals thousands of years ago then buried here in the sands.

I said it was probably the first fancy mirror and comb factory.

Aurora shook her head.

"For the Egyptians, turtles were friends with Set and were the enemies of Ra. They were creatures of the night and symbolised darkness and evil. They would try to stop the solar barque as it travelled through the underworld."

I find it hard to believe in Evil Turtles. But those ancient loggerheads were really sacred in this area, she says.

"This is where an evil turtle cult gathered. Maybe it spread out from here across this whole part of the island. Across the sea, to who knows where else."

I dropped the second shell Aurora handed out. It must have hit a rock or something because it broke open and there it was. The turtle was stuffed with papyrus. Many of the others were too. The treasures we found in those shells included a lost play by Sophocles, quite a bit of Homer, some Virgil, Euripides, and some paintings. Even now, years later, they are still digging and the British Museum in London is conserving the priceless shells.

You see, there are turtle lovers everywhere. But when you talk to one about our slow, beaky friends be aware that not all of these lovers are merely thinking about an innocent life abroad on deep ocean currents.

10

Living is usually for the dying. However, I know for a fact that living is also for the dead.

This was my life.

This was my celebrity life.

This was my celebrity who found the amazing turtle scrolls life.

And this was my celebrity who found the amazing turtle scrolls who someone wants dead life.

After the turtle scrolls came countless newspaper and television interviews, the documentaries, the re-enactments, the job offers, the academic accolades. And before you know it, I have a dream job. Taxidermist to the Stars.

Well, actually, to their puppies, or their cats, parrots or, in one case, a puma.

At first Aurora, with purple and red twists of coloured plastic in her hair, is happy. Then, as first the kitchen and then the bathroom and bedroom fills with the jars and awful paraphernalia of stemming decay day after day, she says to me: "Don't you worry you might be spending too much time with the dead?"

I say to her that's rich coming from her. She should have seen this one coming cos she pushed me into it. I say it is only people's pets.

Aurora says it is not healthy to have dead bits in pickling jars about the house. The neighbours will complain of the smell. She's complaining of the smell and the lack of space anywhere.

"It can take you over if you are not careful," she says.

"What?"

"A fascination for death."

"Well, you are the one who goes around talking to them. Maybe we'd get on better if I was one of the dead."

She says not to say that. "You never know who is listening."

The cooling off between us continues. The more I immerse in my work, Aurora grows listless. She drops her evangelical environmentalism. She goes to The Observatory every other day, hanging about the Meridian line offering to take photographs for tourists using their own cameras.

Or she sits in Trafalgar Square, waiting for it to rain. She shelters in the National Gallery, pouring over Saint Francis in Meditation and searching for Zurbaran behind the cowl.

She comes home and says things to me like: "If life is like loving then I am dying."

After weeks of this, she announces she has a job in a café in old Greenwich, the one tucked in between the theatre and market, where all the freaks hang out.

I may as well be already dead to Aurora. I would stand a better chance of talking to her if I was. All I get is Portia at the Psychic Deli says this, Portia at the Psychic Deli says that. Then Psychic Deli Detective Agency, she says, and laughs that Portia Maxwell has psychedelic hair. Aurora says Portia knows someone in City Hall and that soon they will be official consultants on everything from elections to the Olympics. "The vibe is very important to these people," Aurora says.

Even I can see it is better than pouring coffee. But since she started hanging around with her new friends I have been working late. Usually all night. And on my own. Alone. I stop having my hair cut and allow my beard to grow long. I rarely venture out in daylight and my skin pales. I avoid conversations unless essential and unused my voice fades to a whisper. In keeping with the nature of my work I wear a priest's coat. I am at ease with the Matrix look and the beard is better than looking at my own face in the mirror.

It can only go one way and now I haven't seen Aurora for a fortnight since she moved out.

I stay on past Greenwich to avoid the Deli and get off the train at Westcombe Hill. I immediately head for the newsagents. It never fails to surprise me what a dump this place is considering I've just gone under a world heritage site, home of the National Maritime Museum, and the Royal Park where Henry the Eighth held jousting tournaments. I don't even glimpse the skyscrapers of Canary Wharf. Or catch a whiff of the huge London Dome jellyfish beached on the peninsula. This part of the city tastes of envy and ambition.

It rains so hard down the hill that the magazine shelves inside the shop are wet. Mohammed, the man behind the counter, looks up. He takes mail for me when I'm not home and, never taking his eyes off me, he reaches under the cash register to lift up something wrapped in brown paper. He places it onto the counter.

He calls me Doctor Death. "Looks like a beauty, Doc."

He pushed over a parcel the size of a shoebox. It is addressed to James Tetley Esq.

He taps it on the side. "Maybe one of these days you might let me watch you work, Doc?"

Then he put a small plastic bottle on top of the package and says, "The wife picked up some choramphenicol for you. Oh, say hi to the little lady."

Outside, I leant back against the door and tilted in three drops with rain to each eye. Both are sticky with a discharge. I carried the parcel inside my coat. The thing inside sounds solid and round.

Halfway up the hill, the back windows of our place stare down into the gaping mouth of the Blackwall Tunnel, cars swarming in and out. The walls are roaring with the rumble of a television followed by peels of laughter. Then more deadened dialogue. Laughter is sprinkled in and out of the voices. These days, the people you hear laughing do not exist. They are digitally produced sounds synthesised into place by a keyboard player during post production. The engineer watches the playback monitor in sound dubbing, searching for signs. A little humour, a tickle on the keys somewhere down on the left hand side. A smile can be helped along with a mid range ripple. Full laughter, the sort that comes through the walls from the neighbour, is a crescendo of serious thumping chords.

Coming up through the floor, someone's learning to play electric guitar. They play along to the stereo, going over over and over the same rift. This can go on all night.

Down through the ceiling someone is having a domestic. A man and a woman are barking at each other. Dinner plates are being cleared away. Doors are being slammed. This can go on all night.

These are my neighbours. They are not the dead, only the unseen.

An envelope has been pushed underneath my door, since I've had letterbox boarded over. But even removing your name from the door will never stem the intrusions, the unsolicited bits of paper and the assorted life forms they harbour.

Because of this, with personal hygiene in mind, I have completely modified my surroundings.

Upholstering the three-piece suite in taped together black bin liners introduced me to a readily available recycled material. I pasted the ceiling and walls with more black plastic, closing over the window with decorative bin liner curtains. I braided the yellow tie handles to form an irregular pattern of tassels. I bin linered the table and carpets. Everything is completely sheathed apart from two well scrubbed wooden chairs, the toilet, the sink, the shower. And several bare lightbulbs.

Proving that a hobby can influence your life I now ensure a dust mite free regime by sleeping between a plastic bed sheet and patchwork quilt of supermarket polythene bags. Which is surprisingly cosy.

This isn't what an interior designer will tell you to do. It isn't what a therapist would recommend. Or a girlfriend who wants sofa and cushion covers from Ikea, chintz curtains, wallpaper. But it works for me.

In the bathroom, I turn on the shower and air extractor fan for some white noise to shut out the other lives. The air is bubbling with screams. The people next door are watching a monster movie. Underneath, there's a baby crying, doors banging, someone shouting, and those first ten bars of a familiar song.

You can either turn up the volume of your own life, or let the bombardment slide right on by.

These model citizens who would never dream of dropping litter in the street will leave bags full of their household garbage festering outside your door all weekend. They don't allow smoking in their own home but they will stand in the hall outside your door to do it. These people who would never hurt a fly and believe they are oppressed will try to dominate the neighbourhood by buying the biggest fiercest dog they can find. They will not answer the door. But they will shout into their mobile phone at four in the morning outside your home because the reception is better.

This is what we call modern living. Civilisation's defences are down.

I sit on the toilet with the envelope and package on my lap. I douse them with a generous coating of anti-bug spray then scrub my hands in soap powder for the fourth time that day.

Even after this procedure, putting the mail under an industrial strength magnifying glass with built-in spotlight, more of a domestic necessity than a television, I can clearly see a speck. When I pick it up it settles in the folds between thumb and forefinger. Where the skin is cracked with eczema.

Actually it is in the crevice of a fold.

Something, possibly, wriggling.

There is a discernable pulse.

But I can't figure out if it is my own.

It could be an anthrax spore, or something even worse. That's possible.

Maybe a stray amoeba crawled onto the package while it was waiting to be collected. Then it jumped over.

"Probably just an E-coli," I say to the hand.

The skin tightens after being scrubbed again, this time with a capful of bleach.

I'm not losing it, I'm doing fine. I make a mental note to firm up the procedure for the opening of mail. Microwave is good. I calculate that two minutes on maximum is sufficient for a normal envelope containing a single bill, or bank statement, and up to seven minutes to detoxify the bulk of a larger padded envelope. Problem is, I don't want to cook someone's dead pet.

What I need is a fully oxygenated military chemical warfare isolation suit and an electron microscope.

Aurora threatened to report me to the police for putting her post in the microwave.

"It's an assault on the good standing of the monarchy," she says.

I find it hard to believe the police would be interested in this.

I peel back the tape on the package. What is inside is a rectangular cardboard box, dry and smooth, each corner crumpled. A slip of paper pasted on the front says: The Boss. The return address is London.

The top lifts off and what's inside is covered by a sheet of black slippery paper. Underneath, curled up as if it is sleeping, there is a dead chihuahua.

It is silver. Like a jewel.

One of the long haired variety, with a crazy grey mohican on top of the apple shaped head, the dog still curls his sickle of a tail around himself.

The floor under my seat vibrates from the music. I can feel the guitar through my feet.

I rip, twist and roll the wrapping into a ball and flush it away. The toilet is by far the preferred method of disposal for virtually all household waste. Shredded tin cans, rotten vegetables, chicken bones wrapped in soup packets, ground up milk bottles. Scraps and wrappers. They all get carried out to sea.

Larger waste, intestines and internal organs, may not make it out to sea. These are probably eaten by the pythons and crocodiles that people say live in the city sewers.

I carry The Boss in his box through to the living room.

Out of the box, on top of the table, up close The Boss has pink wrinkly skin. I bend close to his ear and whisper his name.

Those damned ancient Egyptians believed they only had to speak the name of the dead to make them live again. That's why the walls of the tombs are filled with text from the The Book of the Dead, The Book of the Gates, and The Book of the Underworld. The names of the wealthy pharaohs are up there for us to murmur over and give life to.

I stroke The Boss. His hair is soft.

Those Egyptians made Death big business. It took seventy days to treat a corpse. After bathing and oiling the body of their loved one they ripped out the liver, intestines, lungs, and stomach, rubbing in natron salt to dry them out and prevent decay. The treated organs were wrapped in linen strips and placed in canopic jars. After that the body cavity was stuffed with some more natron.

It is not a million years removed from what a modern taxidermist needs to do.

We are not the world's most popular people. The traditional taxidermist who skins an animal, discards the carcass, tans the hide and stretches it over a mannequin. Or the modern freeze dry DIY taxidermist like me.

I started on crayfish, mink, weasels and snakes this way. Even marmosets, those little Gremlin-faced monkeys. I did a rare luminous green Parson's chameleon, native to Madagascar. It no longer changes colour. A couple of cats. A few dogs.

Death. It is all about freshness. And longevity.

People should understand that your average museum yogi merely comprises straw and horsehair. For some reason, the same animal lovers who believe it is cruel to skin their pet, even though The Boss, or Frisky, is already dead, do not worry about freeze-drying them. This is probably thanks to our familiarity with frozen food.

Naturally, as we become more relaxed about burying or cremating, there will be more pet owners who want to have some afterdeath with their little friends as well.

I understand. I am passionate about it.

To remove all the moisture from a pet's body I use a modified Frigidaire freezer, with a custom built quarter inch plate glass compartment and rear fitted vacuum pump.

Something the size of The Boss will take about two weeks.

I tried explaining this to Aurora. "This is crucial. It is vital the animal goes into the freeze-dryer long enough. If animals are not sufficiently dried out, they will rehydrate from the atmosphere. If they decompose they lose their hair. They begin to smell, and ooze fat.

"Nobody but nobody wants a pet like that."

She said, "I have lost you to the dead." Then she got up, packed her bag and left.

As ever, preparation is everything. Before The Boss goes into the machine he has to be prepared and posed. Tonight, straight away, I can't wait. I can't even hold my breath long enough to steady my hand. I cut from the bellybutton down to the bunghole and pull out all the insides into a bucket.

His eyes must be removed or they will shrivel up because they are full of water.

With tweezers jumping to each heartbeat, it is a struggle to have a steady hand. My back is hunched and my neck is curved. A pain at the bottom of my spine is arching up to a headache.

Always, the sound of the community vibrates through the walls, through the table, into my fingers.

Admittedly The Boss looks a bit messy right now. After I rinse him under the shower he will be clean inside and out and looking a lot better.

Plenty of people demand vibrant life poses with lyrical sculptural effects. A salmon leaping over slate. A jaguar baring its teeth at an angry cobra about to strike. But I only do one pose. Eternal Rest. It is why people come to me, the taxidermist archaeologist who found the famous turtle scrolls beneath the true Tree of Idleness.

I arrange him as if he is sleeping all curled up and snug and pop him into the freezer at minus twenty degrees Celsius. The pump sucks the air out to produce a near-perfect vacuum. Later, the ice in the corpse will gradually escape as water vapor ejected from the chamber.

With this job, you understand what a piece of work a life is. Taking it apart is easy. Try putting it back together, you realise it can never be the same again.

We have spent thousands of years building up to this moment. Separating our soul from our bodies.

For the Egyptians, being and intelligence was not the mind. They believed that the heart was the centre of a person. That is why embalmers never removed the heart of the deceased. The brain, on the other hand, was not given any such status. The embalmers went to work there with a hook.

Still it is a rare person who doesn't cringe at the thought of a hook going up the nostrils and pulling bits of brain down.

It is just a matter of time. The person is out there who wants to be freeze-dried so that they can never deteriorate.

Ice frosts the glass cubicle. The Boss disappears from view.

I can tell it must be two or three in the morning because it is quiet. The walls, the floor, the ceiling are subdued. The thermostat on the refrigerator switches off and you can hear the hum of the neon light. You can hear the clock next to my bed. The room is so cold you can see your breath.

To the person who has lost a loved one I want to say they should think about them waiting to see them again, maybe for years and years, floating around out in the icy cold and silence of deep space. That might be true.

Now. Pick up your gory bucket, with all the sloppy stuff that made The Boss what he was.

Bring it crashing down hard on the floor with a scream.

Celebrate. Do it again, and again, and again.

No matter how much mess flies across the room, and your face is streaked with tears and blood, thump it and keep thumping it until the downstairs neighbour brays at his ceiling, the guy upstairs wakes hollering at the top of his voice, or the rest of the neighbourhood, somebody, anybody, starts paying attention. Relax only after receiving existence confirmation.

There are the flames of Hell, a lake of fire of the sort you read about in Paradise Lost. Old as time and still as fierce as the day they were whipped up by a good god to torment a bad god. Then there are living flames, minor tragedies, the kind we see everyday all around us. Aurora says people can be living flames and although they feel they are burning up with some evil desire or greed or cruelty they still appear as cold and tempting as iced beer to the souls of the abyss.

This morning my head is pounding. I don't sleep anymore. Maybe it is because of the emptiness I carry around since Aurora moved out. Maybe it is the silence in the building that is causing it, or the glow from my new green light bulb fizzing around the floor-to-ceiling black polythene. I have been reading Kafka, sweating over the nightmare of Gregor Samsa, and my eyes are burning holes. The bug man would love my fridge. It is the home of decay. The cheese has turned solid and is covered in a blotchy blue mould. The milk has separated into five parts curd and one part slime.

The chaos that parades as life in this city has relented and the walls are breathing a sighful.

The Boss is thawing out on some old newspapers. You have to be careful at this stage. If the corpse has not been freeze dried long enough, it will disintegrate before your eyes.

But The Boss is doing fine, creating a wet patch across the photograph of Mr Hammington beneath the headline running over two pages: REQUIEM FOR TRAGIC MUSIC LOVERS. With the subtext: *Impresario and cancer wife in suicide love pact.*

What exactly is suicide love?

My latest rendition of Eternal Rest is perched on a dissolving platform of last week's front pages.

At his nose is the discovery of the body of Irwin T Corrie, CEO of Flescher Greep Global Investments. Latest in the line of multinational executives to die in suspicious circumstances with unknown women. The room attendant who found the bodies says they died doing it, in bed with him on top. The unidentified girl was blonde, tall, with the muscular legs of a dancer. She was half his age and in great physical shape. It certainly wasn't his wife. She's fifty-seven and cruising in the Bahamas.

Along the curve of The Boss's spine, it is the fire at the newsagent's where I collect my mail.

Mohammed managed to get out. But his wife was trapped by flames in the back shop where she was making sandwiches.

Someone in police forensics has gone public with a theory of spontaneous combustion. This is something they would not normally even whisper about at private parties. That we could just stand up one day and burst into flames for no good reason at all.

The Boss is lucky. We don't all meet our god with a letter of introduction and a stamped addressed envelope for return.

And there is the letter I found pushed under my door. Not a letter in the traditional sense. This has different coloured bits cut from magazines arranged to form disjointed sentences. It looks like a Sex Pistols album cover. LeTs mEEt 4 coFFEE . 2 wEEKs FRISkY café. QuieT SeaT near ToILeT. 5pm.

Coffee is a serrated edge of a word. Frisky makes no sense until I see it is Friday, Sky Cafe. I know where that is, over in Canary Wharf, and I guess this is Aurora playing relationships. I should miss her more. I know I need to ask myself deep questions about my own life and if I love Aurora, maybe I should ask her back, get the rooms in order, have a shave, promise to wash more regularly.

But there is this new obstacle.

First time I met Portia Maxwell in person, as opposed to being bored stupid hearing everything there is to know about her, I didn't like her. I could tell it was mutual.

The front door gets pulled open by a woman pressing a mobile phone to her ear. At first I think she is scratching her ear. Then I realise she is smiling at me but talking to somebody else.

"George," she says into the phone, "you'll just have to come over and see the thing for yourself. I can't describe to you how it sounds."

She motions me in with her free hand, four golden bands around the wrist glint with diamonds. "You can bring a string quartet if you want to." I can barely see her other hand, her long white fingernails, her black phone and a tiny gleaming wristwatch, through the shimmering blue lace agate mist of her hair.

She tilts her head to one side a little, changes from smile to gruel and mouths, *Wait a minute.*

Then back into the phone she says, "It's fab. You'll love it."

She leans against the door closing it with her back, her eyes meeting mine, and nods her head for me to go through.

We are in Hyde Vale, millionaires' row. An Edwardian ten bedroom house with five bathrooms, a library, a waiting room, huge fireplaces, a breakfast conservatory and a seventeen hundred and fifty square foot banquet room on the first floor. It has a separate four car garage, a gymnasium, pool and steam room in the basement which is also where the owner has built a security command centre combining intruder alarms with an array of environmental monitoring devices.

Sutherland Road is the kind of neighbourhood where gardens get vacuum cleaned in autumn.

The people who live here read newspapers with lots of white space.

Hyde Vale is mellifluous.

You ask for directions and neighbours tell you they really don't know anything about who lives in that house.

A woman in a maid's uniform stands in a driveway watching two boys playing with toy pistols. She tells them not to shoot the nice man and shakes her head. She says she doesn't know anyone of that description.

And one little boy says, "That house is haunted. It cries at night."

And the maid says she is sorry. As she is speaking her words are drowned out by the thundering of a huge removal lorry coming down the driveway opposite.

Now, inside Maxwell Mansion, Portia Maxwell walks through sparsely furnished cream coloured rooms.

Her still life is a cloud of crystal hair, a tangerine trouser suit and feet in gold training shoes. Her orange lipstick is thick as crayon wax. She is thin the way rich people are.

Or the terminally ill.

Gold bracelets on her arms. A small white leather purse on a long gold chain over one shoulder. She walks me through an archway of double doors into the next room, then the next.

Into the phone she says, "George. You'll need to make this quick. I've got company."

She places an index finger near her temple and draws little circles in the air, rolling her eyes to meet mine. She mouths, *Sorry.*

Then into the phone she says, "As a matter of fact it is," and her eyes go up and down me. "Black coat, black jeans, black shirt. It's the man in black."

She frowns. She smiles and says, "Thirty something, maybe six feet tall. Brown. Messy. Blue. Wedgwood."

She covers the phone and says, "He wants to know if you're available?" She tells the phone, "Mr T is shaking his head. So that's a no."

Still listening to the phone she takes out a bottle of perfume, Chanel number nineteen. She sprays three times into the air at her head height and steps through the smir of moss and lemon.

The suit is tangerine like marigolds growing next to sweet peas, late evening in summer when the ultra violet is high.

She has a kind of familiar look.

She looks like Barbie might look if she could grow old.

"Uh-huh," she says. "Uh-huh."

She looks over at me and winces. Listening to the phone she mouths, *One second.*

She is looking at the ornate ceiling as she puts her free hand on my arm and keeps it there, holding just a little.

She is saying, "This piano is beautiful. It is sensual. You cannot fail to play something wonderful on it."

She has been deep cleansed, exfoliated and moisturised.

She has been conserved, renovated and restored.

We are standing in a cream coloured ante room with a ornate gilt framed mirror where her dog, I guess it is Bobo, is sleeping on a Victorian mahogany chaise langue reupholstered in burgundy and olive striped cloth.

"Hello, my darling," she says. "No not you, George. I'm talking to my dog."

While studying her reflection she pushes up her hair. Her eyes are amber. She picks at the goo on the corner of her mouth with an ivory fingernail.

I bend my head down to meet her eyes, saying Mrs

Maxwell? I need to see Aurora, this is urgent.

Looking past both our reflections she points behind me towards a door which leads into another room.

I hear her say to the phone, "You will not be disappointed."

Aurora is lying between red satin sheets on a four poster bed in the centre of the next room. The curtains are drawn and the air is tangy with some kind of spicy incense. Red candles burning in tall brass holders mark each corner of the mattress. Enough wax has already melted to form four bloody congealing pools on the floor.

The bed's canopy is draped with grassy pigtails and garlic bulb necklaces. A huge five pointed star in a circle has been drawn all the way around the bed and the grey marble floor is gritty with splinters of charcoal.

Someone has scrawled some mumbo jumbo on the walls, back to front and upside down writing, and the words jump and dance alive in the candlelight.

Aurora raises her hand weakly, but enough to show me that she is clutching the charm I gave her. She has a nosebleed and is pressing with a tissue to stem the flow.

And when I hold her I need to know what has happened and if she is okay.

She smiles yes, now that I am here, and she tells me about the musical Hammington's, Croom's Hill and Linford. She has tears in her eyes when she says, "He wasn't playing the piano. It was playing him."

I heard Mrs Maxwell talk about a piano.

She says, "It was as if it was trying to get through him to hurt me."

I may be a self taught celebrity taxidermist, but I can still ask her what kind of way is this to earn a living?

She almost cries when she says, "It was the most malicious presence I have ever felt."

I know it is really saying something when she says that. And I press my arms around her tighter. I decide I must take her home with me, rip out the plastic sheeting and get on with making our happy life together.

Aurora doesn't cry but now she is sobbing. I can still smell burning. I can see where her hair has been on fire.

The Hammington's. I think of words like love, requiem and last waltz.

Portia has finished her call and followed me into the room.

She crunches some charcoal under her trainer then looks at Aurora and says, "Feeling better honey?"

Then she looks at me and she says, "She came here last week, all a-shiver. She told me all about this haunted piano then turned this place into Dracula's cave. You must be the only person in the world who doesn't answer their mobile. How do you exist without a mobile? I called you. I left messages. I need Jimmy T, I said. And it is urgent. You were needed here. She needed you."

Aurora blots some more blood. She says, "Jimmy T doesn't like telephones when he's working."

Portia wafts her hand through the air under her nose and says, "Or bathing?"

"Phones are an intrusion. And mobile phones melt your brain," Aurora says.

Portia is rubbing the back of her neck, stiff after using her mobile. She says, "It's a necessary evil."

She is talking directly to me. "What if it had been really serious?"

"Really serious?"

"What if this ghoul had followed her here? We could be levitating all over the place, or the house might be burnt to the ground by now."

Portia believes Aurora can do better than me. She

worries I will take Aurora away to research our own tragic newspaper stories, find missing teenagers, or give detectives clues in unsolved murder cases.

I say, "So you bought the piano anyway?"

Portia Maxwell puts her hands on her tiny hips and thrusts her backside out. She leans over into my face, gets disgusted by being too close, then pulls back. She says, "What do you think? Of course I did."

Aurora lies back and groans.

Portia cups a hand to her forehead. "I had to pay a fortune for it."

"And now it's here, downstairs," I say.

There is a discernable pause. Portia Maxwell does not like being talked to in this way.

She looks at Aurora, stretches both arms out and says, "I had to. It was too big for the shop."

"O god," Aurora says.

"It's not for long. George Thalopopakus is coming over. Don't worry. He'll take it. The Academy needs to replace their old Bernstein."

"So, Mrs Maxwell," I say, "apart from the fact it almost toasted Aurora the thought of all those students playing chopsticks on it doesn't bother you?"

"It'll add an edge to their Rachmaninov," she says.

"And your profits."

"I certainly hope so."

Then she frowns at me. "What I need is for you to stop worrying that poor girl, sort out your relationship, and for her to get back on her feet and back to work."

She is on her way out the door when I say I'd like to see it. Her hair flops over like the leaning tower of Pisa.

Portia says it is only a piano five times as the three of us pick our way along cream corridors.

This banqueting room has no table and no chairs. The waxed cherry floor springs when you walk on it. On one wall, opposite the ceiling-high German oak fireplace with carved cherubs blowing trumpets, hangs Man Ray's original Calla Lilies. There is a modern glass light of twisted wire shaped like an exploding star. And there is the piano.

"See. I told you. It is just an ordinary dumb piano," says Portia. "Not that I doubt Miss Spooky's intuition."

Aurora comes into the room, keeping close to the wall. She clutches a red bed sheet tight around herself. She swallows a lump in her throat and nods her head to me. "S'alright. Only don't get too close," she says.

In this light, it looks more ebony than black. It takes me four strides to walk its length, three strides across. And all the while I'm ready for this enormous three-leg beetle to snap into life, try to take a bite.

"It's amazing," I say.

The hardware is solid polished brass, the lacquer barely worn. The pedals are soft, sustaining, and full sostenuto.

"George called it the piano of choice for musicians," says Portia, standing back admiring it like a car.

"In this world and the next," Aurora says.

The lid is open. I hit a key and the three of us look at one another as the low mellow sound it releases dissolves slowly into silence.

"It's flat," I say.

"As if you would know," says Portia.

I need to look inside, study this animal's intestines.

I'm thinking of animals freeze-drying lonely and empty in my apartment.

Aurora says be careful and she and Portia move closer together near the door.

"It's only a bleedin' piano," Portia says.

The ribcage hums with my breathing on the strings and the vibrations ripple through the torso. This animal with no arteries, no heart.

A breathing lung would have disturbed the fine layer

of dust coating the golden brass of the soundboard. Between the black and the gold, I am crawling between the gilded pages of an old family bible. Slithering between Lamentations and Ezekiel.

The sweat of my palm clears a handprint in the dust beneath the strings, revealing a signature painted in gold leaf. JE Hammington.

So he was inside too and thinking of perpetuity.

There is a gap between the soundboard and the case, down inside the throat of the beast, where my hand goes out of sight.

"Careful," whispers Aurora.

My arm is in up to the elbow, fingering among the entrails. Touching with eyes closed. Reaching inside where the wood feels dry and rough. Stretching to where apprehension takes over from expectancy.

And there. Something hard and cold. Next to something soft. It is a long journey, dragging with fingertips from out of the womb.

Portia claims the silver art nouveau frame. "Why look at this," she says. "This must be our Mr Hammington."

The black and white photograph could be a Hollywood still. A thin lipped man wearing black evening suit, white bow tie and starched wing collar shirt, stands in a pool of light. His legs crossed, he rests one elbow nonchalantly on a piano.

"And look, it's this piano," says Portia, scrutinising the image with Aurora.

I have it now. In my hand while their backs are turned. It fits perfectly in my palm, a slim book bound in the softest red leather.

"It must have fallen inside years ago," says Portia, holding the frame up to reflect the light. "It's wonderful fine silver."

"It's a mojo," says Aurora.

"A what?"

"A Mojo. A marker, a personal calling card. Like a personal totem pole. It gives me the creeps," says Aurora.

I don't know why I did it. Something instinctive.

"There's nothing else," I said, brushing the dust from my arm.

Aurora looked at me once then grabbed Portia by the arm. "Come on. Let's get out of here," she said.

As they go marching out, arm in arm, I changed my mind about asking her to come home. In a second I switched off those thoughts about stripping the bin bags and making the place more homely. Already stolen deep inside my pocket, the little book was growing warm.

This morning, while The Boss warms under the green light, the smoothness of the leather binding reveals towering conical mountains with deep glaciated glens gouged by a criss cross network of tramlines. You can feel the great age of the book, sense the multitude of hands that have held it on its long journey through time.

It contains twelve blank sheets of vellum.

Holding the book like this, sizing it up in my hand, idly turning the empty pages, I realise what these lines are. There. The head, life and heart lines of palmistry, curving so genuinely, so almost symmetrically, that it has to be true.

Front and back cover, left and right palm. Two hands permanently bound.

Now there is a man's voice upstairs. Followed by a woman's. Then the shouting match begins again, quickly increasing to normal levels.

I am shaking hands with a dead man. What do you do with things like this for safe keeping? You cannot take it to bed with you, or leave it on the tv.

The book slips in, quite comfortably, between the

stitches on The Boss's belly.

The people that live in this building are like ants. They haul themselves out of the nest and start crawling into fridges, searching for milk and food. They mate on the mattress or in the middle of the floor, without passion or caress. When they are done they kiss farewell with a bite of poison. The death throws last all day.

11

Friday. 5.15pm

What a beautiful night it was. Fresh, but warming. Because I was way, way up, at the fiftieth floor, 244 metres above sea level 235.1 metres above ground level, I enjoyed a great view over London. Yes sir. No doubt about that at all. Amid the electric sea of domestic and office starlight there was the black postage stamp of Greenwich Royal Park, and over there the ultra violet London Eye. Wow. Now, if I just twisted round a little. See around that corner. Yes, there it was, the Houses of Parliament. Bit of Big Ben anyway. What a way to enjoy the Canary Wharf skyscrapers, see the capital of European finance up close. There was a helicopter over there, clapping like rapid-fire thunder. Looked like they were filming. What a wonderful backdrop. Ayeee. And back down thataway, yep, old mother Thames herself. There was the bobbing nun's-head scallops of the Thames Barrier. Was it true they were going to going to scoop out their insides and turn them into a hotel?

My mobile plays the first bars of Yankee Doodle Dandee. Whatever, let it ring.

I looked up through outstretched arms for the night sky. But it was blocked from view by the dark smoke billowing from the shattered windows. A curve of flames singed the side of the building and curled up towards the pyramid roof. I had numb fingertips from gripping the window ledge for so long. It must have been fifteen minutes. Waves of heat boiled over the window ledge and cascaded down the building towards where the shouting was coming from. If I could hang on for as long as the structure of the building remained then I would survive.

The slow wail of sirens drifts upwards from the street. According to the brochure I picked up in the foyer, One Canada Square has, or had, nearly 16,000 pieces of steel like this forming both the structural frame and the exterior cladding. In fact, the exterior is clad in approximately 370,000 square feet of Patten Hyclad Cambric finish stainless steel and on completion this was the world's first building to be dressed entirely in this medium. The 11 metre high lobby was dressed in 90,000 square feet of marble imported from Italy and, surprisingly, Guatemala. The building's floors were of a composite construction with a compact steel core surrounded by an outer perimeter array of closely spaced columns and now my life might depend on them. The building was designed to sway 13 and three quarter inches in the strongest winds that might occur every 100 years. It had 500,000 bolts holding 27,000 metric tonnes of steel. Are they holding now? There were 3,960 windows and 4,388 steps divided into four stairways. And there was the café, at the top, where I was waiting for CoFFEE. Those chairs, the tables and machinery of the café have joined the other customers on the pavement below.

I should have known better. I should have questioned my lack of questioning. When I received the anonymous note, I had hoped it was going to be Aurora, you know, since she was working in a café and making the link between coffee and us all over again. I went straight in and sat as instructed at the table next to the window near the toilet.

Funny. It was neither the time nor place I expected it to happen, but I felt nearer to God. You can go so high, you can leave everything, your doubts, your reasoning, at street level.

Then, from somewhere, a voice. "You there. Hang on. Help is on its way."

If it was the voice of God, He had taken to using a loudhailer.

"I ain't going nowhere."

"They're coming," the mechanised voice promised from somewhere below. "But the stairs are down."

"Great. That's great."

If I let go, without benefit of wings, I would surely die. Oh sure, I would try the breast stroke or butterfly, cavort in the moonlight or strike a Thinker pose on the way down. But I'd be a goner that way. And probably some other poor soul too, who would die in the split second of delusion that he had been hit by a meteor or been struck down by the vengeance of God.

The mobile sounded again. Damn. I hate a ringing phone. It meant swallowing the Adam's apple and almost dislocating my shoulder but eventually I got hold of the short antenna by the teeth and pulled the phone free. The line opened after being hit against the wall a couple of times.

"Whatd'ya waant?"

A shrill man's voice breaking in excitement. "My God. It's him. We got him. We got him. Hang on, sir."

"Whod zi hell iziss?"

"This is BBC, Roving Eye, sir. We're at two o'clock to you sir."

"Rowin Eye? Rowin Eye? Geza fuck ouza hea."

I forgot not to look down. Down Down. Down past the little black trousered legs dangling, the black DMs.

"Orders sir, sorry. Everybody's up here. There's at least three other choppers. There's ITN. Sky. And Five Live. You're headline news Mr Tetley."

As if that made a difference. "Whaza wan me t de? Keep tawkin ondzi way dawn?"

"Sir, can you tell us what happened?"

"Suar. Awazinza woom. A zit doahn anziwaz zis uj fiabah n m xposion. Nox mi deahd onmi feed. Buzt alza winzows cleah ouz, glaz wiz frying everzewah. Ze voom wiz destroyed. Competly. A zot a wazgonadie. A cud heahzisceamz next doah. A zot, fwippin eck, yuz onla chenz iz aut ze winzow.

"Awaza secunz expozon, nearla boo metzo keendum cum. A juzt gabbed zis lej na hunin fuhma deah laff."

The electronic voice crackled back. "Are you injured?"

"Nuh. Juzt zit zcayhad."

Downdraught from a circling helicopter pushed out a choking swirl of smoke. I almost spit out the mobile. But the rotor blades receded.

Roving Eye choppers hover above the city 24 hours a day, ready to respond in a blink to events wherever and whenever. What an irony if it was the downward blast from one of these helicopters that finally caused me to submit, open my hands and freefall all the way to splat. Would the camera pan out, follow me all the way down, or turn a steady eye towards the dark and ruined skyscraper?

The mobile cracked. "I can see rescue teams. Firemen, almost at you. You're going to be alright. Hang in there.

"Mr Tetley, would you like to say anything to our viewers sir, live?"

There was a new pain across my shoulders. The neck, the back, were dead. Embers drifted out of the building and soared towards the stars. I tasted ash on the back of the throat.

"Juzt getza fuahk out oF HERE!" The phone spat out.

BBC viewers heard the voice trail off. Some thought I had plummeted. I believe Cassie Black did a perfect anchor's job when they cut to her without warning. Live pictures of the blaze were being beamed into a box over her left shoulder.

She said: "It looks like we've lost him. That was reporter Jaan Steinweis bringing you an exclusive live link with celebrity archaeologist and recluse Mr T, fighting for his life on a ledge eight hundred feet above the capital, after a huge explosion rocked the financial centre of Canary Wharf."

Black put a hand to her right ear. "The latest we have is that Mr T…has dropped his telephone."

"Jaan?"

The helicopter reporter took up the slack. "Cassie. I can tell you, rescue teams have almost reached him. But he's been hanging out there for more than fifteen minutes. We can't get closer and the flames are growing fiercer by the second. His only hope is a rescue team that is somewhere unseen in the inferno as we speak. This is Jaan Steinweis, reporting live from the air above what's left of Canary Wharf Tower, One Canada Square, where early reports suggest fifty have died in an explosion and fire. TV celebrity, taxidermist and ecological campaigning figurehead, Jimmy T, spoke to us exclusively as he fights for his life just a few minutes ago and had this to say…"

A two second pause, DMs kicking like baby's feet. Then a cracked voice: "A zit doahn anziwaz zis uj fiabah n m xposion. Nox mi deahd onmi feed. Buzt alza winzows cleah ouz, glaz wiz frying everzewah. Ze voom wiz destroyed. Competly. A zot a wazgonadie. A cud heahzisceamz next doah. A zot, fwippin eck, yuz onla chenz iz at ze winzow. Awaza secunz expozon, nearla boo metzo keendum cum. A juzt gabbed zis lej na hunin fuhma deah laff."

Cassie Black nodded solemnly into the camera. Over her shoulder, Roving Eye Two has arrived and is filming Roving Eye One filming.

Cassie shuffled her papers, nodded and smiled. "Thanks Jaan. Dramatic events unfolding. We'll have more as it happens."

A BBC dominated planet Earth flashed up for three seconds, then it was back to the movie. It was Apocalypse Now, again, the bit where Martin Sheen's wasted crew shoot up an innocent family in their boat. They got me down after that. Four big guys in space suits and breathing masks, swinging ropes, sweating and gasping after their assault on the penthouse. They dragged me back into the flame-filled building where three of them tied me chest-to-chest with the fourth.

"Sam," he said. "Name's Sam. I'll get you down."

They looped my feet together and bound my arms behind the fireman's back. It only took a second and I was trussed up like a Christmas turkey. Then there was a speedy flurry of grunts, handshakes and head butting. This got me worried. Then this lumbering great fireman turned and, doubled-up with the weight and the exertion of having recently ran up to the top of this building, leapt straight out of the window. For a few elongated seconds of freefall terror, I screamed against his mask. Falling. Falling. Falling backwards. Behind the streaming condensation on his mask there was a black face, teeth clenched grimacing, brown eyes, no features. Then above him three more space suits leaping, arms out knees bent.

From street level, it appeared as though four spreading rose buds had been spat out of the exploding building. The cameras capture the spontaneous applause as the parachutes open.

What everyone above and below is missing is the snap of a rope caused by the lurch of the chute opening. Deadly as a hairline crack on a space shuttle fuel tank, the combined weight of space fireman Sam and me is too much for the lifeline. Sam felt it go in the instant before it started unravelling. Something changed in his eyes when he realised. Even though we reached out for one another across a Sistine Chapel of night sky and blazing skyscraper, and I tried all my best swim strokes, I had to laugh. It wasn't the bomb that killed me. It was the coming back to earth. Or, in my case, the Thames.

Let me tell you, what they say about that instant when you become an ingredient of the electric soup of life is only half true. The bit about having your whole life flash before you is much more than watching a film. It is like starring in the film, which isn't so surprising, except that it comes at you, this life, from all possible different angles. Through the eyes of your mum, your dad, your lover or best friend. Imagine enjoying your first kiss relived from the other person's lips. Or the kindness you showed a dog from that pet's point of view. What you'll be amazed at what, when the time comes, is the detail. Don't be afraid to have a look, if you can and no one thing is pressing you to move on in any particular direction. Take some time to play around for yourself. It's not always HD quality, sometimes it gets a bit jagged around the edges and the sound reverbs a lot. But there are fascinating things here you never knew had even happened but they really truly went on and you can take them apart, these fractions of a life, pick them open and watch them impact on, shatter, or form, your time.

12

Same Friday. 6 PM.

Fat Vivienne's weekly tarot class has five full tables and the Psychic Deli is unnaturally buzzing. The lessons, usually a jovial warm up for the big séance, are brimming with chaos and disbelief. Already four tables have revealed an identical five card spread complete with Hanging Man, Tower and Death.

It falls to a fat old Russian in washed out Soviet naval uniform, clanging with gongs, to deliver the final spread. He has such a theatrical flourish that Portia has to nudge Aurora to whisper, "Is this a setup?"

Aurora, focussing on an area of ceiling above the tables, shakes her head. She says, "It's a something."

The Russian pauses, worries the red flaky skin on his cheek. He strokes his grey beard. He flattens grey curls on his head and announces to his gawping audience, now standing on their chairs to better see his cards, that this is plenty much more excitement than he had expected when he Dominic Venegris, formerly Chief Starshina of the Russian Navy, popped into this peculiar bistro for a cup of English tea.

Vivienne has told the tables to focus on the symbolism of their cards and forget the fancy instruction book in the box. She toddles around the café, pushing between the tables, her voice booming. "Tarots are individual symbolic pages in a book about symbolism. Remember, your personal images of love, fortune, or despair are all going to be different from mine. So, interpret the artist's symbolic intuition.

"These cards were designed by Aleister Crowley, the occultist, a writer, a mountaineer, a painter, a hedonist, and bisexual," she says. "If he could cram all of that into his life, think what he could do to a pack of cards."

Then bump bump bump bump. The same spread from four tables, four customers at each, four separate Thoth decks of 78 cards. Identical. Not even one card inverted.

Bump 1. Three old women, one in a wheelchair, and their home help gasp. Death is the first card up. "It's alright love," Vivienne smoothes the blanket over the trembling knees, puts a hand on the social worker's arm to stop her leaving. "Death does not necessarily mean death, or doom. For instance, take it another way and it could mean a new opportunity is near." She says how, in this position, Death is the present and the general theme of the reading.

The three ladies don't like the sound of this, but the carer peels them off the top. As they come, with Vivienne's commentary there is

The Lovers

"Interesting juxtaposition. Just put it down there my dear, to the left of Death. There you go. Card two, The Lovers. Here it represents the past and, I am sure, influences still having an effect. Now who's a naughty girl then?"

The Universe

"Card three. The Universe. This is position three, to the other side of Death, and represents the future. How wonderful. The universe, creation, the whole story, beginning, middle and end. See how Crowley visualised the eye of God framed by the Ox, the Lamb, the Phoenix and, I think, the Fool. Strength, Peace, Resurrection and Humility, respectively. Obey the laws of nature and the universe, humility, strength, resurrection and peace will be your reward, as seen in the eyes of God. At the end of all our travelling we shall arrive at that place from whence we began, and to know it again as if for the first time. It's a big story so far. What's next? Let's hope for something cheery."

The Tower

"Oh dear. Doom and gloom. What are you four ladies trying to do to me today? Fire and destruction, high rise hell, the fearful white heat of truth. This is card four and it sheds light on the reason behind the question we are divining away so furiously on, only we don't have a question for this experiment. Or do we? Ladies? Is someone asking something of the cards that I should know about? It helps explain card two, our lovers. These lovers obviously need to get over their differences."

The Queen of Wands

"Ah, the beautiful one. At last. Card five. The Queen of Wands. Were any of you girls redheads? This lady has discovered her integrity through a great period of personal growth. She is a woman who has embraced her destiny by accepting her past. She's the original high-powered girl, passionate with strong opinions and desires. Watch out though, she's protective of her family and her lover, heaven help anyone who gets on the wrong side of this dame. Here, at card five, is what may yet come to be. This is where we find our answers to the question we have been posing. Here is the truth we seek. The lovely queen. She'll sort it out."

Vivienne has a suggestion. "Sometimes, when doing a reading and I need a bit of a hint about who's asking the questions, I ask for a sixth card. Strictly speaking, it's just something I do, but try it and it might work out for you. So, lovely, turn over a sixth card and just put it up there next to the Queen. Let's see who is out there."

The Hanged Man

"Oh dear. This person has no choice. It's a disturbing situation. Still, we best always remember that suffering can potentially lead to revelation, or even more wisdom. In the shadows of all these problems there lie great possibilities. Just glad it's not mine that spread. Phew! Ne-ext."

Bump 2. The table of hippies who run the soap stall at the market, four guys dripping t's with cannabis leaf motif and Rasta stripe beanies. Relaxed. Doodling over lattes and spicy vegetarian panini. The spread comes hot on the heels of their lunchtime spliff, so by the time The Universe turns up their mood is transcendental. When the hanging man shows too, all four retreat to the toilets with their Rizzlas.

Bump 3. Vivienne is sweating streams of dark red on her pink cheesecloth shirt. "Lord," she groans over at Portia. "Hasn't anyone shuffled their cards? Everyone shuffle their cards." Portia and Aurora are statues at the cappuccino frother. Table three are Psychic Deli regulars. Darren and Tim are couple of academics, one lectures in biology at the local poly and the other is doing an MBA at LSE. Sometimes they hold hands under the table but look in opposite directions out of the window. They've come for the séance and are sitting with Mrs Aziz from Sainsbury's checkouts and her old friend Charles, the retired tube driver who now spends most of his time growing vegetables in plastic tunnels in his allotment. He has a loose arrangement with Portia that allows him to trade his fresh vegetables for a coffee. Tim turns the first card and screams an eek a mouse girly scream at Death and grabs Darren by the arm at The Lovers. Mrs Aziz has to fan herself with a napkin by The Tower. "No way," Darren hisses. Tim screams again. "I'm going to die." Charles chews on his unlit pipe. "Rather you than me," he says and takes the deck. At the Queen of Wands Mrs Aziz faints face first onto the table and it takes Vivienne five minutes to make her comfortable. "We can't stop now," Charles says. "We might get the lottery numbers next." By his Hanging Man, Charles is a burst balloon. He says, "Bloody Nora. Anyone got a scotch?"

Bump 4 only really happened because the very heavily

dieting woman in outsize black culottes needed a piece of cheesecake after coming off a busy tube. Her friend, dangling a Selfridge's bag over an arm in plaster, thought a tarot class would be a bit of fun so volunteered them both to make a foursome with two blacked up Goths already sitting, a young man with a nose ring and his pale faced girlfriend with purple hair and orange lips. "Nice," thought Aurora when she saw them come in. Now the purple hair is standing straight up. The nose ring gets spun and tugged until it cuts. The bag falls off the cast. The fat woman pushes herself back in her seat and starts to cry.

Bump 5. "What sort of a something?" says Portia. "Dunno," Aurora says. "But I bet there's another one coming." Vivienne leans her vast buttocks against Mrs Aziz and pushes her off her chair onto the floor, where she lies moaning. "I aint ever seen anything like this," Vivienne says. The four hippies wander in, quite dreamily relaxed. They encourage Vivienne to allow the scabby old Russian to turn the cards for his table - Mrs Pugh, sporting Ray Bans and Chanel topped off by pearls, killing time before the séance, and two Nigerian parking wardens who have had their appeal to be allowed out aggressively hissed down. Death. The Lovers. The Universe. The Tower. The Queen of Wands. "She's a Russina this one with the big bazookies," Dominic scratches. "My Anna Karenina."

The Hanged Man.

The air is like mustard. What's it all about? Vivienne does not know. People start crowding for the door, needing to breathe fresh air.

Mrs Pugh stands, drops the shades and lets loose those bulging white eyes. She points a roving arthritic finger, turning slow across the room, momentarily capturing then releasing those it passes. "It's nothing to do with your stupid Tsarina," she says, her voice calm. "It's her. Her. The message is for HER."

Aurora cannot take being pointed at any longer. She pushes Portia into the office.

"Start the séance. Something big is coming."

13

Aurora is singing in a voice like a German storm trooper. "England England Uber Alles, Uber Alles mit der Wurld, England England, England England, Uber Alles mit der Wurld. England England, England England, Uber Alles mit der Wurld."

"Where are you?" says Mrs Pugh.

"Dagenham Heathway." Aurora slips into a girly voice. "The lads put on a good show but BritRail bobbies sent them scattering."

"What's your name?"

"Babsy."

"Hello Babsy. Do you want to tell us something?"

Aurora has closed eyes to focus inwards. Outside, she can hear the open mouthed anthem. There's a skinhead in immaculately polished ox blood 14 hole docs, Black Watch kilt, ex-Army, and camouflage MA1 jacket. Another. And another. Three of them turn and clench their right fists over their breasts, above their hearts, and launch salutes, flat handed, fingers pointing like arrows. "Freedom!"

Babsy says, "G took a Polaroid."

Several passengers looked away. Two metres tall in his Black Watch, docs and MA1, arrogant as fuck, G has shaved his head like the others but has grown a set of pointy going nowhere sideburns. Specially for this job, he told Babsy.

"Who is G?"

"Our leader."

Aurora moans, twisting.

"Is she alright?" Portia says to the room. "Are you alright Spooky?"

Mrs Pugh moon eyes her. She hisses quiet. "Babsy? Babsy?" she says. "What's happening?"

Aurora barely opens her mouth, like she is trying to be a bad ventriloquist. "We are in a cab," says Babsy. Six in the morning squeezed into the back seat of a black hack cab scooting through Piccadilly, cutting across to Mayfair towards Club Paradise where G says they have to meet someone at seven. The cab hits greens all the way. The black driver speaks some English with an African accent and fixes his passengers with red-rimmed eyes in the driver's mirror. He punctuates the journey by kissing a finger and tapping a Madonna statuette taped to the radio. There's a faint disinfectant smell in the back seat with them and Babsy thinks: That's nice. Here's a black man who cares about customer hygiene.

"What's that smell?" says Vivienne. Everyone holding hands in darkness around the table starts sniffing.

"It's like...Domestos," says Tim.

Mrs Aziz squeezes his hand. "That's right. It's disinfectant. I can smell disinfectant. Where's that coming from?"

"Babsy. Listen to me," orders Mrs Pugh. "Listen only to me. Ignore this chatter. What's happening now?"

Aurora shrugs and smiles a little. Babsy, she feels like singing. "Baby love. My baby love. Oh. Oh. My baby love."

It is early, but G and Babsy are high as kites, bouncing up and down on the Scotch-taped upholstery, leaning a hundred and eighty degrees around corners, giggling like they are on a killer roller coaster ride. There's no hurry so G tells the driver to go around Marble Arch again. The driver taps the Virgin and signals he intends to do a U turn.

An old 60s Motown song, maybe The Supremes, is

playing behind the wire mesh partition. "Musica, uppa da musica," G wafts the warm, strangely menthol, air with his hand like he was conducting the opera at Covent Garden. He tells the driver he will give him five quid to turn up the radio and the driver does so. It is Baby Love, which was actually recorded on Stateside Records in 1964 and was the single after Where Did Our Love Go. The B side is the underestimated classic Ask Any Girl. Together they shout: "Bay-be lo-ve, ma bay-be lo-ve, oo oo oo ma bay-be love."

The cab is vibrating, the driver is kissing and tapping, and the lights turn to red.

A man in a dark green tracksuit top with one white stripe down the arms, who is wearing something that looks like a Hawaiian grass skirt over his legs and two polythene bags tied to his feet, is slumped on the street corner. G slaps the window and shouts "Dirty Bastard." The man lifts unseeing eyes as the cab misses him by inches.

Fifty yards further on and Postreros Primeros is sprayed in blood red lettering on the side of an American Express bureau. G turns after the receding graffiti.

Aurora screams, a man's voice with an accent from somewhere near Manchester. "Will you fuckin' turn that up?"

Then, low with something foreign, she says: "Don't go up none higher."

Aurora devils it out: "Fuckin' faggots, blacks, immigrant baby junkies, Russian commie bastards. Diseases! You never imagined the diseases. Alzheimer, anorexia, bulimia, bollock cancer, tit cancer, cystic fibrosis, cerebral palsy, sick fuck eyetis, leukaemia, multiple sclerosis. You're going to get it here boy. And all over the world. And…all over the world…"

Portia puts a hand over her mouth. Tim is shouting, "My God, it's the thing from The Exorcist."

Babsy baby talks: "We'll show them gratitude."

Aurora spits on the floor and Babsy punches the seat,

looking the driver's tired eyes in the mirror: "Disinfect that, ya Fuck."

They are in Kensington and Babsy just knows there's a puppy round here, somewhere, drinking milk from a crystal cigarette ashtray, wearing a chiffon rah-rah skirt, or an Elizabethan ruff collar, reeking of Rive Gauche and Doggy Pearl Drops toothpaste, soon to be the victim of a cross breed arranged marriage in Alexander McQueen and Vivienne Westwood.

Club Paradise is in a botanic garden on a flat roof up a flight of stairs above a designer boutique. The shutters are up so G and Babsy go on in. It is warm and it smells a bit of cold sweat at first.

A parrot chained to a perch heavy with guano shifts from foot to foot when they come in. Beneath planet earth lampshades a rat faced man is smoking at the bar. He stands, flicks ash off his Ralph Lauren charcoal pinstripe trousers and waves them in. Aurora knows that rat face.

"Come back to us now honey," says Mrs Pugh. "Tell us what you see."

While G and LM have a big pow wow, talk of war and money, Babsy curls up in a booth and dreams of milk and honey.

"No trace?"

G nodded. "No trace. Not him. Not us. Not you."

LM licks along the length of an unlit cigarette, pops it into his mouth, then inhales noisily.

Crisis World, G thinks. There's a real market opportunity. He is going to use his cash from this job to open a theme park with the scariest rides for sick bastards and call it Crisis World. He does not smile.

"Half now, half later." LM crumples the cigarette. "You don't need to know too much about him. Uh-huh."

Mrs Pugh is adamant. "Tell us what you see."

Aurora whispers, "Kill him. They're going to kill him."

G and Babsy register at three hotels a day for a week. When they travel downtown, they hum the famous

Petula Clark song. In Canary Wharf they take polaroids of each other from low down that are full of impossibly angled buildings. Babsy said there was an air of insanity in the photos. G says insanity was "something they put in the air and sprinkled out of jets."

"Who?" says Portia.

Babsy said all the blokes at the Millennium Hilton looked like either Robert De Niro or Michael Douglas. G told her not to fantasize about unreal people.

They make love passionately to the sun setting between the tower blocks and all the time the horns hooting and traffic buzzing in the street below.

G hands Babsy the blue vanity case.

Aurora cries, her voice, is being crushed beneath the weight of the resurrected worlds. "Him. They kill him."

Three blocks later they stride purposefully into Canary Wharf Tower, nod at the front desk without pausing and take an elevator. U2's Lemon blares out. Up to the Sky restaurant. Here a girl wearing a too short for work red lycra dress sees them looking lost.

Babsy put her hand to her crotch and made a swaying movement with her body. "Don't s'pose there's a, hmm?"

In the windowless washroom, chrome walls, black steel floor, polished aluminium mirrors, G and Babsy bundle each other into a cubicle. "Drain it," he hisses, unscrewing a panel to expose the water cistern. Babsy flushes. "Easy fuckin does it," G says, tying off the plumbing with a roll of I LOVE LONDON tape. Babsy has sweat running down her stomach. In one movement G slides the vanity case into the tank.

"There. You do it for luck." He passes the tiny key to Babsy.

On the way down, The Osmonds play Crazy Horses and Babsy feels more relaxed, though they were stopped eleven times and were pushed back in the elevator, silent, separated.

"Easy peasy," G says outside. They find a McDonald's a

block away. G has a Big Mac and fries. Babsy, guts tight as a snare drum, makes do with a vanilla milk shake.

They take a booth near the window. Babsy is thinking, How do we know for certain he's going to be there? G is thinking what it must be like to have an orgasm just at the moment of death.

Then he asks himself if, in time to come, will they both revisit this moment? Could the terrorists be forced to acknowledge their ultimate thoughts were of sloppy daydreams not political incisiveness?

G looked at his watch. "Now."

With a scream Aurora collapses under the table. In the dark of the room, it is as though the walls have come squeezing in, the floor kicks bucking bronco, the table is upended and the air they breathe is on fire.

"That's it," Portia shouts. "Enough."

But when she tries to drag Vivienne to her feet the bulk wont move.

"Sit down, we have to see it through," shouts Mrs Pugh. "We must maintain the energy of the circle if Aurora is to come back to us."

Mr Venegris stamps his feet loud as horse's hooves, his medals rattling. "Da. Together. We hold together."

To Babsy it was more of a rumble, a far away sound at first that rolled out of the sky towards them in a voice that got deeper and more resolute then deepened again. With it came an earthquake out of Revelations. Three cars smashed into one another right outside their McDonald's and had G jumping up shouting "My God! My God!" adding to the commotion. The view from the window frames the panic like a huge television screen showing an 80s disaster movie. A lot of people screaming and running. Others freeze, faces raised to heaven. Some launch themselves into the restaurant, pushing counter staff out of the way. Then giant footsteps came thundering outside. The ground vibrates. "God!" G is shouting, standing up and staggering back, pulling Babsy with him. He is looking across the street, arm raised as if trying to shield himself or, yes, he was pointing and Babsy turned to look from the terror in his face to the area he was fingering just in time to see a unit of three stainless steel wash hand basins crash land out of the sky full on top of a pram being pushed by a pregnant white girl in dungarees. There was a row of friendship beads dangling in a fringe on the pram. G's hand is still pointing when the woman gets pierced by a shard of glass ten feet long that cuts her in two like a melon. Then their own wall is hit by something, maybe a lavatory, the window implodes and the image fractures.

When all the yelling goes quiet, Babsy opens her eyes. She lies twisted in a doughnut shaped mauve leatherette booth beneath G.

"I think I'm dead," she says. And so she is.

A policeman, bleeding and shaking with adrenaline, rushes in, shouts: "Everybody keep calm," then runs out again.

Sirens and alarms howl. Ambulance crews, fire fighters, police. People pick at the rubble.

But all the time the anxiety in people's voices fades, the way things do in London as people realise they are reassuringly not being affected by the cataclysm, or whatever is going on, only a few minutes walk away.

Aurora sits up straight, suddenly tranquil, wide-open eyes fixed on nothing.

"Are you alright?" says Portia.

"I am an everywhere, nothing, something. I can see up the line, I can see down the line."

"What happened?" says Mrs Pugh.

"They killed him."

"Who?" says Portia.

Here I am, Aurora. Didn't mean to make you cry. At this moment I am a former human on a speeding tube train refusing to stop at any station. Aurora is the only person standing on the platform. Our eyes meet for a couple of seconds and then she goes strobing past, raising a hand like a hello goodbye.

They have to catch her when she falls.

"Jimmy T."

Further along the line. Within twenty-four hours a dozen groups claim they bombed London. The City pulses speculation and accusation, mainly targeted at an unknown Arab terrorist organisation intent on bringing death and destruction to the heart of Imperialist Zion-loving UK. Security forces say they remain open minded and investigators are working on the theory that a gas explosion had, in fact, blown the lid off the skyscraper. There were the Brothers of Islam, Anti Abortion Action, Friends of the Oklahoma Bomber, Unabomber B. Red Commando Brigade, the UK Freedom Fighters, the Omega Men, the Colombian Mafia, the Martin Luther Freedom Fighters, the JFK Starfighters, The Iranians, Carcass - an anti meat eating caucus - and the Invincible Earthmen.

Why any one of them would want to destroy this particular building, killing forty-four merchant bankers, two secretaries, a mother and her three month old daughter, a mail delivery boy, a McDonald's customer and me in the process, is unknown.

G compiled a scrapbook of photographs, including several he found on the internet that were taken by satellite, detailing the moment of the explosion in thermal and infrared.

He pasted these next to a chart of seismological readings of the event recorded by quake hunters in LA

Babsy's photo in the Daily Mail

The tired out faces of rescue workers

The interviews with grieving relatives

The President of the United States of America backs the prime minister vowing vengeance

the pall of smoke drifting up from

decapitated skyscraper

It goes on and goes on in the newspapers and in life. And in her forever after Babsy is haunted by the image of the pram crushed by a half ton of toilet and steel. Mary Brown and Joanna. Haunted. Out of her mind. When she longs to sleep, she dreams she is being choked by friendship beads. Her food of life that was luscious as locusts is bitter as coloquintida.

14

Portia Maxwell tugs at Bobo to let him know he has to keep up. All morning, he's been like a dead weight on the end of his blue leather strap. After a couple of steps his legs lose coordination and his head goes down. He wants to sniff every inch of the pavement. He needs to be lifted over the kerb. He wants to sit down, looking up at her with his lugubrious eyes, like he can't go on. Portia's arms are tired out carrying Bobo.

She was going to take him into the park behind the Maritime Museum. Instead he will have to do with a poke around the tombstones of St Alfege's. But the avocado green two piece woollen suit she's wearing has a tight fitting skirt licking her hips. It is not made for carrying dog. Picking him up and putting him down again is a pain.

The still life. Lime green bouffant, dressed with pearls like a swirl of sour cream. Nails like emeralds. Tabasco sauce lips. Honey brown eyes. Her moss green leather heels rattle on the concrete.

At the Psychic Deli she has to push him inside with the side of her shoe. By the time she picks up the mail, pulls up the blind and adjusts her hair, Bobo is under the desk staring at her. Portia runs her palms down her suit.

"You," says Portia, "are in the doghouse. So stay out of my way."

She puts her hands on her hips and looks at the place. Since the séance, since the tragedy, two weeks worth of deliveries are making it difficult to move. Packing cases are stacking up, obscuring several best sellers like the Louis fourteenth ebonised cabinet on a chest with brass stringing inlay. Its two glazed doors enclose three shelves darkly stained with the blood of the aristocratic heads they once displayed. The heads are gone but their screams and the rush of the guillotine remain. Aurora says blood will seep from the two short and three long drawers of the lower section.

Portia can hardly see the top of the walnut card table that she has bought back six times from poker players getting divorced. It deals from the bottom of the deck. It deludes players into believing they are unbeatable, win after win. Until the day they risk everything and the table turns against them. They lose their money, their car, their job, home and family.

Now boxes overflowing with bubble wrap are piled-up on it. One case holds a pair of late nineteenth century continental bronze torches, each with a turned stem cast with stiff leaves and stylized lions emerging from foliage. They stand on a tripod base, the knees modelled with lion's heads, and have paw feet drilled for electricity. The base of one foot is incised W in a three-quarter circle. Ten grand.

Somewhere nearby there is a larger box which holds her highest hopes. A five foot high statue so old it simply has to have seen some misery and be seasoned in blood and anguish.

She read up on the partial gilt polychrome carved wood figure of Saint George. The auctioneer encouraged her to compare the long, fleshy face with heavy-lidded eyes to the work of Gil de Siloe, from around the end of the fifteenth century. The graceful pose and the elaborately executed drapery of the figure placed it among late gothic Spanish sculpture.

George, depicted with his right arm aloft, the dragon at his feet, stands on an integrally carved base. Once he was striking out with his spear, but this has been lost along the way. Thirty grand. There is some minor worming, excellent for authenticity. The gilding is distressed and areas of the polychromy have been refreshed.

Portia knows George embodies the triumph of the Christian church over evil. Hence the dragon.

She has double speculated, spent the money and waited for a change in temperature. But no matter how long and hard she tries she can't see the evil in a statue.

Without Aurora, she has done the best she can.

She tells herself evil is not the only commodity. It is also useful to have several purely decorative pieces, without the haunting, in case an innocent old lady happens to drop by. If they do not sell, Portia can always take some items home.

Only after Aurora verifies them as non-possessed, of course.

She really needs Aurora to assess these pieces. All this mourning has been bad for business. If she shows today, there might just still be a business.

She makes a mental note to call the printer. The poster on the door is selling out of date classes in Astral Projection, Aura Soma and Colour, Plant and Crystal Energy Healing.

This business, Portia thinks, is built on the ghost of a ghost. A supernatural fantasy.

She snaps open the green and white purse on a white leather strap hanging from her elbow and takes out a small gold tube. She better turn the Closed sign over to Open. In the glass of the front door she looks past her reflection out over the churchyard.

A silver limo, windows blacked out, draws up outside. In the reflection of her front door Portia twists the gold tube until a red pepper lipstick grows out.

A chauffeur runs around to the nearside of the limo. He is wearing cream jodhpurs and double breasted jacket with tan riding boots.

She purses her lips and touches the lipstick to the lipstick already there.

The driver opens the passenger door and steps back, pulling hard on an industrial strength chain holding a black dog almost half the size of the car. Then he gets offered a thin white arm.

She rolls her lips together.

A tall woman emerges wearing a black cloud of fur over a full length fitted dress that, when you glimpse it, is like staring into the void of black nothingness. Her hair is black and her skin is white. When she glides over to Portia it is like the night sky has blotted out her reflection.

She twists the lipstick down, she snaps it in her purse and opens the door for this woman scanning the store with her black eyes. The fresh morning air has chilled.

"Can I be of some assistance?" says Portia. "You can see, we're presently rearranging."

The woman extends her arm, palm down, fingers flexed. "Ramana," she says. There is an accent there, eastern european, a daughter of Dracula. "Queen of Evil."

"Oh," says Portia. She doesn't do kiss. She shakes the hand awkwardly between thumb and forefinger, noticing the chunky diamond solitaire. "The Queen of Evil?"

"S'correct. M' card."

Portia presses down the strands of silvery lime hair on the side of her neck, squints at the business card. She says, "Well, nice to meet you. Welcome to the Psychic Deli. Coffee? Croissant?"

Ramana fixes for a moment on Bobo. Then she looks over at the Louis fourteenth. On the wall behind it, the light moves across the school of Rubens copy of The Incredulity of St Thomas, oil on wood, early sixteen hundreds. Not this instant, but at times blood is said to seep from the stigmata. Then the mind goes and the owner forgets everything, even their own name. Insanity forces them to stare at the painting endlessly and they become a babbling wreck.

Ramana says, "The girl is not here today?"

Portia shakes her head. "So sad. An accident. The boyfriend."

"She should not mourn this passing, from night into day," Ramana says. "She knows what is lost can be found."

Portia has heard plenty witchy talk from Aurora and her hippy pals. "Are you looking," she says, "for anything in particular? Some movie props perhaps? Another dalmation?"

Ramana Queen of Evil is ageless. This close, her hair isn't a solid colour of black. Each strand has blue along the edge, with green and almost violet as you look deeper inside. Angry against her white skin she wears blood red lipstick. She has red nails.

She presses these red nails together and closes her eyes. Listening.

Portia looks out the window. The big dog is greedily drinking water from a bowl at the kerb, splashing it around.

"There is a calling here," says Ramana. "It is strong."

Portia frowns. She looks up at the ceiling. She strains, but she hears nothing.

"That which I seek has an association with this place. It is a book," Ramana spreads open her palms, "very small, very old, very beautiful."

Portia says they don't do many books.

"This book holds the mysteries of time itself," Ramana says.

The Queen of Evil looks at her. No, she looks *into* her.

"It is my book of shadows, of memories. It was stolen from me. It contains my life force. It is my pleasure and it is my terror."

She would definitely remember that one if she had seen it, Portia says.

"Maybe you have the secret of eternal life?" says Ramana.

And Portia says no.

"Maybe you have countless lovers?"

No.

"Maybe the wind tells you the secrets of power. You speak with nature?"

And Portia says no, sorry.

"Maybe you can turn sand into gold?"

And she says no, sitting down at her desk.

"You have the power of life and death?"

No, she says, picking Bobo up onto her knee. And feels him trembling.

"Perhaps you can travel through time. Be invisible. Fly?"

No, really.

"Maybe if you can kill someone, you can also bring them back to life?"

No, says Portia. "But if I find this book, I'll certainly give you a call."

Ramana Queen of Evil seems to stall in midair. Then collects herself, sort of starts again.

"It has my telephone numbers. It is so and so, small, bound with the most rare soft red skin. I believe it may have been lost inside a piano."

Portia says, "How extraordinary." But her mind is saying piano, academy, Thalopopakus.

The dog outside starts barking.

"Quiet Sultan," hisses Ramana. "We are trying to hear ourselves think."

Then to the walls of the Psychic Deli she says, "You realise there are many souls here. So many voices."

"Do you know," says Portia, "Now you come to mention it, we did have a piano recently."

She flicks through the filing cards next to the phone.

"But Aurora was dealing with it and, no, no, there's nothing. She's probably still got the details with her, poor thing. She's had such a shock."

She rises out of the seat with her hand extended. "Why don't I get her to call you when she comes in?"

Ramana ignores the hand. Her darkness drifts towards the door where it heaves and swells and blocks out daylight. She takes a last look around.

"You and I," she says slowly, "share similar interests. A body without its soul is no more than a useless piece of abandoned furniture. It is the soul that holds the riches."

Portia watches as the Queen of Evil floats over the pavement and disappears into the waiting car. It cuts across the flow of traffic at the busy junction and veers away towards the city centre.

Bobo stands shivering by the door.

"A fine guard dog you make," Portia says.

15

Aurora digs her fingers into her new henna purple dreads and presses around the temples and top of her head. She's fresh out of the shower and wearing a leopard pattern bathrobe.

Her apartment is this one room where she sleeps on a sofa bed. A breakfast bar partitions off the microwave and fridge. The walls and twist pile carpet are grey. A brass statue of a Hindu god, multiple arms and legs dancing, is on the mantle over the fireplace. Red carnations are dotted around, some of them tied into bunches with black ribbon. Wisps of grey smoke drift up from cones of brown incense. The room smells of oranges. Instead of a fire there are rocks and lavender scented aromatherapy candles in the fireplace.

From the tv come gunshots, explosions, sirens and people screaming that she ignores. It's not for real. She would recognise real.

Real is when somebody you love dies and they can't find bits of the body for the funeral. Real is sorting through that persons belongings, the clothes that smell of them, their bills and personal papers and all the secret trinkets they own. Real is handing over a week's rent to a dead person's landlord.

The doorbell rings. It's a little early for the mourning group.

Aurora drags herself up to answer it, walking barefoot.

On the doorstep, Portia's holding Bobo's face up to the

spyhole, waggling a paw.

"Drink. I need drink," she says, flopping onto the sofa.

Aurora pours out a glass of red wine from the fridge.

"I thought you were one of my mourners," she says.

This is their fourth meeting, more of a bonding session really, and they're holding it at her flat. She's tried most of what the Psychic Deli has to offer. Aromatherapy, reiki, qi gong. Acupuncture, astral travel, colour therapy. Herbal remedies to sleep. Gemstone association for daytime stress. Yoga, meditation and on-line psychoanalysis.

"Get a dog , dear," Portia says between mouthfuls of shiraz.

The pug works his way onto Aurora's lap, a lot more affectionate than usual.

"Strange how they can tell when something is not right," says Aurora.

"He misses you. I miss you too. Truly we both do. My god," Portia sweeps the air with her hand, drains her wineglass. "We had a visitation. Ramana Queen of Evil."

"Wow. How evil is she then?"

"How would I know, Spooks? That's your department." Portia holds out the glass for a refill. "What's weird though is I had this feeling for a minute like she was trying to read my mind. If such a thing is possible."

"No, no, it is," says Aurora. "I mean, she might have been. If she is powerful enough. What did she want?"

Aurora holds her breath as Portia describes Ramana. How she is rich as sin, has a chauffeur, and floats around like a black cloud at night. "Then," says Portia, "she started going on about this address book, her shadows book or something."

Aurora draws up her knees. "That's serious. A book of shadows is like a witch's personal spell book."

"Well," Portia looks over shoulder, "she reckons hers

has something to do with that piano."

"Hammington's?"

"Remember Rainy found that photograph? What if her book was in there too, if it was a hideaway or repository? How much would the Queen of Evil pay to get something like this back?"

Bobo wants to lick Aurora's face. His breath is bad so she pushes him away.

"I tried to buy some time," says Portia. "I said you had the details and told her we'd be back in touch."

The doorbell rings. Portia pours another glass of wine while Aurora opens it.

Standing there is a short bald man wearing glasses with thick black plastic frames. He hands Aurora a neatly folded floral nightdress. The bald man scrapes his feet on the doormat, he looks at Portia and says, "Hi, Dill. I see I'm not the first."

And Aurora slaps herself on the forehead with the heel of her hand and says to Portia, "That's me he means. We take on plant names for the group. I mean, I'm Dill."

She says, "Hyacinth, this is my boss - "

"Rosebud," Portia says.

And Aurora carefully unfolds the nightdress. "We're going to use an item of remembrance to help focus our meditation on the dear departed."

Aurora shows Hyacinth to the bathroom. Portia helps herself to more wine.

The doorbell rings. And Aurora calls from the bathroom for Portia to get it.

This time it's a guy about Aurora's age with long strawberry blond hair and a red chin curtain, wearing blue jeans and a sweatshirt. He steps inside and hands Portia a single white stocking tied with a blue garter. He kicks off his trainers and pulls the sweatshirt off over his head. He drapes the shirt over Portia's shoulder and starts unbuttoning his jeans.

Portia knocks back the last of the wine. The man or the sweatshirt, or both, smell stale.

Aurora arrives and pushes the man back into his trousers.

She says, "Bullrush."

She takes his clothes and the stocking from Portia and hands the sweatshirt back.

She says, "Bullrush this is Mrs Maxwell, who I work for. Bullrush is an accountant."

And the guy smoothes his long hair out of his face and smiles. He has one of those young bodies, with big muscles, that narrows at the waist.

"We're going to try ceremonial nudity," Aurora says, blushing. "But not today, huh? It can, sometimes, help us bond. Complicated grief requires more complex therapies than uncomplicated grief."

"An accountant," says Portia, grabbing his arm. "What do you think of Mondrian's work?"

Aurora nods towards the kitchen and says, "Bullrush, why don't you make us some coffee?"

And then she puts the stocking on the floor next to the nightdress.

Bullrush looks at Portia, winks, and says, "How do you like it?"

Aurora takes Portia into a small hallway connecting bathroom and living space. She says she understands if Portia doesn't want to stay. She reaches behind a curtain where she keeps her clothes and pulls out a long black coat.

"I couldn't part with it. It smells of Jimmy T," she says, pressing it to her face.

"Is that what you mean by complicated grief?" says Portia.

Aurora dresses in her cordons of silver necklaces, the pentacle talisman, chains and pendants, her amulets, and heavy glass jewelled finger rings.

"No," she says. "Really it's the absence of grief I'm

worried about. Someone who avoids any reminders of the person who died, who constantly thinks or dreams about the person who died, and who gets scared and panics easily at any reminders of the person who died, could be suffering from post-traumatic stress disorder. But I'm just waiting for Jimmy to, well, drop in."

In the lounge Aurora spreads the coat on the floor and places the nightshirt and stocking on top. Bobo hops down from the sofa and curls up on top of the coat.

"I'm sorry," says Portia, lifting the dog up.

"That's alright," Aurora says. She rubs behind Bobo's ear with a knuckle. "Animals have to grieve as well."

Portia breathes in, eyes up the ceiling, shivers at the smelly coat her dog is lying on. "Yes. We all have to move on."

Hyacinth comes in. The blubbery white skin of his arms are covered in curly black pubic hair. A mass of hair is sprouting out of the open neck of his shirt.

Portia excuses herself to go to the toilet. When she returns the room is full of people. There is a man called Tulip, who brought a goldfish in a bowl. A policewoman named Dahlia arrives. A Wisteria arrives. A Geranium rings the doorbell. Then a Chrysanthemum. Then someone called Cushion arrives or someone asks for a cushion, it's not clear.

The incense smells like oranges and everything in the room smells of oranges. The wine tastes of oranges.

Aurora lights the candles in the fireplace. Her breasts curve out, her pink nipples trying to touch people through the dressing gown. Beneath the robe Portia can see how Aurora's back arches at the base of her spine and divides into two solid buttocks.

Bobo works his way around the circle of mourners, seeking attention and then moving on.

For a moment the woman called Orchid catches Portia's eye. Dressed in nurse's uniform, accessorised with an art deco leopard turban, smoking a cigarette through an amber tipped Meerschaum holder, she is telling a small group of people all about her past lives. A belly dancer, a milkmaid, a soldier in World War One. Portia studies the sad heap at the centre of the circle. Jimmy T's coat, Hyacinth's wife's nightdress, Bullrush's wife's stocking, the goldfish, a pair of man's underpants, some socks, a wedding photograph, a club tie, a handwritten letter, a handbag. Bizarre fragments of lives being held dear.

And Orchid says, "Does anyone else here believe in reincarnation?"

And everyone starts agreeing with one another that it's a possibility. For certain.

"What about you, dear?" says the woman with the cigarette.

Portia pulls the front of her jacket shut.

The room is so quiet you can hear the vacuum flex dragging along the floor above. You can hear a toilet flush next door.

Then the door goes again and Aurora lets in Mrs Aziz, in overalls straight from work and brandishing a bag of doughnuts. "Sorry I'm late," she says. "I got held up. Not literally, of course, just getting these."

Bullrush sweeps over and grabs the bag from her hand.

"Turmeric, what have you got there you spicy little devil?" He stuffs in a chocolate dream, sniffing and sniggering.

"Hoy. Mr Bullrush. They is for after our mournings."

Deep in the pile of jackets inside the front door a phone rings and this woman called Dahlia runs over and digs it out.

And across the room is Aurora. Dill. She's laughing with Hyacinth, sitting cross legged on the floor, taking turns to stroke Bobo. She's tied her dreadlocks back, clear of her slender neck and small round face.

"Aur... Dill," Portia says, "I'm going back to the Deli."

Aurora lifts Bobo up and skips over to her. "Sorry if this seems strange. We'll join hands in a minute and meditate for a while. And that's it really."

No trouble, says Portia. "And if you want to come back, I need you. There's this Ramana Evil majesty person to deal with and a missing heir I need you to find. And we've a lady who is convinced her husband is playing around."

"I miss you too," says Aurora. She's already decided she'll go back in the morning. Then she hugs Bobo. Poor old pooch. She holds him up and looks him in the eye.

Up this close, Aurora's eyes are not just grey. They are diamonds with ribbons of emeralds on a bed of gold.

"And this old boy," she says. "Strange, how he makes me think of Jimmy T."

"Probably because it's time to get him stuffed," says Portia.

No. Aurora says. There is something more.

And all the time I am waiting.

Aurora says she feels hot and sticky.

I am praying harder than anyone has ever prayed.

Aurora says there's something not quite right going on here.

It is the vertigo feeling you get on a cliff edge high above the ocean, with nothing between you and the endless sea. That weightlessness you get when you fall down a tunnel in a dream. First steps on a suspension bridge over a deep gorge. Playing hide and seek when the seeker is almost on top of you. Having only one hope.

And a voice says, *Jimmy?*

Faith and prophecy, of Messiahs and martyrdom, thousands of years of life after death arguments. The saints, the reformation, Palm Sundays. It all comes down to this. One minute I was flesh and blood, now I am hurtling around the universe sharing the wire free energy of mobile phones, bouncing off satellites, reflecting off clouds and dancing with sunlight. I thought my destiny was to be stuck on that tube forever until it suddenly screeched to a halt and I was ejected into an electricity cable, racing effortlessly across the national grid. Then I got stuck in a light bulb for a week until my electric self could surge again, this time into someone's laptop. From there, the internet stretched out, sweeping global lines of communication that have allowed me to win a little control over speed and direction.

In this hallucinatory Mondrian universe, every straight line is infinitely extendable, the open ended space between two parallel lines infinitely expandable.

So I try to seek out Aurora. And then, you can imagine the surprise, when I open my eyes I am this dog. There are two small brown legs where my arms used to be. My hands are inarticulate bony feet almost as long as a hare's but not so round as a cat's. The fingers are black nails. My legs feel strangely connected to this hairy stubby body and that tail curled around is the oddest feeling.

It isn't reincarnation. This fur ball is no puppy. It is a possession. Despite much hasty soul searching, there is no trace of a previous occupant. Then the bridge comes down. It falls away from under you into the roaring seas. The line gets cut off. You are stranded. Alone again. On the other side.

Portia touches Aurora's shoulder as she sways for a second. "Are you alright dear?" she says.

And Aurora hugs me close and whoops, spins around and around, goes dancing in and out her wine glugging guests. I can smell her perfume like I never smelled before.

While Hyacinth gets the meditating started Portia lifts me up on the kitchen table, holding my head behind the ears, squinting deep into my eyes.

"Are you sure he's in there?" she whispers.

"It's him alright," Aurora says.

Portia is looking and searching and seeing nothing. Up this close, she has little cracks around her waxy lips.

"His breath hasn't improved any. You'd think that would be different," she says. "Jimmy? Jimmy? If you're in there, give us a sign."

I understand. I hear the words and they all make sense. But when I try to answer, my words get blocked and lost.

I visualise them in my mind, giant simple words like yes, help, or me. My cry comes out a whimper.

If I concentrate as hard as I can, shout as loud as possible, it's a yelp.

Aurora pours some milk into a new red plastic bowl. It says DOG in black letters. I can read.

Uncontrollably, I offer her a paw. Then the tail twitches.

"Jimmy T," says Portia. "If you can hear me, give us a sign."

I managed to bark. Once.

"Can't we get him to bark once for yes, twice for no?"

"It doesn't work that way," says Aurora. "We've got to think of him as a prisoner, wrapped in chains and gagged and stuff."

"Well, if that's him," says Portia, straightening up, "then what's happened to my Bobo?"

Aurora folds her arms over her pinafore. "Dunno about that."

They both study me so closely I can feel the red embarrassment under the fur. I can feel their gaze on my nakedness. Especially down there, I mean, in those parts I can't bear to look at.

Aurora says, "I suppose the old Bobo has just moved over a bit to let Jimmy T in."

Portia doesn't buy it. "Is that possible? I mean, I know none of this is what anyone would say is probable. But is it possible that there's two of them in there?"

"I have to say that anything's possible in this world," says Aurora. "There might be millions of people, just like him. Stuck in animals."

Portia shakes her head in disbelief. "Maybe we should get an exorcist?"

Aurora looks shocked. "I don't think that's the answer. We need to figure out how he got in there and how we're going to get him back out."

Portia clasps her hands over my ears. "How can we get him out when his body's gone? There's nothing left for him to go to."

Aurora spills out her bag and spreads around her collection of dream catcher earrings, yin and yang beads, I-ching coins, lucky rabbit key ring, quartz crystals, rune stones, her pentacle choker, Tibetan prayer beads and incense cones.

She doesn't think there's anything there that can do the trick.

"None of it's got any clout, apart from the pentacle really," she says.

Portia remembers Ramana. "Don't you have a book of shadows?"

Aurora sighs. "Nothing for this. My witchy spells are all to keep the bad guys away."

"Maybe the Queen of Evil could help?"

"She gives me the willies," says Aurora.

If only I could make myself understood instead of dribbling at them like a dumb dog.

Portia says, "What we need is a receiver, a television set for thought waves."

Aurora tells Portia telepathy with animals is something we do all the time, only we're not aware of it because it tends to be with human animals. When a friend tells you she is fine, but your gut says it's not right, that's telepathy. The thought of the animal blends with your consciousness. It becomes your own inner thought for a flash of a moment. It happens so quick and unexpected that we don't know how to tell the difference from our own thoughts.

"Then do it with Bobo. Jimmy T," Portia says.

Aurora says she'll try. But Portia has to appreciate that setting up telepathy with a dead person who's living in a dog is a lot different from anything she's ever done before.

There's bell-tinkling going on between Mrs Aziz and Orchid as Aurora lights two cones of incense and wafts the jasmine scent around a bit with her hand. "Sometimes," she says, "it helps to use a mirror."

Portia snaps open her gold and cream shoulder bag and hands over her turtle shell compact. Aurora angles the mirror so that she can see my face and I can see hers.

Bobo stares at Portia with his watery eyes. "What is it?"

"What's what?" Aurora says.

"I'm talking to the dog," says Portia. "You cannot need to do your business again. We'll need to get those kidneys seen to."

Aurora asks how old Bobo is.

"Fifteen," says Portia to the mirror. To the dog she says, "Choking with asthma and a bladder like a wet Sunday. It just goes on and on. He doesn't get around much now. Does you my darling?"

Aurora says, "Fifteen is a hundred and five in dog years. He's ancient really."

"What's the difference between dog years and human years? The world goes round just the same speed for both of us."

"I think," says Aurora, "it has something to do with the size of the brain. Or maybe it is the heart. A little thing, like a hummingbird, lives this all fast and speeded up kind of life. We have to film it and watch it in slow motion just to see its wings beat. Its tiny heart must be pumping ever so fast." She drums her fingers. "To them we're big lumbering animals that creep around ever so slowly."

Portia says, "I don't think Bobo has ever lived that fast." Then she says, "Does that mean small people or people who run around a lot live shorter lives?"

Aurora flops back. "No. Growing up is different. Time is relative. Now hush. This takes time. And I need quiet," she says.

Portia leans against the wall, admiring Bullrush's torso. Aurora wriggles loose her shoulders, joins thumbs and middle fingers to form two small circles, closes her eyes.

Spooky has had some crazy ideas, Portia thinks. Things Portia would never have believed possible. And she does have a witchy talent. But Portia can't help thinking, this time, the girl is freaking over the death of her boyfriend.

Aurora starts breathing raspy deep lungfuls. When she breathes in, she says a drawn out So. When she breathes out, it is a long sigh and she says Haun.

Portia says, "What's with the heavy breathing?"

Aurora opens one eye. "It's mantric breathing. You're supposed to be being quiet."

Portia says sorry.

"That am I. I am that. That being the immortal spirit," says Aurora.

"Oh. Nice," says Portia. "I thought it was meant to be I think therefore I am."

Aurora sighs. "If being is the result of thinking, what happens if I do not think? At a deep level most of us are scared to allow the mind to stop because that is the absence of ego, the absence of self. Yet it is only through the absence of self, that the power and mystery of the great being can be experienced."

"What great being?"

"*The* Great Being. It's a zen thing. Now hush."

Aurora wriggles her shoulders, settles again, shuts her eyes and resumes her mantric breathing.

Come get me. Come get me, I'm thinking. My tail is flicking. I'm searching around inside my head, which still feels as though it belongs to me even though it looks like Bobo's.

I'm expecting a flash of light. An explosive breakthrough. What actually happens is like the first outdoor broadcast from the moon. Inside, on the scratchy black and white film screen of my mind's imagination, pixels are dancing here and there. They are rearranging themselves around a bit. Tuning into the signal. Almost taking shape. Almost connecting to sound.

Portia worries about Aurora's breathing. It was very shallow and now it has virtually stopped. Bobo is very quiet too. He has this bemused air.

Then, as if from out of nowhere, Aurora sucks in a great So. Her eyes pop wide open, focussing somewhere through the other side of the mirror. Her dreads are up like Medusa snakes. My fur is standing.

When Aurora's thought beam bounces through the mirror and into my head, the crackly screen in my mind's eye starts holding together better.

First a blur, then a glowing amorphous creature.

Then an outline.

A golden light. Then a face.

Up there, in here, it's Aurora's face on my screen. All wispy.

She has this echoing voice. She says, "Jimmy T, you've been a very naughty boy."

I say she's my angel. I only have to think the words and she hears them. "You've got to get me out of here. I don't want to be a dog forever."

She says, "How can we get you out if we don't know how you got in?"

And I say I don't know how but this is all about that

damned piano. Our connection crackles and fades. The echo voice gets lost in the surf.

And then Aurora, the scratchy silhouette of Aurora, says, "She's a witch, and not a very nice one. The book is her book of spells. Her book of shadows. She'll do anything to get it back."

"Well, I know where it is," I say.

My voice is all chopped up. Any definition in Aurora's face has gone.

Aurora is stressed. She says, "Jimmy T, quickly. Tell me where the book is."

"Inside," I say. My mind buzzes with interference. I focus, shout out my thoughts. "The Boss. The chihuahua."

And the link drops. Dead. Before I can say how alone I am, or can tell Aurora how much I long to be in her arms, or ask for vegetable soup and ice cream instead of chopped up meat and biscuits, the only door there is to the outside world has been slammed shut.

"Blimey," says Aurora. "That was something else."

She is rubbing me behind the ears, making comforting noises. My chest is wheezing, out of breath.

"Well?" Portia says. "Is he in there?"

"Definitely," Aurora says. "It's him alright."

"Is it?" Portia stares into my eyes again.

"Yes it is him," says Aurora. "And he's told me where to find Ramana's book of shadows."

"Did he say what he's doing inside my dog?"

"He didn't. But. There's a chance, if we find the book and give it back to Ramana, if she's the Queen of Evil she will know how to do this sort of thing."

Portia steadies her hair, lifts the turtle shell compact and inspects her lipstick. When her eyes meet mine in the mirror she blinks uncomfortably then turns away. She could live forever. Fly. Make anyone love her.

"If you really think it's necessary Spooky," she says.

"Of course it is," says Aurora. "Only problem is... "

"There's always a problem."

"Jimmy T hid the book inside this dog."

"Inside Bobo?"

"No," says Aurora. "There was a dog called The Boss. He was dead. Jimmy was preserving him for someone."

When I hear the words, I want to jump up and kiss the marvellous Aurora all over. Instead, I lie down with my chin on stretched out paws. There is a pain in my chest and Bobo's breathing is all over the place.

"I think we can safely assume Ramana is looking very closely in our direction. She'll do everything in her power to find her book. She'll be mad as hell, do all sorts of nasty things."

Portia says, "Dark riders, shadow demons, yucky things that suck your blood out?"

That's kid's stuff, Aurora says. She means really nasty.

"The other only problem is," Aurora rolls her eyes up to the ceiling, brings her shoulders up to her ears. "I don't know where it is. I only put the lid back on the box and posted it, didn't I? All I can remember is it was somewhere in London."

Portia moans. She slaps a hand against her forehead. "Spoo-ky."

Aurora is saying how there has to be a way to find The Boss.

Portia is groaning. All hope is lost.

And I'm thinking, what about me? This might only be hell's waiting room. It could be the fire next time.

Bobo's breathing gets faster. I can feel the fist tighten in his chest as life melts from his body. When I demand that the dog stands up, order him to stand up, reach out and shout for Aurora with the last gasp of my consciousness, Bobo rolls over into the approaching shadow.

And dies.

Dahlia puts down her phone and says, "If anyone's

come by car I'd avoid the city if I were you."

Portia puts her hands on her cheeks and tilts her head to one side, watching her dog.

And Dahlia turns, showering breadcrumbs from her plate of sandwiches, and says to everyone, "There's been a huge fire at the music academy. There's burning bodies and everything."

16

Portia Maxwell is stuck in afternoon traffic. Aurora is lying across the back seat of the car pressing a patchouli scented pillow to her face. The leather smell of Portia's big Cherokee makes her feel sick.

The radio is playing Chopin's Nocturne in D flat as a tribute to the late pianist James Earnest Hammington.

Aurora has just been saying funny, when music is called sad it is humanity it brings to mind.

They are waiting for the policeman directing things to let them go. Every set of traffic lights in the city appears to have broken down.

Portia picks through the gold tubes and shiny bottles of her lipstick and makeup, her cosmetic case spilled open in her lap. She unscrews little boxes of eye makeup, looking and smelling at their blue or grey or pink dusted with gold insides.

Today, this is Portia's still life. Hair stacked up like a Gainsborough, two golden ringlets springing up and down either side of her face. Deep blue eyes. Portia's suit is red, like marinated strawberries in lavender custard. Matching red loafers. Her finger jewellery is a large piece of amber set in a silver ring. Up close, what looks like a flaw in the amber is actually an ancient mosquito with straggly legs and veiny wings.

Aurora says it is eighty million years old and might have a bellyful of dinosaur blood.

She twists up an orange lipstick then changes her mind. She looks in the rear view mirror and bounces the hair. She looks at her watch, tapping its face with her index finger. Then she twists up a red coloured lipstick and draws it heavily across her lips.

She grabs a can of hairspray, shakes it, protects her face with the other hand and atomises the top of her head.

Someone behind is blasting their car horn. Up ahead, three lanes are narrowing into two. There is a coach full of school kids on the outside and an articulated lorry on the inside.

Aurora moans when they start to move.

"I told you not to have it done honey," Portia says into the mirror. "If those things were made for wearing rings they'd be at the end of your arms."

"It only hurts when I move," Aurora says, bringing one arm across the blue Indian cheesecloth covering her breasts. When she bends over, Portia sees they are restrained by a fine gold chain that loops through both nipple piercings.

"Anyway, the pain is good for me."

Portia thumbs the corner of her lips with a perfect nail. "I can understand. You see the world different when your in mourning. Well the world wont grind to a stop you know. Mutilating yourself wont do you or Jimmy T any good."

"I'm not mutilating."

"Jabbing metal through your nipples isn't?"

Aurora, painfully slowly, pulls herself up in the seat. Plenty of cultures do self harm in mourning. But she is not in mourning.

"I'm not in mourning."

"No?"

"No. I thought I was but now I'm not. I'm in melancholia."

"Oh?"

"For a start I wouldn't be coming to work if I was in mourning. Ask Freud."

"What's the difference?"

"Both are triggered by the same thing, that is, loss. The difference is that mourning occurs after the death of a loved one while in melancholia the object of love is not irretrievably lost."

Portia thinks of her little Bobo. "And Jimmy T is...?"

"Exactly."

Portia looks at the bus of school kids. Looks at Aurora.

"But he is dead," she says. "I don't want to be hard, but nobody comes back from the dead."

Aurora has this faraway look, under the scented pillow, so that Portia decides not to speak.

"Anyway, it's a fashion thing," Aurora eventually says. "I don't expect you to understand."

Portia smiles at the nice young policeman waving them on. She can do without the traffic and she can do without sarcasm from the back seat. She brakes for the school bus pulling in front of her and she says, "If it's a fashion thing then what do you do when it goes out of fashion? It's not like buying a hat you can simply throw away."

Aurora puts a finger up her nose, pulls it out and examines it. "Fashion is what fashion does," she says. The next thing she wants is a spider web tattoo on her neck.

One of the kids at the back of the bus is watching her so she pretends to flick her bogey finger at him as they pass on the outside.

They are travelling over Blackheath in slow moving traffic, late for an appointment with the Queen of Evil.

They think it is for the best, to make a pact with Ramana and help find her book in exchange for a spell to bring back Jimmy T. Portia researched the phone directory and there it was: a Queen of Evil listing under acting and model agencies. On the internet, she finds thirteen million four hundred thousand hits including one for a Queen of Evil who represents a number of unidentified horror movie stars, stage extras and musicians. Mad, Bad or Simply Evil, says the web page. Other credits include animals trained for acting. Stars include the single most vicious pig in Pork Revenge, the pack of killer dogs in Hounds of Blood and the eye-pecking crows in Black Birds.

This person definitely needs lunch in the Psychic Deli.

Aurora reaches down in front and drags a canvas bag onto the backseat. She takes out a notebook.

It is caught in a tangle of silver wire and feathers, they look like chicken feathers, died yellow and green and blue. Some of the wires have little glass beads on them and hooks. "These are the funky earrings I'm making," she says.

She rummages around until she finds a pencil at the bottom of the bag then sweeps the bundle of wires and beads back in. Loose feathers float in the air and she says, "I think I'll make them more spiritual, use Pa Kua or Yin and Yang beads."

Portia looks in the mirror then looks ahead. In all this traffic, it's dangerous not to concentrate.

"It's not as easy as it looks," Aurora says. She opens her notebook. There are columns of numbers, significant dates, calculations with arrows pointing up and down in different colours of ink.

Portia nudges the mirror, shifts the angle. Aurora is scribbling at the numbers, scoring some out and drawing lines between columns. "What's with all the maths homework?" she says looking ahead again.

Without looking up, Aurora says, "I'm reducing."

"Reducing what?"

"Numbers," Aurora says. "What year were you born?"

Portia says 1950. January twenty first.

Aurora runs her fingers through her hair, jangling with little beads.

It is difficult to properly visualise Aurora's still life. A stab at it, at this particular moment, would be dirty blonde hair with rats tails, studded with yellow and blue glass beads. A blue shirt. Black pencil skirt down to her ankles. Second hand commando boots. Grey eyes. Some freckles on her nose and arms.

But these are just the trappings of something deeper.

In the mirror, Portia tries to figure out what is going on, decipher the upside down scribbling.

"I'm not much older than The Beatles," she says.

"Who?"

Aurora has added together the digits of Portia's date of birth and is now changing her name to numbers. She clucks her tongue against the back of her teeth. "Your life path is the number one. That's who you are, decided at birth by the numbers, and the traits you carry through life."

Portia indicates to move out then cancels it. "Number one," she says, almost turning around. "That has to be good news."

"Depends," Aurora says. "Maybe good. Maybe bad."

Portia screws up her eyes, talks to the mirror. "What's maybe bad about it?"

Aurora taps the page with the pencil. "Number one drive is a lust for personal gratification, independence, and the need for personal attainment. There is inner strength and potential greatness in a leader. Ambitious, though you may hide that for social reasons."

"Such as?"

Aurora is flicking through the pages, turning the book around to find something. "Well this is nothing personal," she says, "but with all the self interest around, the negative side of this number means you are likely to be unhappy with your circumstances, egotistical and impatient."

"Let's not get personal," Portia says. The traffic is moving again.

"The other thing is the destiny number. I can add

together the numbers associated with your name."

"I'm not sure if I want to play this game anymore," says Portia.

Aurora is frowning, counting out Portia's destiny on her fingertips. She says this isn't a game. Numerology is one of the most ancient prophetic arts.

"Right," she says. "You are a number seven for destiny and that's good. It means you are the type of person who really searches for wisdom or hidden truths. You are very rational, in fact you can almost seem to lack emotion sometimes."

Portia slaps the steering wheel. "Spooky, that's such a hurtful thing to say."

"But that's not so important. It's like there is a balance, always a Yin and Yang, good and bad. You're an Aquarius and that's great. Honest and loyal, perverse and detached."

"Well, that covers everything," Portia says.

"These are only traits. It's the same for everybody. I'm Pisces, sensitive and unworldly yet idealistic and easily led if I don't watch out."

She holds open the book so that Portia can see her writing.

"There I am. Aurora. Ten three seventy eight. Life path eleven, destiny eleven. Spiritually aware visionary, nervous and crap at relationships. Psychic talents. Willing to sacrifice self to save others."

"I see you use your Sunday title," Portia says. "What about your real name? Maybe you should do me again using Margaret."

Aurora stifles a yawn. "It depends how much you want to think that person still exists. Personally, I prefer Portia."

They are overtaken on the inside by the school bus, the rear seat crammed with children sticking fingers up their noses and waving. Portia sees a gap in the traffic and moves inside, three cars behind the school bus.

"Spooky, you're an Einstein," she says.

They are coming up to a roundabout and everyone slows down to a crawl. The kids at the back wave their arms in the air and stick out their tongues. One teenager drops his trousers and flaunts his bare bum.

Traffic turns in all directions. Portia wants to take a left. There is a gap after the next car.

Two large houses away Ramana waits for her guests. Her still life at this moment is a night sky blue long dress with sequins shimmering like stars.

When Portia looks back in the rear view mirror she looks back in time. Twenty years. She is the same age Aurora is now. Where she sits, smirking in the back, it's her husband. For once he's not smoking. Big Al's rocking their baby. Little Al is sleeping, making contented gurgling noises.

She's driving this car, this Capri she always hated even before Aurora was around to sense the mood of spirits lurking in things.

This Capri, this devil car, was the only thing she had ever got a feeling about.

She can't remember where she is driving to. The road is black, black, black.

This car, the evil in it, wrestling out of her hands. Twisting free, taking control, tyres screeching, screaming. It was one of those amazing things, a miracle someone called it, that anyone survived.

What do you think when doctors say they want to turn off the life support for your husband and baby son?

Maybe they should wait five, ten, twenty years until medical science catches up?

Maybe. But what does a baby look like after twenty years on life support?

Survival isn't enough.

You keep those kinds of thoughts to yourself.

At times like this she usually reaches for the soothing organic peppermint and starflower vitamin E enhanced scalp balm. How she regrets getting dressed this morning in the Kylie Minogue underwear she really is too old to wear. Pink with black lace trim. She fumbles around the glove compartment. She heard it rattling around next to the boxes of contact lenses, under the custom made eastern european human hairpieces. It has not rolled inside the champagne pink tiers, the bouffant, or today's silver crystal tips. It isn't underneath the Mary Quant jet black bob, the long brown ponytail, or the lime green smoothie. Or the blonde Monroe or the ginger Fergie.

At last she finds it, tucked inside the grey ghost with purple rinse that she hardly ever uses. "Now how did you get in there?" she says.

What on earth is she thinking? Tomorrow she is going to put Spooky right. Poor girl. She will tell her there is no such thing as evil that sneaks into furniture, just people that are highly strung. Jimmy T is dead dead dead. There are no such things as dead humans living in dogs or computers or anywhere else. No magic spells that make you live young and beautiful forever. She will even offer to pay for Spooky's medical fees. Hell, if it means getting her sanity back she will even sell the Psychic Deli.

17

Dr. Bedlo croaks. Ramana swishes the raven a nightsky bat sleeve that sends him spiralling into the rafters, trailing a cosmos of sequins. She throws a rat fat seed ball after him, and says, "Get out of here, you damned road kill. And don't even bother coming back down."

Dr Bedlo does this thing with his neck and wings like a shrug.

A midget in silver lame pantaloons and matching turban pops out from a shadow to brush and shovel up the sequins.

"Not now, not now you fool," she says. Kick kick kick. It is the big moment. Ramana has her guests to look after. "Get out of here. Do something useful. Prepare The Pendulum."

The Pendulum. The look on the man's face is an aghast cameo of horror. When she snaps her fingers at him he gets going.

The blue shadow of Ramana, Queen of Evil, rises like smoke. Spreading, magnified, clacking giant Nosferatu fingers up the wall, across the ceiling, clawing at the inverted crucifix hanging from beams.

Where we are is the throne room of the Queen of Evil. Built on a plague pit, this villa and its bricked up windows is dark and dank as a dungeon. The interior design is Incarceration. Only this room has any daylight, a pale radiance that limps down through a north-facing window of lead glass squares. The walls are faux sandstone blocks hung with medieval tapestries of monks dancing and celebrating around crosses of burning witches. Flames of latin Deo's lick around the victim's body.

Propped up against one wall is Ramana's quilted coffin of a day bed. A dusty rag covered skeleton dangles opposite, manacled in the gloom. Despite the urn of smouldering frankincense the air is heavy with the stench of decayed fruit that spills from a half open marble sarcophagus. Sultan chews the remains of a cow skull on flagstones next to the blazing fire. Splatters of fat hiss in the flames. The corners of the room are lost in shadows. Somewhere there is water dripping. The heart beat of pigeon wings whistle momentarily in the beams.

The Queen of Evil's throne commands the centre of the room. Ramana leans forward on it, grabs a carved goat head armrest in each hand and spits into the fireplace.

"Charming," says Portia.

"Insolence," says Ramana. "You are in no position." Her eyes are black mirrors that reflect the flames. "One more word from you and I will close the door."

Dr Bedlo drops out of the shadows, flaps at Ramana around the head, then finally comes to rest on the horned devil head armchair beneath the window. He tugs a peck at a nearby string of yellow and blue glass beads. These beads, and the loose tussle of dreads beneath them, shake in retaliation. Aurora has started working on these straps around her wrists and ankles and the last thing she needs is Portia being used as a pincushion.

She says, "You best be quiet Portia. Most iron maidens are made so the sharp points don't pierce vital organs. The idea is not to *immediately* kill a person. Ideally, you want to drag out a torturous death, really."

"I don't believe this," Portia says. On the inside of the door, with spikes inches from her face and throat, a typewritten label says American International Pictures.

However, the chains holding her in this cage are really hurting. And those small guys in the lame pants totally mashed her hair when they crammed her in. She tries to sound convincing when she says, "Your B movie horror props, don't frighten me."

A low, swishing noise starts up somewhere along the corridor. The swish sounds solid and sharp.

"Then you shall be first to face The Pendulum," says Ramana. "Since you think evil can be laid to one side and forgotten, I expect you will find the experience of being sliced open illuminating."

Where Aurora is rubbing, the leather ties are burning on her wrists but at last there are signs of loosening. What on earth was she thinking, that she and Portia could simply drive right up to the door of the Queen of Evil and ask a favour? And those swarming little midgets, allowing them to separate her from Portia and then snap on these straps and locks with their chubby fingers, it was as though she had helped the hangman put their heads in the noose.

Aurora says, "I only asked if you could kindly bring my boyfriend back to life."

Ramana kicks a chair. She screams, "You want me to beg for what is mine? My book – give it to me."

"You know," says Portia, "I thought you were in public relations or something. This is no way to treat a guest, or to get whatever it is you want. If you ask me you should "

And like the world loses sound, as if all the words dried up, she cannot finish. She can think the words but for the life of her she cannot move her mouth. Ramana had only lifted an index finger and wiggled it in her direction. Was it something hypnotic, or she has just had a stroke? Portia cannot prevent the saliva drooling from her mouth and trickle onto her jacket.

Ramana stalks around. The door of the iron maiden is a fingertip away.

"Woman," Ramana says. Actually she says woo-man. "If I tell you, I can close this door with one thought, then you should realise there is no more than a flicker of an eyelash between you and your fate. Perhaps the girl is correct and you will not die quickly. Not even of fright. Then, perhaps, we shall still bury you, screaming and clawing. For a time, you will be terribly alive. I like this idea."

"No," Aurora says. "I thought you were going to use The Pendulum."

Portia suddenly has real horror in her eyes. Her eyes are screaming at Aurora.

And Aurora says, "I mean, she's being quiet now. Please, if she bothers you again, you have your pendulum."

"Yes. I have my pendulum. Only it is not quite simply, *my* pendulum. I do not own the horror of it anymore than you, or she, can ever hope to own my book. When evil is no longer invisible, it must be very horrible. Even cruel."

Ramana fishes about under her chair. She spills out some knives, a leather whip, a brass knuckleduster, and finally holds out what she has been looking for so that Aurora can see. "You know what these are?"

Aurora studies the wooden screws. "Cork openers?" she says. "It is a bit early. But under the circumstances. Do you have any champagne chilled? Doesn't have to be Dom Perignon."

When Ramana snaps her fingers little servants appear. They pop out of shadows, the walls, from behind chairs and under tables. The place is full of them.

Ramana puts one of her own thumbs under a screw and twists until the head flattens the nail. "Pain is unbearable."

"You don't frighten me," says Aurora. She tilts her head at Portia. "Isn't this the bit where you put them onto her anyway, cos you know I wont talk and she's a lot older and more vulnerable than me so you think I wont be able to stand the guilt of watching her go through the pain of being tortured?"

"Wrong movie," Ramana says. The midgets grab Aurora's hand, not the one she has almost worked free, and prize her thumb from her clenched fist. They hold it up for Ramana to squeeze it into the thumbscrew. She gives it a little twist and it bites tightly but not yet painfully. "I think we know what happens now."

"Sure. I tell you everything you want to know."

"No," Ramana's smile, up this close, is disgustingly white behind blue lips. Then she shouts, "Amigos! The Pendulum." And half a dozen more little guys appear and drag Portia out of her cage. Ramana slumps purring onto her throne while a new team of midgets lift her shoulder high and head out of the door. Then Aurora's chair gets lifted and the whole bizarre circus traipses out along a candlelit corridor. Ramana's mad laughter trumpets off the stone walls and rolls towards the source of a low mechanical percussion. They reach a room that is more than a room. Where they have come in is high up on a balcony with a narrow staircase running down the wall into the sunken pit of a cellar below. A huge suspended axe blade swings over the Y shaped table standing in the centre of the pit. When the axe swings, it cuts lengthwise over the deep gorge of the Y, where a squad of the little guys get busy strapping Portia down. She cannot take her eyes off the slashes on the table. The butcher's block.

"This is crazy. We don't have your book," Aurora says. "A friend had it. But he's the one who is dead."

The blade sweeps down with a whistle and slows up with a sigh.

"If you are the Queen of Evil, bring him back and you'll get your book."

Ramana bangs her fist on someone's turban, knocking

the person down with a single blow. "It is my life's work."

"Can't you use the internet?"

"My contacts, not every site is listed."

"Contacts with the living or the dead?"

"Both."

Ramana raises her index finger to one little guy with a twisted black moustache and the pendulum gets cranked lower. The blade curves up over Portia's head and the backdraught ripples her shirt. From chopping board, the axe head swings up almost to disappearing before making its charging descent. When it comes thundering down, between her loafers, she closes her eyes but feels the punch of air. In her head she is screaming. At least, she thinks, she is wearing red for the occasion. And it could have been worse than The Pit and The Pendulum. It could have been a Driller Thriller.

"You cannot do this. We've told you everything," Aurora says.

"Everything?" Ramana is leering.

Aurora cant bear to watch as moustache midget obeys The Queen of Evil and slips the blade even lower. One more drop and it will dissect Portia.

"As far as I know it got hidden in a dog."

Ramana lifts her hand.

"Honest. My boyfriend put it in a dog, a dead chihuahua, and it got posted. To somewhere in London. That's all I know. " Aurora thinks, she really is going to do it.

From the table in the pit, Portia fixes on Aurora and Ramana and thinks what a ridiculous way to go. Her down here in the pit and them being carried shoulder high on their thrones by a dwarf troupe. The blade swings so close now she can smell the steel. When Ramana's hand goes up, she thinks, *that's it*. She can see the look on the face of the nearest midget. He is also thinking, *that's it*.

Aurora at last works her hand free and then it happens. She is up, and from what Portia can see between strokes of the pendulum and lying as flat as she can, Aurora is floating not standing, her hair twisting in a localised tornado.

Whap! Portia is almost decapitated trying to look.

Aurora's eyes are closed but in the middle of her forehead blazes a new golden eye.

Whap! Portia has to lie down for the pendulum to swing.

A yellow energy ball blasts out from her fingers and smashes into Ramana's throne forcing the midget team to unceremoniously drop it to the ground. Another energy ball ripples across the room and scatters the midgets away from the pendulum lever. She makes a fist and when she opens her hand she releases a searing light and the force of a soundwave bursts across the room. A third blast aimed at Ramana gets neutralised by a purple coloured energy ball from The Queen of Evil.

What's happening? She can't see. Whap! Portia has to lie flat out.

Sparks are flying in all directions almost as quickly as the midgets. Ramana fires off handfuls of purple flash bombs that Aurora blocks by sweeping a circle of her own golden force field in front of her. Then Ramana's eyes are black holes that suck at Aurora's force. Next the room shudders in a firework explosion of gold and purple whizzbangs, as Aurora matches Ramana's strength.

Whap! What is going on?

Aurora has her hands up on the sides of her head, like she is in pain or focussing, and then the golden eye goes pure white and a searing light beams out lasers into Ramana's black holes. There is smoke from Aurora's hair and flames from Ramana's eyes and together they smell of burning flesh and the smoke fills up the room like a pressure cooker. The world inside the room is being opened up and the forces of good and bad, of nature and time, are bursting over until the structure of the cosmos can take no more of it and the room trembles, quakes and buckles in on itself and knocks the pendulum half of the last notch closer to Portia.

Whap! Whap Whap!

Whap! Whap Whap!

The damaged pendulum is wobbling and chopping, a crazy broken down arm of death, and Portia is too afraid to lift her head. From here she cannot see a thing, so she closes her eyes and screams. The return of her voice surprises her. So she does it again. And keeps it going. Until a voice tells her to stop.

"It's me," says Aurora. "Stop that noise before you burst my ear drums. And we can do without this."

Portia cannot see how, but Aurora does something that freezes the pendulum mid swing. "How did you do that?" she says. "Magic?"

Aurora looks at her. "Simple. I pulled the brake lever."

"No," Portia says.

They clamber out together through the rubble that was Ramana's cellar, finding a hole where the wall has exploded and where daylight now streams in. A pall of smoke and dust gathers above the villa.

Portia wants to know what happened. "I mean, look at this mess. What on earth happened? Did you kill her?"

Aurora shakes her head. "I don't think so. I don't know what happened. Maybe we got hit by a train?"

Portia stops dead. She wants to go back inside. "Let's go back and make sure she's dead. Let's kill the bitch."

"None of that," says Aurora, fishing the car keys from Portia's trousers.

"We've got a chihuahua to find."

18

Once out of that fur ball, I went whizzing all over the national power grid, through dales, over Scottish mountains and under the Irish Sea. I've crossed the Atlantic in telecom cable, been everywhere from Aberdeen to Zanzibar via Beverley Hills and the Pentagon. I've even been the torch in the statue of Liberty.

It is a lonely existence. Perhaps it is because space feels so vast when you are almost nothing, maybe no more than an electron or two. Soon I began to feel less out of control and gained confidence. I can cross continents in the blink of an eye. I can go on up the line and I can go back down the line.

Back down the line.

The hamster is kicking its legs as hard as it can, twisting its head up, not wanting to look down, running like mad in mid air, going nowhere. It spins a full circle around the axis of its own tail.

Ramana, sitting on her burned out throne, holds it up. Her black eyes meet red eyes, her thin white arm straight out between them.

"Anyone I know?" she says.

The hamster bends double, almost bites her finger.

"I don't think so." She snaps the fingers of her free hand.

Two bare chested midgets in scorched Aladdin pants sprint over, steadying equally fire damaged silver turbans onto their heads. Between them they carry three coils of prime handbag material thick as a child's neck.

"Go say hi to Piggy," says Ramana Queen of Evil.

The python reaches up and takes the freefall hamster in one swallow.

The midgets bow. As they back away, Ramana smiles at the wriggling lump in the snake's belly.

Ramana's throne. One of its carved goat head armrests has been blown away.

Ramana wears a full length black satin number, painted around her hips and bust, opening out with bat wing sleeves. It smells like it came from a fire sale. The fringe around the bottom is reminiscent of her blueberry hair. Uneven, with bits missing.

She's had a headache for months. The smell of this place is making it even worse. Since she lost her book, nothing goes right. This pounding in her head, the incessant tribal drums, is driving her insane. Dr. Bedlo shifts from foot to foot on top of the empty iron maiden. He obviously hears the same distressing beat.

The chauffeur, now dressed as a butler, pushes open the two big wooden churchy doors. "Your majesty," he says. When he bows his penguin suit creaks. "A miss Trudi Wanton has arrived for audition."

Ramana clenches the arms of the throne. Digs her fingers into the goat. She ordered all appointments to be cancelled.

The chauffeur butler makes a little bow. "Evidently this woman did not receive notification."

"Fools," Ramana says. Her voice is hollow. "I am surrounded by incompetent fools."

The midgets take their chance to scuttle out the open doors, weaving past the chauffeur butler and a tall woman with a red bob. She strides in. Trudi Wanton's still life is high heels and a short leather skirt. A pink faux fur jacket. Chewing gum. She smells of cheap au de cologne, a leftover from the eighties, a Charlie girl.

There is nowhere for the red haired woman to sit, so she stands, honed legs apart, toes pointing forward. "Some place you've got here," she says. "Midgets and everything. It's mental, innit?"

Ramana beckons her forward and extends her arm, limply, forcing her visitor to make a little curtsy to touch her hand. "Forgive me Miss Wanton," says Ramana. "I am unwell. You should have been informed."

Trudi Wanton acts all pale and surprised. Appointments take two to cancel, she thinks. Dancing laps for a hundred a time isn't doing it for her. Executive massage in Soho hasn't done it either. No way does she cancel. She is determined to get that break. She's twenty seven and needs it yesterday.

"Oh, I was out of town. Working," she says. "It's been so hectic, you know? My diary is mental. Just you wait till I get my hands on my flatmate. She must have forgotten to leave a message."

Ramana hears the raw desperation. All the others had it too. "So you don't mind working out of town?"

Trudi Wanton puts her hand on her hips, thrusts her chest out, strains the zip on the pink faux fur jacket. "What? Get out of this place?"

Ramana smiles her perfect white teeth. "Well, you look like the sort of girl I have in mind. There may be something."

"What is it, a film? I can sing, you know? I can dance," says Trudi Wanton, starting to take off a shoe.

"That wont be necessary," Ramana says. "I can see you have all talents that are required."

Trudi Wanton clasps her hands to her face. She can't believe her luck. "What? I got a part? Just like that?"

Ramana lifts one hand off her throne. Lets it fall. "It may be that I can arrange for you to meet someone. Very soon," she says.

She snaps her fingers. "I'm certain there will be an

opportunity for you to do great things," she says.

The chauffeur butler returns and takes Trudi Wanton by the arm, leading her out. She's hobbling, putting her shoe back on, looking anxiously over her shoulder at the throne. "So you'll be in touch?"

Ramana nods, " Be prepared. At all times."

Pretty girls are so easy. And so useful. So profitable.

Debbie Heartache made ten million. Four hours with Gill Bates, managing director of Schwartz Grunsted bank, now in liquidation. All that cost was a flight to Los Angeles. There was Sophie Golden, Bayern Assets. Ramana made three million one hour after Ms Golden's one night stand with Lyndon Hessie the chief executive. Cost? One flight to Tokyo. Tammy Bluebell, another three million. One night with Marvin Applewood, director of New York Insurance after a launch party for their new London bureau. She even travelled by coach. Sal Lovechild and Irwin T Corrie, CEO of Flescher Greep Global Investments. Didn't have to leave town so no travelling costs incurred. So far Sal has made Ramana two million and rising.

In less than the time it takes to have a night of sin, a reputation can be remoulded. Corporate confidence is a stream that flows into the ocean of the global economy. It can be easily diverted with a well placed digital camera, preferably in a light above the bed or in a wardrobe with an unrestricted view. Sex is a great investment. You simply have to know where and when to take advantage, accept that nature is also chaos and eternal night. She can be a dark mistress.

Ramana pounds her fists. The fire's flames rise. She is on her feet, arms outstretched towards the rainbow of light breaking into the dungeon.

"I want my book," she howls book like a wolf.

The raven, the pigeons, splutter up into a dark corner among the frazzled beams.

Ramana has contemplated. She has cast the runes, read

the flames, and consulted her almost all-seeing mirror. She has cried to the moon goddess and summoned the spirit of the winds.

The veil is impenetrable.

Up the line.

"It's all a bit Hollywood," says Bullrush, blowing cigarette smoke over Portia's silver curls. "I mean nobody believes in magic in this day and age."

"Spooky has hidden depths," says Portia.

They're in a hotel near Heathrow, a one nighter for travellers, an upgraded YMCA.

Portia does not expect to be seen in a place like this.

The barmen are all Italians and the walls are plastered with cheap posters. A night shot of Rome. Christ on Sugar Loaf. Liberty. Istanbul. Venetian gondolas tied up opposite St Mark's. A white house with a blue dome on Santorini.

There's only one other customer at the bar apart from them.

All the while the whine of jet engines, the noise of the nearby city of an airport, drifts in on the night air.

Bullrush leans over and clunks his half full bottle of beer against Portia's. At the last moment she turned her bottle to protect her French manicured nails.

He takes out a cigarette and does his flashy thing with the Zippo.

"I love London. Wouldn't want to live here forever though," he says, as if he has seen it all.

"Business is business," Portia says, taking a sip.

"Too many crackpots. Too much pollution. Twenty years from now we'll have people flying around on jet packs that run on cooking oil."

The girl on the end of the bar, with the red hair and big lips, a skirt far too short for a bar stool, takes a handful of peanuts.

She looks over at Bullrush, flicks a peanut into her mouth.

Bullrush is saying, "They'll put a mirror in space to give us daylight all night."

Portia says, "Yeah? Why bother?"

"Yeah. And babies will have gene chips implanted at birth to sort out disease. Heart disease, cancers, cot deaths, things of the past. They'll learn Chinese or any other language through these chips. And maths, and rocket science."

"Great."

"Yeah. And we'll all have dream machines instead of television. You wire yourself up at night and have these adventures in your subconscious dimension. You can either create your own movie, or have one zapped in."

"Wow."

"Yeah. You could be kissing Bogart in Casablanca one night, dancing with Sinatra the next."

"Or the Exorcist."

"Yeah. The Boston Strangler, or whatever. This chip will record the whole thing and play it back like a movie in your head anytime you like. You can fly around the solar system in your dreams then share it with your friends. Beats the hell out of going to the cinema."

Portia says, "Will people still be able to sleep with all that daylight?"

And Bullrush puts his hand on her hand. His tanned skin on her white skin. Like he has been waiting for it, he says, "Who needs sleep?"

Portia pats the champagne hairs tingling on the back of her neck. She checks the time on her tiny gold wristwatch. She takes another sip of beer.

Portia says, "Wait till you get to my age."

When Bullrush wants her to tell him about herself she thinks Big Al Little Al. Only she has come this far and says, "What is there to say? I run a café. I sell antiques. I collect art. Or I collect antiques and sell the art."

She shrugs. "Anyway, I live by myself."

"Aha," Bullrush says, smiling as if he has just found out something.

"I live by myself and I like it that way," Portia says.

"I'm a post modernist when it comes to these things," says Bullrush. "There is no such thing as the truth. Everything can be true from a certain point of view. And, according to FBI profiles, most serial killers live alone."

And he says there's something particularly nasty about women doing the killing. Genene Jones was a nurse who killed babies in the intensive care unit where she worked. Aileen Wuornos went on a killing spree of white males with a point two two calibre gun. Amy Archer-Gilligan poisoned the patients who stayed at her home for the elderly. She even poisoned her husband. But they don't always fit the profile. Myra Hindley, crazy girlfriend. Rosemary West, weird wife. Gwendolyn Gail Graham and Catherine Wood, two lesbian lovers who killed elderly patients at their nursing home.

"How are you on the McDonald triad?"

Portia shrugs her shoulders. "Never heard of them."

Bullrush says, "Them's an it. Serial killers have usually done at least one of the McDonald triad. That is bedwetting beyond the age of ten, committed arson, or the torture of animals."

"Not guilty," Portia says, one hand on her heart.

Bullrush is smiling. Putting one hand over his heart, holding the other up in the air. Beneath a grey stack of cigarette smoke and messy blond hair, he says, "Hey, don't get me wrong. You know, the world is full of lonely heart killers."

So, apart from being a financial genius, Portia wants to know some more about him.

"I'm just your typical work hard and play hard single guy."

The still life of the redhead at the bar is black leather boots that fit tight over the calf, a black leather skirt and a red satin plunge neck blouse. It drinks vodka on the rocks and smokes menthol cigarettes.

She's supposed to be waiting for someone but keeps looking over at Bullrush.

There is a delay in the conversation, a blip, a dip that lasts no more than a second. "Did you say single?" Portia says. "What about Aurora's mourning club?"

"Oh, that. That," says Bullrush, waving the smoke in front of his face, "was an aberration. I was thinking, singles bars are such a messy way to meet people. Mostly they're fucked up. At least there's something honest about mourning."

Portia blinks twice. "You faked your way into mourning group therapy?"

"At least it wasn't naked group therapy," says Bullrush.

"Is that legal?"

Bullrush blows his smoke in the direction of the girl with red hair. She has surprisingly long legs.

"And what about the wedding garter?"

"Hey, babe," Bullrush says. "Anyone can buy those kind of things. It happens all the time. I'm being honest with you. You don't think the sado's with the hats, the goldfish, the love letters, all got together in the name of mourning, do you?"

This is different from the picture of serious grief painted by Aurora.

Bullrush screws the cigarette into the tinfoil ashtray. "The bald guy, Hyacinth, and Orchid the Mata Hari with ten lives? Biggest swingers in town."

And Aurora?

Bullrush pushes himself back in his chair as far as it will go. For a moment there is a hint of remorse. "Cooky's genuine about some guy or other, I can see that. There was a time. I mean who wouldn't be interested? But not now."

This time Portia does not want his brown hand pawing hers.

She picks up her silver purse. He grabs her wrist, holding her down, saying, "Come on. I like you. We can still be friends. Have some fun."

Half standing half sitting she says, "I don't do fun. You're a predator. And I don't like that."

Bullrush has both hands on her wrists, pressing hard. All of a sudden he looks like someone else. He sounds like someone else. "Stay. You know you want to. Why else are we here?" this somebody says.

Portia drops to her knees, pulling out of his grip, sending beer bottles crashing to the floor, her chair gets knocked over, the table rattles. She cries one little scream when her knees hit the floor.

Bullrush is brushing cigarette ash off his shirt. "Stupid old bitch," he says, looking down at her.

Portia's hairdo is split open and wiry strands hang in her eyes. Her pink lipstick is smudged. Her nylons are ripped. Her knees bloody. And slowly, freeze frame slow, she rises to her feet. Her face is red, as red as the blood running down from her knees.

"Great idea, darling," Bullrush says loudly. He half smiles. "You go up first. Get warmed up, babe. I'll join you in five."

Standing up, she says, "People should be allowed to have their own dreams. They should be allowed to switch off the light and sit in the dark."

For the benefit of the waiter fussing around their table, to the girl with red hair at the bar, Bullrush says, "She's upset because I wont have her children."

Portia steps up close and slaps him hard across the face, dragging with her pink and white nails down his cheek. A heartbeat later, there is more blood.

A stigma. A warning.

A second after Portia pushes past, the redhead is over

dabbing her napkin around Bullrush's face making cooing, soothing noises.

"Lover's tiff?" the redhead is saying. "A bit mental, isn't she? Nobody deserves physical violence. Not in public anyway."

Her lips are full and red. She smells of dry roasted spices, smokes and peppermint. And she is standing intimately close.

"Better let her sleep it off," she is saying, dabbing.

Bullrush takes in her freckled skin. He feels the energy of her body surge across the millimetre that separates them.

"Crazy thing is," he says, "I only met her a couple of hours ago."

The redhead says, "Really?"

"Yeah, she was struggling with a suitcase. I was in the foyer and couldn't get past her. So I offered to help."

"The perfect gent."

"Yeah. And this is the thanks I get. From a complete stranger."

And the redhead looks him in the eye, takes a step back, and jabs out her hand at him.

"From one stranger to another. Trudi Wanton."

She is pressing his hand warmly.

"Bullrush," he says, smiling his white teeth, flicking his blond hair off his forehead.

"It was a hippy thing. You know, like River Phoenix? My parents were into travelling around in camper vans. They had me and Buckwheat, my little sister."

She says really like she is Really surprised.

"Yeah. They were surf bums, I guess. We went all over the place in that thing. Cornwall, France, Spain, Islay."

Trudi Wanton slaps her forehead. "Hey. I love surfing."

Now they can both say what a small world it is.

The waiters are clearing up the mess, so Bullrush lifts the bottle with most beer in it and pulls a stool over to where Trudi has been sitting at the bar.

He's down in London for business. She says amazing. She is too.

He's helping a friend, this art dealer, find a particular rare dog. A stuffed dog.

She screws up her face and says, "Like one of those pregnant cows, the ones they cut in half?"

"Nope. Just some old chihuahua."

He says he hates London but business is business. She wraps her feet around the legs of her stool and says that's exactly how she feels too.

She's got an audition tomorrow for a part in a big movie.

"I've got this great agent," she says. "Fantastic contacts. There's going to be loads of stars. Then little old me," she says.

She has these green eyes. And her smile breaks into a laugh.

He has some pink lipstick on his mouth. Off the bottle. Portia pink .

"You know," she says, touching his mouth with her fingertips, "it's really not your colour."

"No?"

Trudi shakes her head.

"No. You should try a little red."

*

Bullrush is trying red. He has her with legs over his shoulders. He has her sitting on top of him in a chair. He has her face down on the mattress. He has her swinging from the doorframe. Pressed naked against the plate glass window. He has her looking up at him on her knees. He makes her do things with some fruit that he has only ever imagined anyone would actually do.

He puts her underwear on to have her. He puts the tv porn channel on to have her. He cranks up the volume of her i-pod and has her doggy style.

At two thirty he calls room service for a case of iced beer and a four seasons pizza.

Hell, room 512 at this Heathrow hotel is bursting with red.

They left the water running when they were in the shower and now the ceiling, the walls, the windows, their bodies, are streaming. The bulb in the little bedside lamp is sizzling. The trail of clothing they discarded when they came into the room, shoes, socks, pants, shirt and trousers, they lie damp on the floor. Trudi's leather skirt is perspiring.

This big shot, this entrepreneur, this money machine, he asks her to dance for him. And she does this shimmy thing around the room while he spreads out on the bed, guzzling pizza, smoking a cigarette. She takes little steps, pointing her toes down, lifting her skinny knees up thigh high, swerving her hips with each prance. Her shoulders are seesaws. She zigzags her hips down low and comes back up again slowly. She holds her bottle of beer like it is a microphone. She doesn't sing. She makes shapes with her mouth around the bottle. She doesn't spill a drop.

And when he begins to fall asleep she is on his back, demanding to be taken for a donkey ride around the room.

The whooping, the thudding, the screaming, the shouts and the laughter vibrate around the hotel.

Trudi tells Bullrush sex this great means they were fated to meet.

When she drags him back onto the warm wet bed, she is surprisingly strong. Her fingers, when she rubs his shoulders and the spine at the base of his neck, are like iron. Bullrush groans, the master of the universe has had a devil of a night.

Trudi has one hand pressing hard on his back, the other bends his knee back.

Somewhere, probably in the States, there's a team working on delivering this kind of pleasure, he says. They've got a frogman suit wired up to computer sensors. It zaps the pleasure neurons. Electrodes pulse the nipples. The rubber ripples with delight. An aromatherapy mask drifts sensual pleasures up the nose.

Trudi digs her iron fingers into his buttocks and says, does it do this?

Bullrush says yes, though with less oomph. They need to take the infirm into consideration.

Trudi pulls back his other leg, almost bursting the knee joint.

People might get addicted to it, she says.

Bullrush says he hopes so.

People might prefer to lounge around all day getting orgasmic, Trudi says. Nobody would read books, go to the cinema, go dancing, play sport or *do* anything. People could overdose on pleasure. They could even die.

Bullrush says well, nobody wants an orgasmo suit that only tickles a bit.

Trudi blows on the soles of his feet, pressing the joints, stroking between the toes. The best thing about pleasure, she says, is the knowing when to stop.

So she clambers off the bed and goes into the bathroom.

Uh-oh. Maybe she stood up too fast, or it's the alcohol, she's light headed and somehow her legs don't feel properly connected. In the steamy cauldron of the bathroom she's breathless, uncoordinated, making useless movements. She's dying of thirst but where the cold water tap should be is a towel rail. Where the towel should be, beneath the neon shaving light, is the toilet. She stumbles in the direction of the hissing shower. Her arms, windmilling, her hands, flailing. Blind in the swirls of suffocating steam. Where the shower should be is the sink. The taps sway out of reach, her fingers closing like pincers on liquid nothing. Up is like down and down is heaving up. The only way she can be certain of finding a solid anything is to surrender and fall.

It takes way too long to slap onto the wet floor.

It is a human thing. Cowering under the sink, beneath the chrome piping, against the streaming with condensation white tiles. Like it would make any difference. She wants to see her face.

An arm reaches out from where she didn't have one before, low on her ribs above the hips, swishes at the porcelain and clears some of the condensation.

Trudi Wanton, who always screams at this part in horror films, wants to roar but she can't. Her throat, her mouth, overflows with mucous. It runs down her face and neck and arms. It chokes her breathing and her tongue doesn't move properly. She can't form the words, she can't make a sound.

That is her reflection, but it is not her face. Not the gaping jaws or the six bug eyes blinking back at her.

Next door, Bullrush is lying face down on the jagged edge of the light from the bathroom, half asleep, listening to the shower running, the cartoons on television, the three am flight to San Francisco racing its engines, when the bulb sizzles one last time and expires.

What he doesn't hear is the scuttling on the ceiling. The creeping above his head of an upside down something in the darkness.

He's thinking how the shower sounds like surf and how in the morning he will phone Aurora and tell her how her boss tried to hit on him.

He's not thinking that something terrible has its black eyes burning on his flesh. Or that his warm body glows, it even radiates in the half light. If he could think, and turn around at that moment, he might have seen the shadow move towards him. Then lowering itself, dropping from above, a broken backed figure more insect than naked woman.

He is surprised when he feels Trudi's weight on his body, her arms and legs sliding around him, cocooning, her breathing on his neck. Her arms seem everywhere. Touching. Arousing. He is almost awake again when she lifts him off the bed and easily flips him over onto his back.

He raises his head to kiss her lips and then there is an instant in the half light when he thinks, maybe he has fallen asleep again after all. And he starts to cry out in the hope that it will shock him out of the nightmare and back to consciousness.

But life is being sucked out of him faster than he can wrestle with reality. Dreams, moments, holidays, telephone numbers, history, colours, loves, hates, lies, sunshine, winter surf, the taste of a cigarette with a glass of wine. They flash past with the clarity of the periodic table. Corporate clients, his shoe size, the time he broke an arm falling from a tree. Trudi Wanton. Pleasure. Portia. Aurora. Finally, indescribable pain as the thing that was Trudi Wanton empties his soul.

All this without a look of horror on his face. All this, and a last lifeless erection.

There is one more penetration to perform and she does it by arching the bottom segment of her body down on top of him. She lowers herself onto him, feeling the ebbing pulse of warm flesh fill her.

Perhaps the black eyes give it away, the full mouth, or the perfume that fills the room. Perhaps an airline passenger, half asleep heading for California, glimpses the carnal scene - the white skin of the dark haired woman, the tan skin of her blond lover.

Through the darkness outside, the steam inside, for a moment it is Ramana Queen of Evil who rides the husk of Bullrush.

This is their eternal rest. The red haired woman slumps on top of the man, embraced in deep penetration. Her face is contorted in ecstasy. One of her arms snakes under his shoulder the other stretches out and disappears beneath a pillow. He throws his arms out. Impaled. Impaling. His feet are crossed. His head is back. His mouth gapes open.

Forensics will find there is not a scratch on either of them. It is a pieta abandoned to pleasure, this eternal orgasm.

It is a brief moment of disbelief for the half asleep airline passenger, strapped in for take off.

There may have been someone else in the room. Perhaps a movement in the shadows.

But before this passenger can refocus, the aircraft banks away through a cloud in the dark night sky, hungry for the Atlantic Ocean.

19

Aurora has only prayers for the dead. The Ma she never knew and the Pa who ran away. Fitting him in every night is an affirmation that the bastard is dead.

Tonight she also prays for Jimmy T and she is praying full blast to the thing she always sets her sights on when she kneels beside her bed. She needs to open a direct line of communication to the Great Being herself. She has prayed ten minutes each to Saint Michael, Saint Peter, Saint Paul, and the Virgin Mary, and fifteen minutes to Saint Jude the patron of lost causes, pleading with them to get the great one to tune in. She tried crossing herself and evoking the holy ghost. She sat cross legged for an hour saying Om. She has lit candles, burned incense, offered rice water and spun miniature prayer wheels. She moved around the bed to face Mecca rather than Manchester. She made a voodoo doll of Jimmy T, with an empty toilet roll for a body and a bar of soap for his head, and spread her yin and yang beads around him. She is certain that the Great Being will know who it is meant to be and will breathe life back into him if she can be bothered. She spread her tarot cards out in a great circle of life on the floor then dribbled blood on them from a cut she opened in her breast. She went on the internet and posted Jimmy T's date of birth to madam LaBelle at Dial A Medium. She stared at a flickering candle in the mirror for three quarters of an hour until her eyes burned, waiting for a devil's face to appear. Yes, she would even ask for his help in bringing him back from the dead. She split a chicken carcass in two and offered half each to the deity of night and day. She persuaded room service to deliver a bag of smokeless coal and she poured it into the bath tub and lay on it naked until her skin was dried out and sore. Then she turned to flagellation, whipping herself with the toilet bowl brush. She wished on the stars and she closed her eyes and concentrated as hard as she could on Jimmy T's face. Until she can take no more.

20

The man opens his front door and there's Portia and Aurora in the vestibule, Aurora pulling Portia's Louis Vuitton nubie over her shoulder and Portia holding up a tin of Chummy dog food bought in the local supermarket.

She says, "Hallelujah. It's the new religious sensation for dogs."

She draws a cross in the air with her other hand and says, "My daughter," and she steps back. "My daughter and I would like to share with you and your pet the joy of Chummy and the Lord Jesus Christ. For free."

Portia's hair is a Mary Quant black bob. Her new red trouser suit has a safari jacket and flared trousers. She has green nails, tortoiseshell Raybans.

The man is holding a can of beer. He is wearing unfastened rubber sandals. His towelling bathrobe hangs open and beneath he's wearing a grey T-shirt splashed with something like chilli. He has boxer shorts on with a teddy bear motif.

He sticks the can to his mouth. His head tilts back and he gurgles the beer. The little teddy bears are rolling a beach ball. The man farts and says, "Come on, you're kidding?"

He has black hair hanging over a crumpled forehead. He has grey sad baggy eyes. He says, "Dogs don't do religion."

Aurora makes a move, her hand reaching out to shake his. "Mr Papandreou," she says. "I can see that it is urgent that we share God's love."

And the teddy bear man squints at them and says, "How do you know my name?"

He points the open end of the beer can at Portia and says, "Did Hellena send you to talk to me?"

And Portia angles around him, looking into the hallway. She looks anxiously at her wristwatch. She puts an arm around Aurora, pushes her forward, and says, "May we come in?"

The others were easier than this.

They made plan A during a sullen drive through one of those yellow mornings in London, the pale lemon light and swollen grey sky. Portia is steering, an open street map propped against the windscreen. Up front next to her, Aurora balances a map of greater London on her knees. She uses felt tips to trace the route she makes touching pinpoints kindly provided by the English Kennel Club for Chihuahuas named Boss. Connecting the points on the map Aurora has coloured a pentacle. It's what she does. They drive along the circumference enclosing Aurora's pentacle. To Portia there is a giant, smiley, rainbow coloured snowflake threatening London.

Portia wants to know, what sort of person has their pet stuffed? A person whose today is more yesterdays than tomorrows, she answers herself.

"The kind of person who lives here," she says, "in concrete lah-lah land." She taps the windscreen as if it is the glass of a fish tank.

Aurora turns around and stares back at the distant skyline, to the tombstone tower of Centre Point. She puffs up her cheeks and says, "It still feels…"

Perhaps it was condensation from the building's central heating rising against the concrete lemon skyline. Or the dark plume could have been a vampire wraith.

Aurora tries not thinking. She rummages in her canvas

188

bag, finds her bottle of black nail varnish. Then she scrapes at the edges of the day before's black and smoothes on a fresh layer. After painting a finger she purses her lips and blows. Ten little puffs on each finger. Ten little angel kisses she calls them. Altogether, her heavenly army of blow dry manicurists get to work blocking out guilt.

She's guilty that her today nails are the same as yesterday's. And she's guilty about Bullrush. She was supposed to mourn with him over coffee this morning but Portia woke her early and insisted they leave him behind, without even a message on his answering machine.

Portia touches the sore area below her knee. "Don't worry about him," she says. "He's big and bad enough to look after himself."

Aurora scrapes the sole of one para boot across the toes of the other. "I know he's a pain. It's just,"

"Don't say bad karma."

"Well it is."

Portia is looking at the map, steering the car, searching for street names. "Spooky dear, karma is what karma does," she says.

"It just doesn't *feel* right, you know?" Aurora says. "I have this *feeling*. He wanted to help us later. Now, I don't know. I just have this *feeling*."

Portia puts a finger on the street map, traces a white line northwards on the orange page, and says, "What is this, a Julio Iglesias convention?"

"A bad feeling," Aurora says. "We should have said something."

Portia almost tells Aurora what she knows about Bullrush. She really needs to put Aurora in the picture about a few things. But the time had to be right. For the time being, she shifts her sunglasses. "Look, how do we explain it when we find The Boss? If we find him. It."

"The owner doesn't need to know the details."

"So we rip through the guts of this thing and pull out a book. And you say, Oh wow. Look. A book of magic spells. I wonder how that got there? Never mind, I'll use it to bring my boyfriend back from the dead."

Portia indicates to turn left, changes her mind, turns right into a broad avenue of red brick houses, neatly trimmed privet hedge, ornately painted chess piece chimney pots. She says the words and instantly regrets her lack of conviction. You don't bring back the dead. Not even Aurora can make her change her mind on that one.

Those spooks Aurora finds trapped in the bubbles of glass vases, ghouls swirling in the flecks of oil paint or spirits bursting the grain of some ancient piece of wood, they're never coming back.

The most they can do is growl and grumble, make a bit of noise about the way things have turned out.

Personally, she has never been moved much by the mystery of faith. Mysterium fidei. If Aurora says there's a spirit trapped in a piano, then Portia reckons some other way-out sensitive type of person will probably see it too. Sooner or later every investment comes good. But no way she is going to say credo. Her articles of faith went hurtling out the window with Big Al and Little Al.

They are following signs for Watford Road, passing the entrance to Sudbury Hill tube station.

Aurora presses her forehead against the window. She hates the smell of leather in a car.

She thinks, did I fall asleep for a second there, did I imagine the air hiccupped?

And then the fencing, the pavement, the streetlights on the corner, the bricks, slate and cement of the buildings, swell and make a ripple. A blue faced boy swings down from a streetlight straight at their car, dangling by the thick fist of a noose around his neck.

Windows turn slits for eyes, the station doorway melts round into a gaping black mouth that consumes commuters, glugging them down into the underworld. It spits out a fiery snake of a tongue, smacking the window near Aurora's face. Several pedestrians are incinerated in the flash of flame. A newspaper vendor is sizzled to a crisp by the hot sharp edge of flame. The smouldering bodies are hoovered down the bloated frog throat.

Aurora shields her face with Greater London and presses back into the car seat.

She's making these terrified squealing noises.

But when Portia looks around anxiously, there's nothing.

Someone takes advantage of the clotting traffic to run across the road to buy a magazine at the newspaper stall. Portia stops, allowing several more commuters to weave past into the station.

She looks up and down the street. The traffic. The pedestrians. Nothing unusual.

Aurora is moaning, slipping through the seatbelt, sliding off the car seat, squirming under the dashboard. Eyes rolling upwards into the back of her skull. A white froth on her lips.

Portia hits the accelerator, twisting the wheel. They lurch into Harrow Road, veer around a couple of corners, scatter a group of schoolboys in black tails and multi coloured waistcoats. She guns the Cherokee and the back end swings out. She swerves past the pale faced boys, runs a red light on a filter lane, turns towards empty playing fields and comes skidding to a stop in a car park near bricked up changing rooms on municipal playing fields.

The noise Aurora makes is called groaning, but it is more than this. Half on the seat, half on the floor, she is making animal sounds. Portia wipes the drool from her chin, strokes her hair for reassurance. She never considered that Aurora might be seriously ill. She might have epilepsy, a brain tumour, some psychological dysfunction. She might be suffering from some thing she has not told anyone about. Or, she might be possessed. Like a demon in a piece of furniture. She doubts it. But Aurora might think she is. It could be delusional.

Whatever it is, it only lasts a minute. Then Aurora opens her eyes like nothing strange has ever happened. "So we're there then," Aurora says, as though she is coming round from a nap. She wipes her mouth with the back of her hand, taking in the deserted football pitches.

Clockwise on the map, in circles drawn around Sudbury Hill, Palmer's Green, Forest Gate, Beckenham and Wimbledon, Aurora has written, Boss Boss Boss, Boss Om, Boss Anova, Boss Scat and Boss Y. Across the square that is really the dead grass of the recreation area she has scrawled Boss Boss Boss, Sunnyside Nursing Home, The Elms.

Portia looks out the windscreen into the undergrowth, at the hand painted sign crawling with ivy lost behind overgrown rhododendron.

She tilts her head sideways to read the writing, pleased at the way her expensive bob of hair seems to hang naturally. "Well, so we are," she says. "You'll feel better in five minutes Spooky."

Aurora shakes her head, gulping deep breaths. "No. Let's go. Sooner we get out of this place the better," she says.

First she thought she had urban claustrophobia and was suffering karmic exhaustion. Now, she says, she feels she is being deliberately targeted.

She cups her hands over her eyes. "London's doing my head in. There are so many horrible things."

"The streets were never really paved with gold," Portia says.

Aurora's voice is trembling. "They're paved in ghouls."

She says, "Didn't you see the boy with the blue face hanging from a streetlight? The buildings eating people?"

Portia reaches down behind her seat and hauls over her nubie, picking through the silver and gold tubes, the shiny boxes, the lipsticks, eyeliners, perfumes and makeup.

"No dear." She hands Aurora some tissues.

It comforts her to unscrew the little round boxes of eye shadow, to open and sniff at their peach or tan or brown insides.

Aurora says the combined howl from art galleries and museums drowns out the noise of traffic. These buildings, full of blood and horror and anguish, she says, they have shadow spectres looming over them. She plots them across the horizon. The Victoria and Albert Museum, purple phantom squatting on blood red pillar of weeping souls. Nearby, the Science Museum, a great fiery eye and whirlpool of banshees. A black spectre squats on top of the British Museum. Two vampire ghouls squabble over a pile of bloody bodies stacked high above the National Galleries and the National Portrait Gallery. A cloud of doom drizzles medieval martyr's blood around the Tate. Sickness, pestilence and agony moan and wail outside The Royal College of Surgeons, craving a return to feast on the thousands of dislocated organs and dismembered body parts inside.

Aurora says she can barely look at the terrible curtain of howling evil that consumes itself, and then gives rebirth a hundred times more terrible, half a mile high astride The Tower of London and the Bank of England.

"I know you can't see any of it, but that doesn't mean it isn't real. It's unbearable," Aurora says.

Portia feels surprisingly motherly in the midst of all

this panic.

Aurora fishes around in her canvas bag for the rabbit foot, spilling I-ching coins onto the floor, tipping out her one black eye liner pencil, one bottle of black nail varnish, a length of leather cord and two eggcup sized frosted plastic pots of ylang ylang anti stress balm.

Her heart's going calypso. She's pressing the rabbit paw tight to her breast as they step into the dining room of the Sunnyside Nursing Home.

They don't do security.

In one room Portia puts the palm of her hand flat across her chest, the mass of sparkling gems and pearls and sleeve of golden bracelets rich against the red suit. To the three old crones staring into space there she says, "Ladies, we're from Fantasy Facial."

It is the starting signal for a shuffling zimmer of a Le Mans. Portia throws her palm open towards the three white haired women rumbling towards her in carpet slippers. "My name is Mrs Margot Daniels," she says.

She jangles her bangles with a flip backwards of her wrist, saying, "And this is my wonderful daughter Miss Melanie Daniels."

And she says, "We have a wonderful free makeover gift for everyone today."

Aurora opens up the leather holdall, spreads the cosmetics over a table.

The air is sharp with the smell of fried egg and urine. "Oh, sisters," the first woman says. "Beatification."

Her still life has cherry lips and black eyes set in saucers of baby blue eye shadow. Her trembling hand tugs at her thin white curls.

A zimmer shunts Cherry Lips out of the way, the pilot leaning the weight of her humped shoulders into the frame.

"I come, Graymalkin," she says.

Then the toothless one shoves her in the back. "But my Paddock calls first," she says. And she thrusts her

194

bearded chin at Portia.

These weird sisters, dribbling yolk, dancing with Parkinson's, are vicious for a handful of Portia's tubes and phials. Questions are lost in the incoherent babble. But the more Portia and Aurora ask about Boss Boss Boss, the more they are ignored.

Hump Back inhales a collagen enhancing overnight face crème. Gummy grabs a bottle of free radical neutralising advanced night repair cream, pumps it a dozen times and massages it through her hair. Cherry Lips tugs the sleeve of Portia's jacket. She says, "Have you any chestnuts?"

Portia stands in the doorway and looks along the corridor towards a room bursting with the noise of people trying to talk over the sound of a television. She points at the tiny face of her golden wristwatch and spreads out five fingers to Aurora. Then she jerks her thumb in the direction of the corridor.

Gummy, her mess of hair standing straight, smears advanced night repair cream onto Cherry Lips' hair.

"Here you," Hump Back says to Aurora. "Where have you been, sister?"

"Killing pigs I'll bet," says gummy.

Aurora says she would never ever kill any animal whatsoever. She takes the tops off more pots of moisturiser, empties tubes of foaming cleanser, pumps mascara, rolls up lipsticks.

The room is heavy with the promise of rejuvenation by plant extract.

Cherry Lips has had her thin curls slicked flat. Now Gummy, the sister with the most pronounced beard, begins working her fingers through Hump Back's white hair. They have a clucking language all of their own.

Hump Back, the blown knuckles of her curved spine, she wants to buy all of Portia's cosmetics. She has no money, but that doesn't matter. There are more important things. "You may have the devil's teat soon enough," she says.

Gummy stops her massaging. She tilts her head up to the ceiling and howls, "Bow wow. I'd like it now."

Yes, that's good, Aurora says. Bow wow. Bow wow wow wow. Where is the bow wow?

"You," Cherry Lips says to Hump Back. "You're all dried up with cursing and madness."

Aurora presses a tube of Portia's favourite golden lip gloss into the clawed-up hand and she says, "That's for you. A gift for you. For you."

Portia is flat against the wall, moving sideways along the corridor. Then her mobile rings. Portia Maxwell, spider flat against the wall in red Armani. Holding her breath. She might be here to raid the pharmacy, empty the drugs cabinet of any Halcyon, Prozac or dopamine shifters. She could be a maniac out to attack old ladies. She could shout fire, but no one would hear over the television.

So she answers the phone and she says, "Portia Maxwell." She takes the pocket diary from her silver purse and writes a name at today's date. Into her phone, she says, "You don't need an exorcism. We'll put the painting straight back on the market."

Aurora and the weird sisters have started barking.

Into her phone, Portia says, "Really? Your bedroom smells of sulphur?"

Echoing along the corridor, under the downpour of noise, the barking is a distinct new voice. Not alarming, but attracting the grey outside, pink inside ears of a chihuahua trying to sleep.

It slips out from the television room into the corridor and stops, vibrating from ear to toe nails, staring at Portia.

"Well. You must be Boss Boss Boss," Portia says, closing the phone.

The sisters get the dog, Aurora keeps the little studded

collar as an ankle bracelet. Remarkably like the real Boss, she says.

"Only this one's still alive," says Portia, scraping the cosmetics into the holdall.

Then she says, "Remind me never to use any of this makeup again. If I'm not mistaken those women had herpes."

Aurora insists on riding in the rear of the jeep, hidden beneath a tartan rug. She says she can feel the eyes of something wicked searching for her. London is not a safe place, she warns Portia.

The next couple of dogs, no problems. Boss Om was chewing a tennis ball in the garden outside the address in Palmer's Green. Om it said on his nametag.

On the way to Forest Gate, Portia had a false alarm when she saw a toddler playing with a dog on wheels. She screamed, jumped out of the car, and reduced the boy to tears by grabbing his toy. Closer examination, Portia holding it against the rear window so that Aurora can study it from beneath her blanket, revealed that the dog was a worn out wirehaired fox terrier. Made in China. Further along the pentacle curve was Boss Anova, who spends the day in a trendy hairdresser's window in Forest Gate. His quiff is tinted vibrant pink, worn in a centre parting, and he prances back and forward along the length of the shop window to the Joao Gilberto cd the owners play constantly.

It is a long drive across London to Beckenham. Aurora complains about every pothole they hit, every bend she slides around, but she refuses to come out from under the rug. She tells Portia not to talk to her, or even look in her direction. She is to act like Aurora does not exist. Of course, she'll be right there, in the back. But it's no good asking her to help with directions. She does not want a sandwich or a coffee break. She wants them to find The Boss and get straight home.

"Fifty fifty now," Aurora says. "Boss Scat or Boss Y."

So Portia pretends she is alone, making this dangerous drive from north to south of the river under the eyes of, and perhaps between the legs of, the evil Aurora is so worried about.

Outside the car, it's raining. The big city. The whole mess of life gets wet. For whatever reasons, Portia's husband comes to mind, her husband and son.

Big Al isn't the friend, the nice person you've known for years. He's a threat to your existence. He tells you what to eat, how to dress, what books to read and where to shop. He tells you that you are fat even when you have been starving yourself. He says you are ugly when you believe your hair is sitting pretty. He says you wear too much eye makeup when you try to cover the bruises he gave you. To know him is to understand when taking the beating is in your own best interests.

What he calls love makes you bite your lip until it bleeds. This is better than screaming out in pain and hurt at the violation. Swallowing rage is better than having a crying baby in the equation.

You don't even really understand how the baby got to be there. How anything meant to be born out of love can happen just the same in hate.

This relationship, this marriage. This battlefield where your soul is under siege. And you know all battlefields have casualties.

Margaret Maxwell has the Capri going flat out. In the headlights, through the gold of autumn trees, the black waters of the loch flashes momentarily negative. *Where me and my true love will never meet again, On the bonnie bonnie banks of Loch Lomond.*

Big Al and Little Al.

The first idea was that none of them should wake up. Then she prayed, but only for Little Al. It wasn't selfish. Any reasonable mother would have done the same. How it worked out that she was the only survivor, with this metal plate in her head, she will never know. Pure bad luck, you guess. Something to do with trajectories.

She wants to believe that. And belief is more about hope than faith.

Now, when she closes her eyes, she sees Little Al with a set of brussel sprout angel wings on his shoulders. He zips around, playing these pan pipes perfectly. And he is not coming back.

Big Al never shows his face.

Talk about reincarnation. If it could happen it would have by now. Meeting someone you used to know in another life would be a regular occurrence. She's waited twenty years and still there's nothing. She's read every book on the subject. She went through Science. She researched Religion. She looked up Philosophy. Poetry. Children's stories. Portia went right through Fiction.

Nobody brings back the dead. Bottom line.

"Some things proclaimed as true have absolutely no proof," Portia says out loud to herself.

Aurora's stifled voice from behind says, "Remember, I'm not here."

Portia has no proof of blood running down the walls, haunted pianos, two way mirrors into another dimension, hands that grab at you from nowhere in the shower. She cannot explain why she has a terrified girl hiding under a blanket in the back of her car.

It starts to rain harder.

And hitting her as fast as a shiver, Portia biting hard on a knuckle, she starts to cry. Breathing between her fingers, hard sobs that hurt her belly.

She has held the power of life and death in her hands. She has learned you don't go to hell for the things that you do. It's the things that you don't do that take you

199

there in this life.

Portia wipes the snot from her face with the back of a hand. When they find this book, if there is some way of raising the dead, maybe they better burn it.

"That's my point," she says into the rear view mirror. "I know you're there."

"You can't see me though," says the bump of Aurora. "So you don't know for certain that I am here. You can only believe."

"No, I know for a fact that you are back there."

"Meiaow. I'm Schrodinger's cat," Aurora says, wriggling around beneath the blanket. "If a tree falls in a forest with no one to hear it, does the tree make a noise?"

"Yes. All large objects that fall make a racket."

"But how do you know for certain, if there is nobody around to hear it?"

"Well, you just know."

"I could be dead and you wouldn't know unless you looked to see."

"Spooky, we *are* having a conversation here."

Then Aurora says, "Do you believe in aliens?"

"Yes."

"But not in God?"

"No."

"Heaven?"

"No."

"Hell?"

"Hell, yes. Right here on earth."

"Do you believe in fairies?"

"No."

"Elvis is alive?"

"Maybe. They spelled his name wrong on the gravestone. That could be a clue."

"Penicillin?"

"Of course."

"That appearances count?"

"I suppose."

"Time flies?"

"Yes, in a manner of speaking. But time is time, isn't it? Steady. Plodding."

"Well," the muffled voice of Aurora says. "Imagine you were a scientist waiting for a radioactive atom to decay. Say it's a carbon 14 atom with a half-life of 5700 years. You know that this incredible thing is going to happen. But since the probability of it decaying in any given year are only about one in ten thousand, the chances of it actually doing this amazing thing before your very eyes are really, well, enormously far out. That's statistics. And it doesn't matter whether the particle is one year old or a million years old."

Portia thinks maybe the world is mad and it was always meant to come down to this day and these people, Aurora and Jimmy T, her and Little Al.

This is the day they are destined to change the world. To conquer death.

Or maybe it is their duty to the universe, for the whole forever hereafter, to destroy this book, keep things just the way they are.

It is probably her duty to drive Aurora right now, straight away, directly to a private psychiatric wing. The thing is, god knows, what if Aurora was to be left believing that the spells would have worked? To be always waiting for the half life. Treat that.

The others were easier than this.

Plan B. Plan B says if there is a man at home, it is plan B.

The teddy bear man is in the kitchen. There's the hiss of him tugging a ring pull. When he comes back into the living room he says, "Sure you don't want a beer?"

In the living room there's just a tilt-back chair. There's a small flat screen television sitting on top of it's own new cardboard box. In the thick green pile of the living room carpet there's the outlines left by a sofa. There's the outlines left by a hi fi, one big flat square and two small ones where the speakers crushed the carpet. There's depressions left by the feet of a table and chairs. On the walls, there are shadows where there were once framed prints and photographs. There are no curtains on the windows. There is a stinking ashtray on the mantelpiece, full of doubts.

The teddy bear man waves Portia at the chair and says, "Sit down." He takes some beer and says, "Take a seat and we'll talk about God and my dog."

Portia asks if her daughter can use the bathroom.

And he moves his head to look at Aurora. With his free hand he rubs the stubble on the side of his face, saying, "Go on. Down past the kitchen," and he points into the hall with his beer can.

Aurora steps over where the beer slopped out onto the carpet and says, "Thanks."

She disappears into the house. The bathroom fan comes on. A door closes.

Portia hands the man the tin of Chummy. The teddy bear man smells of beer and sweat. He stands so close, the teddy bears are at eye level. Their backs are bent over at right angles, it looks like the beach ball is too heavy for them to shift. He looks at the Chummy, swills some more beer, and says, "So how does this work?"

The chair smells like him. It has worn grey velvet stained dark from dirt along the arms. It is warm.

Portia says God is the definition of everything good, a moral hardliner but forgiving and generous. God is the eternal, all present, all-powerful, supreme creator and sustainer of the entire universe. God is loving, kind, merciful and wants to share his magnificent existence with man. That's why he gave us a soul. And when our soul was in danger, this loving father sent down his only son from heaven to die for us on the cross. He cares for our pets just the same. That is why Chummy puts a prayer in every tin.

"Crap," the guy says.

He puts the Chummy next to the ashtray and goes to look out the window. When he lifts his face up to the sky his eyes are reflected in the glass.

Portia puts on her best religious sermon voice and says how God understands that man will have doubts. But remember he is also father to all the innocent little animals.

"Crap!" the guy shouts, spraying beer down his reflection.

Aurora appears in the doorway, one hand covering her mouth. She looks at Portia and shakes her head, then disappears back down the hall.

Sinking into the dirty warm velvet, into the smell of the man, Portia says God is a genius of unlimited power and is a beacon of hope for those lost in a world of cruelty and sin, an angel of strength for the weak, for those who are battered and oppressed by a world of selfishness.

With a sigh, the man says, "My dog is dead." He turns, pointing his beer can at the Chummy, and says, "Tell me how your holy dog food works."

Portia looks down at her knees. "Every can is sealed with a prayer," she says.

The teddy bear man screams, "Who to? Dog God? Will it convince my wife that what happened was an accident? If Chummy can do that then I swear I'll eat it myself right now."

Portia says it is not meant for human consumption.

The man drops his arms by his side. The beer foams over his hand onto the carpet. "I lose everything because of one mistake, one stinking night with some secretary, I don't even remember her name. I lost my wife. I lost my kids. Tell me where God says that just because I put down rat poison I did that deliberately to kill her dog and get back at her?"

He shakes his beer at Portia, crushing the sides of the can and says, "I asked God to love this family. And that dog, I never meant to kill him."

Portia says of course God would like to listen to every single person who prayed. But with his popularity, and all the demands, the machinery gets clogged up. Think of the years and years of getting the same prayers about family problems, divorces, unwanted pregnancies, sick pets, people losing their jobs or pleading for the winning lottery numbers. He has to prioritise. But that doesn't mean God is a bastard. Chummy with a prayer is designed to take some of the strain out of the relationship. Give God more time.

And the teddy bear man says, "I even got the dog preserved. Now she doesn't want it." His breath is pure beer and he says, "I get the dead dog. She gets the kids. My two beautiful children."

Down the hall a toilet flushes. A door opens and a bathroom fan clicks off.

The man swallows the dregs out of the can. He has a light froth of beer moustache.

Aurora appears in the doorway.

Portia stands up. Maybe, she says, he should have thought about that before committing adultery with some whore at the office.

And the teddy bear man crushes the empty can between his palms, twists it together until it is the size of a hamburger. He says, "You better go."

Outside, it is raining harder.

Walking to the car, Aurora says, "That was one of the most awful experiences of my life."

Portia says yes, he was totally strung out.

"No," says Aurora. "I meant that guy's toilet."

They don't look back at the man watching from the window. "Messy?"

"Blimey, yes," says Aurora. She's looking straight ahead, starting to smile on one side of her mouth. "But you should have seen the bedroom."

Her smile gets wider and she walks faster over to the car. She says, "You'd think he had a dead dog in there."

21

While Aurora has her hand stuck up the arse of a dead chihuahua in Beckenham something much worse is happening in Wimbledon.

A limo is parked under a tree in a neighbourhood of tidy little homes. It is a pink flowering tree and for several hours petals have fallen onto the car, sticking to it in the rain.

Ramana's car is pink as a bride's covered in confetti.

Inside, the chauffeur is sleeping in pink light, his grubby cream double breasted jacket unbuttoned at the collar.

Ramana is visiting the house with the double row of toy garden windmills and crazy paving. The trembling border of red, yellow and blue plastic sails leads to freshly whitewashed walls, a red tiled roof, the laminate frames of the reproduction Georgian cottage windows.

The panelled front door is blocked by a rustic effect watering can, brimming with rain, and a row of flowering red geraniums in clay pots. To the side, there's a gate painted with creosote. This allows you around the back of the house, where there's a neat patch of grass dominated by a rotary clothes drier. Dotted about there's a dirty tennis ball, a chewed out rubber bone, a headless doll .

The rotary groans, heavy with rain sodden shirts.

The back door is open and inside the kitchen is clean and tidy. A washing machine is spinning towards the end of its cycle. A radio presenter is talking about the impact of war on foreign travel. A handful of dog biscuits are spilled around a saucer of oily milk on the ceramic limestone effect tiles.

You go through a door and you're in a small hallway, with orange shag pile carpet and brown hessian wallpaper. Next to the phone there's a mirror with a Southern Comfort transfer, which means it is useless for inspecting your appearance. In the crevice between glass and frame someone has slid a photograph. Whoever took it was standing too close and the flash has bleached out the details of an overweight woman wearing a tent sized purple blouse. She's laughing, you can see her red retinas through her spectacles, and she's turning her head away from the dog she's holding up to her face.

The dog, this blue chihuahua with a mop of hair, it has either been licking her mouth or is just about to. The dog's tongue, its pink tip, is almost inside the corner of the woman's mouth.

When you look closely at this photograph, you can see there is a smaller pink tip of an erection under the dog's belly.

You are directly facing the front door and from this side you can see it is bolted and locked. On the right there's an open door and the shag pile continues into the front room. A Jaeger trench coat, tan with green tartan lining, makes a surprisingly lifelike corpse lying on the floor.

To the left, leading upstairs, the orange carpet is peppered with these brown leopard spots.

You follow these up and there are three doors, a window and mesh curtains at the top of the stairs. From here you can look out over the garden, over the trees, down to the pink float of the limo. Or you can pop into the pine panelled bathroom and enjoy a deep soak in the white ceramic Victoriana bath tub with polished nickel ball and claw feet. Blast yourself with the period porcelain showerhead. Choose from a range of toiletries designed to stimulate, relax, or turn you on, up, or off.

You can go into the study. The computer isn't on but you can still mess around with the neat piles of paperwork, household bills and bank statements. Add some bogus appointments on the crowded wall planner. Erase a few genuine ones. Put some stuff in the empty to do tray, for Christ's sake.

Or you can follow the leopard spots, that are really splats, which trace a crisscross pattern about the carpet. They could have been dabbed on by a paint brush. A trail of Yves Klein's.

Only, it isn't paint. Paint doesn't dry like this, still wet under a crust, binding the nylon strands of carpet.

Paint doesn't smell like this.

The splats, some of them are little heart shapes, are most concentrated around this door. The one closed door in the whole house.

Standing here, outside this door, making the choice between going in or turning back down the stairs, you're straining to sense what's on the other side of impenetrable.

And just when you begin to accept that there is nothing, the door opens.

It opens wide and the room sucks you in.

Ramana, the shadow of night, raises a hand. Not in greeting, but to pump the gore from a yard of intestine down her throat. She is having breakfast in bed. In fact, breakfast is on the bed.

Every day, your heart beats about a hundred thousand times at an average of seventy two beats a minute. Your heart pumps a total of eight thousand gallons of blood twelve thousand miles through your body. It mainly comes in four different flavours, A, B, O and AB. Each minute, about a quart of blood passes through your kidneys and comes out clean. That's about one million gallons of blood in a lifetime.

Not this chihuahua lover's.

Your brain has three parts. Your cerebral cortex, the inner area, governs involuntary muscles. The cerebellum, the middle part, controls balance and muscle coordination. The cerebrum, the outer part, governs thought, the senses and movement. It is, some believe, where the sense of individual resides.

Only, not this individual.

Although your bones are hard, inside they are light and spongy with marrow. They are about seventy five percent water. Most people have two hundred and six bones. They have six hundred muscles.

Not this body.

What job does your appendix do? Nothing. It is a little dead-end sack that dangles three inches from the lowest part of your large intestine. Food particles sometimes get caught in this tube and bacteria grows. This irritates the appendix, so it swells up and needs to be removed.

Ramana, on the other hand, finds it something of a delicacy. A pope's nose. It gives momentary relief from the agonies that torment her. To retrieve one, she finds it helps to place something like, in this case, a shoebox under her host's back. This causes the chest to protrude outward, the arms and neck need to fall back, and this allows the maximum exposure of the trunk. Ramana always comes prepared with her Rambo serrated athame. In this case, the case of the fat lady now before us, Ramana curves a Y-shaped incision beneath the heavy flopping breasts. The arms of the Y extend from the front of each shoulder to the bottom end of the breast bone. She takes the tail of the Y down to the pubic bone, doing a roundabout to avoid the navel.

She cuts very deep, down to the rib cage on the chest and completely through the abdominal wall below.

She could hack the heart out. Rip the stomach open. There are plenty of ways to go about these things. This is simply how she prefers to do it.

It is also a necessary preparation for one of Ramana's favourite moments. With the Y incision made, she peels the skin, muscle, and soft tissues off the chest wall. Then it's just a flick of the wrists to throw the chest flap up over the face. This way, she gets rid of the ugly visage and exposes the front of the rib cage with the strap muscles of the front of the neck.

She finds that the edge of the blade goes through the rib cage with a little bit of elbow grease.

One cut is made up each side at the front, so that the chest plate consisting of the sternum and the ribs still connected to it can be separated from the adhesive soft tissues and lifted clear.

She calls it the fleshy spider. Lifting it clear reveals the lungs and the heart, if the beast has one, nestling in its pericardial sac.

Slicing the abdominal muscle away from the bottom of the rib cage and diaphragm allows the flaps of the abdominal wall to fall off to either side, neatly exposing the main organs.

There are titbits here and there. If she is peckish, and is not in a hurry. Her favourite morsel is the brain, either as a cold snack or as a takeaway.

Today she has no time for such niceties. She is too busy for epicurean delights. Not for her the leisure of augury, leconomancy, or the stupid flaming straws of sideromancy. Give her a good length of intestine any day, preferably followed by cabernet sauvignon. She has always believed you can't beat entrails.

The oesophagus, the lungs, the heart, trachea. The thyroid. Sliced like loaves of bread. The liver, a spotty familiar. A nasty deflated gallbladder there. The spleen. Intestines bloated with faeces and undigested food. The bowel. The stomach gritty with that morning's cereal. The unforgettable smell of gastric acid. The pancreas and the duodenum. The bladder, the ovaries, the uterus. Those kidneys look delicious.

Really, for Ramana, best enjoyed before an evening at the opera where she can wolf howl through the loudest chorus.

Tonight, nothing in this library speaks to Ramana of her book.   Like Rembrandt's Dr Tulp, she's found zilch.

Trudi Wanton expired too fast. She could have delivered details, yet she only provided an index. Wimbledon, Beckenham, Forest Gate, Palmer's Green and Sudbury Hill. Of course, she placed Wimbledon first since the English lawn tennis club was the only place she recognised.

Lucky for Ramana, London is not a chihuahua city.

And it is a strange thing about dogs. How they enjoy human company.

It only takes a click of her fingers and Boss Y is over, jangling with affection, his bony feet prancing in the slops of butchery, nose pressing at the stranger's hand reaching down to lift him.

She looks him in the eye and she says, "Please can you end this misery and tell me where my book is?"

You can see by the twitch in his tail that he is happy.

At last.

Now it is his turn to get some attention.

22

Each time the Psychic Deli's neon fizzles, that's me getting a jolt from the national grid. It is trying to move me on. But I am determined to hang around these little scarlet loops of glass in the café window. Aurora is particularly sensitive to static and if one day she comes close to the multicoloured tubes I hope to attract more than simply dust. My dream is to reach out, touch a hair on her head and hold it close.

Tonight, though closed, the café is full of shadows. The paintings are alive, dancing to the ripples the streetlights and car headlamps make on the walls. The Portrait Of A Woman 1892 looks ready to step down off the wall if it wasn't for the entrapment spell Aurora put on the painting to keep the lady in her place.

Aurora and Portia arrive on foot. They loitered for a time like smugglers, hidden under St Alfege's pillars, before making a jog across the road. Portia does this peculiar on tip toe run, due to her heels.

Portia opens up, Aurora bundles in. Portia locks up, scans the street, then follows Aurora in. In the half darkness, the beat of the neon, they drag stools over to the counter. Portia lights a peppermint scented aromatherapy tea light and Aurora pulls something out from inside her underpants. Straightaway she falls purring over a familiar looking little book, like a cat over a saucer of milk.

Portia says, "Come on. Come on. What does it say?"

Without lifting her head, Aurora scrapes an orange

from a nearby fruit bowl and says there is a process to understanding the mind of another witch.

She says some witches write their spells in secret symbols, or backwards. Some write them line after line, snaking them across the page from left to right then backwards right to left, like steam rising from coffee. Some witches use spirals to twist and hide their most powerful spells. The more twisted the sinews of the spell the more it will confuse and possess the victim.

A rap at the door makes Portia jump. Aurora folds her arms defensively over the book. Vivienne raps at the door again. This time, Mrs Pugh presses her white eyes against the window. She searches the blackness, looking beyond seeing. When Portia opens and closes the door, they have to be quick to wriggle inside.

Vivienne breathlessly tells Portia she has had this idea for a Psychic Deli web site.

"Powerful spells cast on your behalf," she says. "Spell casting for love and relationships, money and jobs. Aura cleansing, Black Curses, and Emergency Spells. Tarot readings down the line."

She says the web surfers point their browsers at the Psychic Deli and place their order on-line.

Aurora does not lift her eyes from the book. At first she felt the evil in its pages. Now Seduction is the word she cannot get out of her head.

"We'll deal with the web later," says Portia. "I need you here because we might need some help. Why is she with you?"

"We were in the middle of a spread. Really interesting cards, Portia. There's something weird going on here."

"You can say that again."

A clatter at the door and Vivienne gets the full beam of a flashlight in her face. A hooded figure, details hidden behind torchlight, fills the doorframe.

"Who's that?" Aurora hisses.

"What is it?" Mrs Pugh says it with affection. "Who else are you expecting?"

"Not a who. A what," Aurora says. "A wraith, a mummy, an evil of the night. A bloodsucker, a zombie, a living dead."

"Oh good," says Mrs Pugh. "I could be doing with a bit more excitement before it finishes."

Portia makes the door open and drags the thing, or person, inside. The way they spin around together they fall face down onto the floor. Portia wrestles the torch free and whacks the person over the head with it. "Queen of Evil? Go to hell," she shouts.

Vivienne slam thumps her massive body down on top of the stranger, causing the tremor of a localised earthquake.

"Ty chyo, blya? It is Dominic. Dominic. Get off. Otyebis! You mad women."

And when they pull back the hood, turn the light on his face, pained and breathless, there he is. Beneath the duffle his naval jacket bears a chest full of medals. He is wearing red white and blue striped pyjama bottoms and slippers.

"Dominic. See who am I? It is Old Starshina your friend."

Vivienne peels herself off, blushing neon. "Sorry."

"It is all right," he says, giving his ribs a rub. "Russians like women who give such big crushes. I have flat nearby. I saw something, movement, I thought you were the bad guys after the cash. Old Starshina was ready to defend the good ship."

Portia helps him back to his feet. When he takes her hand, in this light, it could be Big Al brought all up to date and grey and flabby like the rest of his generation. Would she be offering her hand to him? No she would not.

Dominic is about the same height as her, but built like an ox. Eyes grey like the Atlantic his boat sailed across, she thinks. Beneath the twist of grey curls and full beard she suspects an appealing sad compassion. She was lucky to have caught him off guard this time. "Come in. I'll make some coffee."

"English tea, please. The one for breakfast."

There is code for living, a code for dying and codes for everything else in between. More than anything, death codes are words that need to be said out loud. Which is the thing frustrating Aurora as she stares at the blank pages. She cannot make the words take shape. She shuts the book. In places, the dark red leather of the binding is polished almost mahogany with handling. She steers the outside edge of her little finger along the life and heart lines on the cover.

"A life. A love. Can you imagine," she says, putting her small hand flat into the man's palm of the book, "the lifetime of this person?"

Portia puts her hand to her face, fills a kettle. She says, "I'd rather not."

Dominic wants to know what it is.

"A code book," Portia says.

"Let me see. I am cold war code cracker."

"No use. Pages are blank," Aurora says. "It could be a thousand years old. Some kind of sacrifice maybe. Or a homage."

And Portia looks at Aurora and then at the book in disgust. Aurora's delusions are getting worse. The way they huddle around the book, in candlelight, staring at blank pages. It is not natural.

Balancing it open in one hand, leafing through the pages, Aurora says to the book, "A thousand people might have died because of what's in here. Maybe another thousand who should have died are still walking about the place. If only I could see."

Mrs Pugh says, "Hold it up. Sometimes the blind can see better than anyone using eyes."

Aurora holds the red leather of the book wide so the

café's neon light shines through a single page.

"See anything?" says Vivienne.

"Still blind. Been like this for 30 years," says Mrs Pugh. Aurora squints at the page, and from where she is sitting, the angles of light and shade fall into place. "Of course."

You can see a pattern in the paper, faint words, transparent sentences and ghostly paragraphs.

"Invisible ink," Dominic says. "This is espionage."

"On children's television," Aurora says, "they tell you if it is vinegar or milk you hold the paper over a hot light bulb to turn the ink brown."

"If it is lemon juice, you boil a red cabbage and spray the paper with the water," says Vivienne. "I remember reading that once."

"Or you can use crushed blackberries, or red onions, or a solution of hibiscus flowers," says Mrs Pugh.

Aurora says, "If it is semen, you can read it under fluorescent light. That's what this is."

Everyone looks at one another.

Portia says, "They tell kids how to write spells with sperm?"

And Aurora looks exasperated and says, "Of course not. Anyway, it is only the most especial sort of powerful spells you do that way.

"When you think about it, sperm and life and everything, you can see how it works."

Aurora harvests a selection of berries, grapes lemons and red cabbage from the help yourself to as much as you can eat salad bar. If it is corn flour, she says, you smear on iodine. For baking soda, you need to daub on grape juice.

"Looks good enough to eat," says Portia.

And Aurora slaps the book shut. "This is an ancient witch book with chopped off hands and pages probably written in fossilised sperm. Not a sandwich."

Portia says she takes her point. But if it is a health

hazard maybe they should burn it now.

Aurora slams her fist into the table, spilling the tea and coffees Portia made. "I'm the one who decides what we do with this book," she says.

She tells Dominic to find a bottle of iodine in the first aid box. Vivienne rummages for the cotton buds in her handbag.

Portia unhooks the ultra violet insect killer that lures bugs away from the sandwiches to their deaths. This one has a cable long enough to reach the front counter. It also has an adapter to power off a car's cigarette lighter. If you believe the advertising, it is a portable death ray cleansing the campsite, the campervan, and the countryside, of pests. Only, because it attracts every insect flying in a five miles radius, you have to ask yourself if this bug magnet of a death ray is really the best way to avoid being plagued?

The Psychic Deli is Aurora's ultra violet sterilised neon lit laboratory. She uses cotton buds to smear indigo cabbage juice that paints invisible symbols purple. Iodine brushed across a blank page reveals a trail of red and brown words. Grape juice has no effect. In the bug light, one page glows pink with a tightly packed spiral of words, a mixture of Greek and Latin, astrological symbols and gargoyle faces.

Aurora's fingers, the countertop, the leather seat, are stained yellow. The place stinks of vinegar and iodine and lemon juice.

"This is clever evil, very clever," says Aurora. She turns the book upside down, reads pages from behind, follows spirals and waves of words that intersect and lose themselves in a jumble before they emerge in unexpected new directions. Most of the handwriting is different, but the last four pages are crammed with the same scrawl. The final page is a list of names. There is a column of these in the middle of the page. One new line starts at the top, runs clockwise all the way along, down, around and up again. Little spiral clouds of names. Starbursts of identities.

"Aha." In one cloud Aurora finds what she has been looking for. Her Rosetta Stone. *Hammington*. It has to be Ramana's handwriting.

She tells Portia it is fantastic.

"I think," she says, "that this is Ramana's flying spell. And this is a spell for astral projections and out of body experiences. This is how to summon a succubus."

She runs the violet light down the page of sperm writing. There are details in the writing Aurora does not understand. "Something this complicated has to be for demonic possession, maybe with some eternal life thrown in too."

Then there is crack, as a moth comes out of nowhere and hits the bug killer, and Aurora screams. "I can't believe it," she says. "The evil bitch. She's locked the spells."

Portia says what does she mean? She looks into the weird glowing whites of Aurora's eyes as another bit of moth spits in the ultra violet and she tells Aurora that words cannot be kept under lock and key.

Aurora shakes her head at them. "Evil is personal," she says. "Ramana has purified the essence of the evil in the spells and then made it personal. It's all disguised in numerology and scenes from movies. If I try it, they are only useless words. Watch."

She places the open book in her lap, spreads her arms out, then brings her palms together at her chest. She reads a flying spell, as revealed by cabbage juice.

'Fly in Never Never Land, Peter Pan. By Hook or by crook. Director Clyde Geronimi, four million to animate in nineteen hundred and fifty three. Mr and Mrs Darling's Wendy visited by Disney Bobby Driscoll. And loathsome fairy Tinkerbell.'

And she does not fly.

She says, "Need a female demon to have sexual intercourse with a man while he sleeps?"

"Not I," Dominic says. Vivienne elbows him.

'James Polakof shapes Satan's Mistress. Lana Wood is taken by the spirit lost in limbo. Britt Ekland tries to understand the mysticism in nineteen hundred and eighty two. Beware! Once the Fury of the Succubus is levelled next to you.'

An evil nubile does not appear in the deli, howling for sex.

"And look. Here's one for you Portia. To put evil in art."

'Daughters of Satan, Tom Selleck. Loves the art of our sisters burned at the stake. His wife Barra Grant was burned long before. Sellek the judge seeks vengeance once more.'

"Or," Aurora says, "What about possession of an infant?"

'Rosemary's Baby, Polanski's second Repulsion. Mia Farrow's vague vague dream, supernatural metaphors make pregnancy scream. Dix neuf cent soixante huit, Satan's holy child the world does meet.'

Aurora says there is also one for causing perpetual pain and misery and other things she needs more time to understand. In the lemon juice she recognises George Romero, Night of the Living Dead, probably a spell for zombie consumerism. Stained in cabbage water there is Ringo Starr, Son of Dracula, nineteen seventy four. There's Omen, antichrist, Armageddon. Vampire's Kiss, Nicolas Cage, eat cockroach. Witchboard, possession, Peter Svatek, yuppie greed. The Bride Wore Black. Truffaut.

Aurora concentrates, runs the bug light over the semen again. She turns the book around and around and around. "This one is the most complicated. It starts in the middle with *'Henry Portrait of a serial killer, John McNaughton, eighty nine, green impala, Rooker with Towles. Henry and Otis. Videotaping.'* Then it gets lost in

219

Greek stuff. Then, over here, it says *'Cabinet of doctor Caligari. Until tomorrow's dawn.'* And then it's all tangled up again. And then here it says *'Werner Krauss.'* And there's *'Willy Hameister.'* Over here it looks like Henry again and it says, *'There is no good to counterbalance evil.'* This is powerful twisted stuff."

Aurora punches her fists into the seat. She feels her eyes filling with tears. "It's impossible."

It reads like horror film reviews to Portia but the way Aurora says the words has her mouth dry with fear.

"I don't understand," says Dominic. "What are you looking for?"

"She," says Portia, pouring herself a large gin, "wants to bring the dead back to life."

The chill in the room, the look on their faces, their pulling back, Aurora knows what they are thinking.

"She wants to bring her boyfriend back."

Dominic hoots in astonishment. Vivienne cannot believe her ears. She says, "That's not natural."

"No, it's not *not* natural. Just not normal," Aurora says.

Mrs Pugh surprises them when she stands up, her blind eyes searching for where she guesstimates Aurora's face is.

"Not natural, or normal," she says. "But understandable for someone in your condition."

Everyone, everything, skips a beat. The blood drains from Aurora's face.

"Don't you know my dear?" says Mrs Pugh. "You're having a baby."

Aurora looks at Portia. She looks at Mrs Pugh. Her black Chanel dress, her white eyes, the world's biggest pearls.

Both hands unexpectedly on her tummy Aurora says, "Am I?"

"Yes." Mrs Pugh has a pumpkin smile. "A very special baby."

"When?" Aurora says it like, this is a joke isn't it?

"Tonight."

And Bam! Just like that, the Psychic Deli sign explodes, pinging shards of glass all over the floor and blasting me back up through the fuse box and hurtling out onto the grid on a crazy resistance free surge that closes the Dockland Light Railway, takes out the radar at Heathrow, crashes the internet and fries mobile phones across the capital. Some kid in an internet café couldn't believe his eyes when my frazzled face flashed up on his You Tube download. When he couldn't find me on rewind he put it down to tricky subliminal imagery.

I've been keeping close for so long and now, exactly when I need to be there, I'm all over the place.

Imagine. Aurora never said she was having my baby.

This rush is all about losing control and by the time I put the brakes on I'm halfway down Tokyo's Ginza. I manage to take a steer into someone's mobile, then hitch a bounce off a US military satellite over the South Pacific that points me dangerously close to Disney World until, at the last moment, I make touchdown at Cape Canaveral. There the boost from NASA systems kicks me out over the Atlantic and then it is easy down through the UK network, searching, searching, covering the grid, sprawling so fast so fast it is almost instantaneous.

In this lonely electric world of particles, microprocessors and nanoseconds, my tentacles are spread into every corner of the beast, touching every processor, reaching into every memory cell and sim card.

And outside, in the underground car park of St Thomas's Hospital, the turbulence from Portia's jeep ruffles the black tail feathers of a mashed up raven.

They spill out into the corridors. Portia steering Aurora, pushing aside her complaints, Old Starshina has Mrs Pugh on one arm and Vivienne on the other.

"I never thought it was meant for you, Aurora. How could anyone have ever have seen that?" Vivienne is saying.

"The cards don't lie. The cards have their own secrets. The first card was the Empress in the upright position. The Empress appeared at once, in a place symbolizing the present situation. When Mrs Pugh asked me about her miscarriage, for some reason I just thought the cards were saying *she* was pregnant.

"I'm seventy five, dear," says Mrs Pugh.

"Ten times we did it. And ten out of ten, there she was again. The Empress. Urgent preggers."

Aurora moans. She hates hospitals. Now she feels sick. On the way to radiology, these tan coloured tiles and daisy yellow walls, the neon strips, it is a stroll along the yellow brick road of misery.

Vivienne says, "She can represent pregnancy or actual birth of a child, or some special involvement with nature. Negatively The Empress can also symbolize infertility or unwanted pregnancy."

Dominic says, "Yes, yes. Ten out of ten for the pregnant lady. But why does this mean tonight?"

"Very urgent preggers," says Vivienne.

Portia's tumbling golden curls are urgent bouncing ribbons. The way Dorothy's pig tails flicked in Munchkin Land. She flops open another pair of swing doors for Aurora to shuffle through, waves her hand back at Vivienne to hush her and says, "We just need to be on the safe side. Get Aurora checked out straightaway."

Past colonoscopy, between haematology and neurology, is pathology with a laboratory that doubles as a classroom for outpatient group therapy. A timetable pinned on the door says testicular runs back to back Monday with cervical. Tuesday, bowel is paired with urinary. Syndrome day, an angry dry-eyed screaming foul-mouthed itchy twitchy hell of a Wednesday, is aspergers, sjogrens, turners, behcet, and tourettes. Breast has all day Thursday to swell and suppurate. HIV does Friday. On the timetable someone has written Breast Is Best.

"Hospitals should be in alphabetic order," Aurora says. "At least we'd know how near we are to antenatal."

Portia says following this green line on the floor should be simple enough.

It was a blue line for Little Al.

Keeping her thoughts close, she feels the weight of the peculiar, red leather book tucked under her arm. Buried in the herringbone armpit of her tweed jacket, Portia can feel it rise and fall like a breathing lung. A pressing. As if the palms are pushing open, forcing out against her ribs and arm. Wanting to be opened, to spill out the evil. Touching the book, even wearing gloves, makes Portia feel queasy. She had to prize it from Aurora finger by finger. She wouldn't let go even though she complained it was making her puke. Vomit, she says, because her stomach squirms to be so close to the evil she is resisting but desperately wants to own. Aurora says it is like shaking hands with the devil it is so evil.

Portia Maxwell doesn't know what she thinks any more. Pregnancy causes some strange behaviour. This could explain everything, really. Maybe they should forget radiology, go straight to psychology. Maybe they should get Aurora's head x-rayed.

The way she peels an orange, strip by strip, clawing tramlines a fingernail width from north to south pole. It is a cry for help.

Portia pushes open the door into radiology. At a desk in a room with no windows a woman wearing a white shirt, blue ski pants and a leopard skin turban looks up from eating a sandwich.

"Orchid," Portia says straight away. "You're such a great swinger. Swing this for me."

Now Orchid is leading them through the corridors, heading for a room somewhere in antenatal. Her complexion is embalmed skin. She has Mediterranean blue mascara and her lips are way too red. "Dahling," she says. She blinks three times at Aurora, three times at Portia. "You never said you had a baby."

"It's just a theory," says Aurora.

"What we want is a simple scan, to see what is in there, " Portia says.

Orchid makes a little cough with a smile attached to the end of it.

The green line stops. Where they are is a holding area outside the actual neonatal area. Orchid presses a button on the wall and talks to some person at the other end. She says, "Richard? I have a personal party needing attention."

More doors swing open and more marching along corridors led by Orchid. Finally everyone crowds into this dimly lit room with a bed, a wash hand basin and a desktop. Aurora, naturally, takes the bed. But before the others get organised a man in a white coat appears, pushing a trolley load of computer parts, cables, plugs and what resembles the stripped down parts of a tumble drier.

"Meet Professor Heinz," Orchid tells Aurora.

"Frauline," says Heinz. He almost clicked his heels. "This is most unusual. But we do have to test the equipment. So."

He leans into Aurora's face, peers at her over the top of his little round spectacles, adjusts the knot in his black tie decorated with little gold fleur de lis, ruffles the thin grey curls drifting over his ears. Talking to nobody, he says, "I take it you are familiar with the principles of ultrasonic imaging?"

Aurora says, "No. But I hope you are."

Orchid punches some letters into a computer terminal to power up a screen. "The Professor is a technical expert rather than medical. We can trust him."

"So," Heinz says to Aurora's tummy. "What exactly is the matter with your little friend?"

He says vot, der mattar, vis and leetle.

Aurora gets a shrug of the shoulders from Portia. Heinz twiddles something on the mouse and the computer monitor jumps into life.

In all the cosmos of electrical discharge, I am aware of the minutest change.

"So, you think a little bit of god is stuck in there?"

"Err, no," Aurora says. "I'm not so sure if there's anything."

"Good, good," says Heinz. "It is good that there is not a god inside. This at least proves your sanity. There is no supreme being."

Heinz drags the mouse, edging a parabolic curve into position on the monitor.

He says, "I may have awe for the universe. But here, we save cancer patients. Not prayers. We do this. The sons and daughters of monkeys."

Aurora says, "Well, even the catholic church accepts evolution these days."

Heinz bends down under the desk, powers up another computer screen. "Accepts it yes. But believes it, no. You see the difference? They want to steal science. Take the ownership. But science is already there, you know? Virgin birth is easy peasy."

Heinz orders Orchid to lock the door.

He says people who believe in god may as well believe there is a sofa bed in orbit around a distant star. "Thor, Poseidon, Apollo, Ammon Ra. We are atheists about most of the gods people once believed in. So. Now we must go one god further."

Orchid lifts up Aurora's shirt and squeezes some blue coloured jelly onto her tummy. "Which trimester did you say you are in?" she says.

"Dunno," says Aurora. Portia has a very numb shoulder now. "You tell me."

And Vivienne says, "She's late. It is very late. Imminent."

Heinz moves a scanner over Aurora's tummy and the parabolic curve disappears from the screen. It goes black with lots of snowy streaks. He asks Aurora her name and as he is typing it in he says we are these amazing monkeys who have come from dissecting rainbow's light into different wavelengths, who arrived at Maxwell's equations on electromagnetism and the existence of radio waves, and then went on to special relativity.

Orchid checks the screen is refreshing at a steady pulse. The professor's computers make a constant electronic murmur. It is like angels singing.

Aurora fingers the pentacle around her neck. Eventually she says, "What do you think happens to us when we die?"

Heinz clears his throat. He says there are three criteria for clinical death. One. The absence of spontaneous breathing. Two. No heartbeat. Three. The loss of activity in the brainstem and cerebral cortex, areas of the brain responsible for sustaining life and thought processes. "We are all atoms, of course. The dust of stars. The physical part of us dissolves into dirt or blows into the ocean. Some of us might become particles in a glass of water."

Portia takes Aurora's hand and says, "Scientists do not believe in any sort of life after death."

But Heinz lifts his hand, the one holding the scanner. "Now that is not absolutely true. We understand very little about the relationship between the brain and the mind. Think of an out of body experience."

He taps his head with a finger.

"The consciousness is this whiz of brain cell activity

sparking around in here. What is not known is how all this becomes an individual. Some people believe, or should I say think, that the mind, or consciousness, is produced by quantum processes in brain cells. The mind may itself be a separate entity."

Aurora says, "A soul."

"Well, perhaps. Or an alien computer," Heinz says. "So. In our heads, our minds are these itsy bitsy microtubules that work like quantum computers. If you can accept that consciousness is a some kind of thing separate from the physical flesh, then somehow we create consciousness, or we tap into this quantum field which we have chosen to call consciousness and which already exists. Ja?"

"What does all that mean?" says Portia.

"What you call the soul may be a physical attribute which science only now is on the threshold of understanding. The medicine of the conscious."

Aurora puts it into her words. "Like astral projection."

Heinz squirts more blue gel. He apologises if it feels cold. "Muddled up along with so much nonsense over centuries and centuries, I believe it may be so."

Heinz says think about the woman who is blind from birth who dies on the operating table and who returns from her near death experience able to describe the most startling visual details. The man whose heart has stopped for twenty minutes then, when they revive him, recounts his rendezvous with relatives on the other side.

"And don't forget the tunnel of white light," Aurora says.

"Yes, almost always. It may be stimulation of the optical nerve. But even so, very interesting," says Heinz.

Aurora believes in Buddhist astral projection, swears by the Hindu idea of everything being connected to everything. She grasps the concept of Chi in Chinese philosophy. Now she hears a soul may be all in the mind, put there by itsy bitsy quantum computers within brain cells. "I bet that's what happened to Jimmy T," she says.

Everyone stares at the black screen. Heinz rolls the scanner around again.

"When my boyfriend was killed he must have had an out of body experience. And his quantum consciousness, or soul, or whatever you call it, is still hanging around."

Professor Heinz is nodding. "So. Maybe you are right. Quantum reality is a very out there topic. Theories do permit this."

Orchid says she is not seeing anything on the scan. Everyone stares at the monitor.

Orchid says she is not seeing anything on the scan and she still has half a sandwich waiting.

"Alright," says Heinz, tapping the scanner against his palm. "I'll try another."

The atomic hum drawing me to this room is now a garbage can being beaten with a golf club.

That pain under her arm is burning and now Portia's eardrums, her skull, are bursting. Her neck and shoulders are numb. Her eyes can't focus. It feels like someone pummelling inside her head. Her legs are buckling and even while Old Starshina catches her and lays her gently onto the floor her nose starts to bleed dripping rosebuds on the tiled floor. The curls on her head roll off too and there she lies, bald as the day she was born.

This is my infinite requiem. From wherever I've been to wherever I'm going, I know now I am one of the lucky ones. Most people never get to die because they are never born. The potential people who could have been standing in my place but who never saw the light of day must outnumber the atoms in the universe. All those unborn ghosts. Greater poets, greater scientists, greater musicians.

I realise in that moment that to understand life we have to turn to mystery, to strangeness beyond our wildest dreams. Magic beyond witchery and illusions.

I'm me, only I'm not Jimmy T the person, not Jimmy T the dog, but Jimmy T the being now floating around the ceiling of this room above Aurora.

From somewhere, everywhere, there's a tinkle of wind chimes. Little glass ones like your grandmother used to have, not the modern bamboo tubes or aluminium pan pipes.

Down below, Vivienne, Old Starshina, Mrs Pugh and Heinz are crouching over Portia. Heinz is taking off his white coat and folding it under her head like a pillow. Orchid is shutting everything down as fast as she can. She is pulling out cables, kicking at computer sockets under the desk.

Portia looks up at people and she says, "What on earth is going on? Am I dead now too?"

Aurora bites the back of her trembling hand. She reaches over to Portia and touches her, like she has made her decision. Then she starts looking around the equipment, searching everywhere, under the bed, under the computer. She finds Ramana's spell book and goes ripping at the pages. As each one gets shredded it burns with the fluttering flame of an incandescent butterfly. She stares right up at where I am floating next to the ceiling. Me, this essence of me who is glowing with rainbow light, rolling over playfully, arching, floating on my back. Way up beyond the ceiling, the cone of a diamond-lined tunnel is gradually opening. No one else is watching with open eyed amazement, so I am guessing that only I can see this. But Aurora stares so hard that I have this feeling. I just have this feeling that it is not over yet.

Mrs Pugh prods Vivienne and says, "Is Aurora's baby coming yet?"

The book is in ashes and now Aurora rips the leather binding itself, separating hands that have always been together.

It's *Aurora's* baby.

I was not forced to make any decision. Neither would I say it was preordained. It just seemed the right thing to do in the circumstances.

The tunnel of diamond light closes in on itself, receding upwards until it is a star in the dark sky beyond the hard cement of this building as I turn to drift slowly down. It is like being in an elevator, except the machinery is all in your mind. In fact, you are all in your mind. There is no body.

I feel the touch of Aurora's dress as I go seeping through the weave of the fabric next to her warm skin. I hold it there for a moment. Skin deep.

Portia is crying. Aurora is too.

Penetrating effortlessly, infinitely undetectably, I absorbed myself into the warm darkness of Aurora's womb.

What I remember are the fading wind chimes.

Then the sound of two hearts beating.

23

The Psychic Deli in spring is a wonderful place. The constellations overhead and the paintings on the wall are beautiful distractions. The smell of coffee and the constantly changing ebb of customers make it the favourite place for Aurora and me to pass an hour or two after a stroll in the park, or before taking a nap.

I am held in the arms of a woman. She pledges her undying love to me and perhaps I can grow to love her too, in a way.

As Aurora's womb baby, our minds as well as our blood and flesh were one. Call it a graft. Call it making a clone. We grew to know each other more intimately than any couple ever could. From the very moment of conception, if that is the word for it.

Quantum physics or magic, Aurora can't decide. Only one thing is certain. She knows it has nothing to do with artificial insemination.

Orchid says why on earth did Aurora want to go and do that, bring a child into this world?

Aurora says because this is the only world we've got. But then again, she's not so sure.

Every so often she blows on a charm she wears around her neck and uses it to tickle my nose. "Jimmy T," she says. "I love you."

We are the first major miracle of the millennium.

There used to be a beach I could go to inside my head. It was protected by a slender coral reef and the waters were sheltered and warm. But a great storm has washed that barrier clear away leaving me exposed and vulnerable. There is no protection from what's out there, lurking in the unknown deep. Even for the ones who think they still control their destiny, who invite some kind of spirit to manifest itself. The spirit of evil. Spirit of good. A slogan. A politic. A creed. A love. A hate. We are all ghosts of our former selves. The haunting is right here and now. We understand this when we go past the certain point and look back at what we have learned. You cannot kill a vampire with an MDF stake. Werewolves do not fly. In a straight race, anyone can outrun a zombie. Illusions are real.

To amuse me, Aurora invents elaborate new pretences that shock and confuse people into wonder or disbelief. For someone with a home video camera, Aurora has learned to casually appear to fly. She positions herself at forty five degrees to the camera and floats off the ground. The trick is only going up on tiptoes on the rear foot, lifting her front foot a little off the ground. But she's got it off perfect. To heighten the effect she cut the sole out of an old pair of baseball boots and wears black socks.

Or she frightens Portia by eating razor blades and string. She winces in pain, she groans with every inch of string, every blade she eats. Then she pulls them all threaded together out of her stomach. Only I know she spent an hour that afternoon painting a skin coloured latex pouch onto her belly, filling it with threaded blades.

And I know the ones she eats are made of sugar.

When she brings a dead fly back to life, the kids run screaming to tell their parents about the resurrection.

She picks the bug off a windscreen and she usually says, "I give you the breath of life." Or I once heard her say, "I am the life, the power and the glory."

Then she clasps this fly in her hands for a minute. When she opens up, it veers off.

The kids don't see her swat the fly unconscious in the Psychic Deli, or beg Portia to put it in the deep freeze for her to use later.

The bug never has a chance. In the insect world, there is no medical examination to detect critical mental or physical damage. No lawyers to seek punitive compensation.

It is a protection thing, these illusions that she is more powerful than she really is, more capable of standing up for us both. All this because, like everyone else, we're expecting some one, some thing, some evil, is going to arrive. Sooner or later. Not that we are hard to find. Aurora says I radiate like an unearthly lighthouse and this beacon is something that evil might easily home in on.

Portia makes a funny voice, her Countess Dracula. "The book is mine," she screams. Crying with phoney frustration, she says that one day soon she is going to be the most powerful force alive. Live forever, she cackles. Have people build shrines to her. Be served by diminutive followers in baggy silver trousers. She will fly about the world in a magical wisp of cloud. We will have mountains of money.

Until then, she says in her normal voice, the whole world needs a detective. Everybody has lost a treasure, believes they are being cheated out of something, or needs to find a lost lover or fix a broken heart. If we sometimes need to speak to the dead, or consult the cards, we can work it out.

People spend so much time theorising about what happens in death and all the time the important thing is what happens in life.

Aurora picks me up and blows cool air on my face. She says she loves me. That I am so special, that she can't wait for me to grow up. The things we are going to do. The love we are going to share.

Only this time I am not so sure. My memories of the here before I was dead are fading. Soon they may be gone forever.

This close, even Aurora's face is blurred.

Mother? She could be anyone.

At least the spring sunshine is full of hope. The smiles of Grandpa Starshina and Aunty Viv promise more love than I can ever forget. Aunty Portia does great animal impersonations. And the noise from the deli's coffee maker is like waves crashing on a distant shore.

Jim McLean gained an MA (Hons) in English Literature from Glasgow University where his personal tutor was Professor Edwin Morgan, Scotland's first poet laureate.

In a media career spanning 20 years he was twice Journalist Of The Year for investigative reporting, won national awards as Health and Science Correspondent of The Daily Record, was Arts Correspondent for The Herald and has written for national newspapers, tv and radio.

He lives with his family in London and is currently working on several new writing projects.

www.ingramcontent.com/pod-product-compliance
Lightning Source LLC
Chambersburg PA
CBHW030327130626
46554CB00011B/189